In Defiance

Illyrian Invasion

VC Sanford

Illyrian Invasion: Defiance
V C Sanford

Published in the United States of America

By 341 Enterprise
Rossville, Georgia USA

Dedicated to

Bonnie Ann Moulder.

For teaching me there is no such

thing as "I Can't."

Only that

"I have not yet found a way."

Never Give Up

Chapter 1

Corporal Akins watched the blip flash across his screen for the second time, then slapped the button on the com and requested a supervisor ASAP. He closed his eyes for a moment, then backed up the readout and reviewed it one more time. He had been working long hours and it was beginning to show. It was easier to request an evaluation of the recording from an unbiased and hopefully fresher set of eyes. There was a ninety-seven percent certainty the blip was nothing more than a code anomaly. The class had endured extensive training on mass hallucinations and psychopathic delusions during the six month training period. He knew that after eight hours of staring at the screen, it would be easy to imagine a weather balloon on an unusual trajectory was something unidentified. It was going on ten, with no relief in sight. The virus had reduced the normal schedule into a scribbled mess of call outs and hospitalizations, so pulling a double was not unheard of, even when SOP specifically called for a mandatory shift change every eight hours.

The Naval officer that watched the recording glanced at his cell phone, pulled it out and texted someone. Then he hit replay and watched the recording in slow motion, using the computer to chart the trajectory of the object. He set up a formula for triangulating the theoretical landing location, ran the calculations and made a notation on a pad. He sat back and closed his eyes for a moment.

"Corporal. Have the mess send up coffee and sandwiches for at least six. Soft drinks too. And have someone bring me a laptop. Make sure its secured, level 6 or better. Better make it two, just in case one of the others didn't bring their own."

The corporal felt a shiver run up his spine at the sudden realization that the situation must be more serious than he imagined when he called for a second opinion.

The Majors next words stopped his in his tracks. "Fuck. There are more of them!"

***

Why do I have to work every Friday?" Erika looked around the building, counting on her fingers the number of chores she would have to complete before she could getaway. The number was discouraging. She rolled the bus cart into position beside the table and began stacking the dishes inside the plastic bin, mumbling her complaints under her breath since no one was close enough to hear them.

Mona, her mother allowed the briefest frown to show before replacing it with her public happy face. "It could be because we own the restaurant. We can't afford to pay someone's salary for such a trivial matter. We know you want to go to the skating rink and hang out with your friends. However, we have more important priorities, like keeping the power on and buying needed operating supplies. Besides, we close at nine o'clock. The skating rink doesn't close until midnight. That gives you three hours to hang out after you finish your chores. And don't whine about it not being enough time. I know Diane drops you last when she brings you home." Her mother turned to take the check from a customer, thanking him for his patronage with a smile.

Erika did not say another word until he had left the building. "I know… I don't … it just doesn't seem fair." She thought about the pile of dishes waiting to be washed and put in the steam sanitizer. Jose was already done with the pots and pans. Jason was working on the food prep for breakfast tomorrow. Once the restaurant closed Jose's wife Maria and her sister would arrive to do the daily cleaning. All she had to do was buss all the tables, wipe them down and fill the shakers and napkin holders. Fifteen minutes…tops.

Unfortunately, the Red Hats were dragging their meal out as long as possible. She sighed. Sometimes it didn't pay to be a teenager. She was finally old enough to date but had no time free to go out with anyone, and too old hang out with most of the kids at the skating rink. Luckily, there were three or four girls whose parents were just strict as hers were, so she could always find someone to hang out with.

She glanced at her phone hoping there would be a text from Thomas. Nothing. Not that she expected it. She had shared her lunch with him earlier at school. In between bites, he had hinted that he was interested in talking to this one special girl, but no names were mentioned. She hoped he meant her but at the back of her mind, she figured it was probably Savannah.

All the boys liked Savannah. Who wouldn't? The girl was gorgeous. She probably weighed a hundred pounds soaking wet. At least fifteen of them were her boobs. There was something about a tiny body with oversized breasts that drove the boys in her school wild. Not that Thomas had a chance, she only dated seniors.

The flavor of the week was the Co-captain and B-team quarterback of the football team. Coach Marks had made a spectacle of her in gym class by announcing that she needed to make sure Ryan showed up for practice on time or he would lose his position on the team. Supposedly he'd already reamed Ryan in front of the other football players. That hadn't made a bit of difference, Ryan still stayed up half the night talking to Vanna instead of sleeping.

Erika stuck her tongue out at the reflection in the mirror. It wasn't that she was ugly. She was only five foot five, average height, and maybe 110 pounds. Her mother claimed she was too skinny, but she liked being slender since women in her family tended to plump out in their thirties. Next to Savannah, she looked long-legged and gawkish, and possibly a little bit too slender. At least she would never have to worry about finding a bathing suit that fits. The last time she went to the Mall with Brianna, they had run into Savannah and noticed she had to buy separates or two suits. That was a small, petty victory but Erika could not afford to let even the tiniest ones slip by.

Combine that classical face with a golden umber complexion and almond-shaped eyes, and Savannah reminded the boys of something out of a fairy tale. With her pale skin and freckles, Erika knew she would never be considered exotic but her auburn hair was beautiful and the sun brought out the red highlights. It had just about reached the middle of her back. Her mother was beginning to make noises about chopping it off so that she would not have to wear a hairnet in the kitchen. Of course, it would have something to do with the restaurant. Her mother had kept it shorn most of her life. Short hair made her look like she had giant ears. And her face was a little bit too square to wear it that way, not that her mother cared. To keep the peace Erika kept it braided most of the time.

She stood at the door to the kitchen and stared at her last table. Three women remained after the meeting and of course, they all took desert. They were drinking coffee and eating their pie as though it was the most important thing in the world. She wanted to tell them to get a life but realized driving off some of her parent's best customers would not enrich her own miserable life.

Until they paid their check she was stuck. It was already a quarter after nine. Time was ticking down. As though the Red Hats intended to personally screw up her social life they were the last table in the restaurant to leave. Erika commenced to clear it as soon as they headed for the cash register, almost running over one of the stragglers in her rush to ger the cart to the table. She apologized over and over but the old woman continued to mumble something about the lack of manners in the younger generation. Cleaning it off so fast would probably screw up her tip but at this point, she could care less. She just wanted to get the table bussed so she could finish her side work and leave for the rink.

She had the table cleared and wiped down before they finished paying their check. Wheeling the awkward cart before her, she quickly rushed into the kitchen, turning sideways as she passed through the swinging doors to avoid hitting Jose. He was stacking glasses for tomorrow's breakfast crowd. The beverage area needed an overhaul, it was a pain to rotate the different sizes needed for each meal. That was one of a bazillion things that they didn't have the money to do.

Heading directly for the wash area, she shoved the last few cups and saucers into the hot soapy water. Seconds later the dishes were washed and the final rack was in the sanitizer.

The clock on the wall said five minutes to ten. It was gonna be well after ten o'clock before she got to the rink. Hopefully, Eric would be in a good mood; sometimes he didn't want to let anyone in after ten. Usually, he would make an exception for her because he knows she had to work but occasionally he locked the door and headed to his office. There were a lot of things that could set him off, and if the younger kids were terrorizing him he could be a total jerk.

"Bye, Mom. I'm taking off," she called out as she passed the cash register.

"Don't you want your tips? I have them right here."

"Hang on to them I'll get them in the morning." She didn't exactly run the two blocks to the skating rink but she was walking as fast as she could. Even so, she was fighting to catch her breath when she reached the parking lot below the rink.

Eric was standing in the parking lot outside talking to one of the fathers when she arrived. From the conversation she could hear, two of the boys had got into a fistfight on the skating rink floor over one of the girls. Both of the boys were eleven and the girl was twelve. She laughed, remembering it wasn't that long ago when her friends were doing similar stupid things. No one was bleeding and a few bruises might teach them a lesson. Doubtful but stranger things had happened. Eric waved her in and turned to say something to the boys. They would be banned for a weekend or two and then everything would go back to normal.

Erika grinned. Not only would she get inside, she would not have to pay. There was not much of a crowd inside anyway. Joey, Eric's son was showing off in the center of the rink. She stopped to watch his intricate footwork. It was a shame that he was two years younger than her. In a couple of years, he was gonna be one hot fox with that creamy complexion, dark hair, and baby blue eyes. There was not a girl under fourteen that didn't swoon whenever he skated by. Naturally athletic with the perfect balance that comes along once in a generation, Joey was not only an expert skater, he could dance to anything.

No matter how hardit was to accept, she had two left feet. She could get around the ring without falling but that was about it. Only a blind man would call her graceful. Someone could paste her picture over the words *white women can't dance* and no one would be surprised to see it.

Erika waved at Diane as she passed by the concession area while searching for Brianna. She had a pretty good idea where she would find her. Most of the older teenagers had claimed the bench that ran along the backside of the rink. They were all hanging out listening to Casey. Casey had a really good voice, clear, deep, and smooth. That deep southern drawl that would have made a great country song but sounded strange when he was trying to rap out the hooks and bars of the latest top forty.

An avid athlete, Casey was into most physical sports, the result leaving him with a fantastic body. Which helped to make him very popular. He had been dating the same girl through school, a really pretty blonde named Kim who had dropped out of school at sixteen. Casey graduated in about 6 weeks and everybody expected them to run off and get married shortly afterward.

Some of the snobbier girls we're always gossiping about the reason Kim quit school. Of course, her being pregnant was the favorite story. That wasn't true. Erika knew it was because her mother was sick and she had to go to work to help take care of her brother and sister. Her mother had been coming to the restaurant to eat for years. The other day when she came in she looked like she had lost about fifty pounds. She was wearing one of those portable oxygen tanks that people have to use when their lungs go bad. Mama said she smoked since high school and believed she'd developed cancer lung cancer. After three years in the same school, she still didn't know Kim well enough to ask her. I didn't know anyone that might know the real story, …except Casey and he wasn't talking.

Sure enough, Brianna was sitting nearby, present but not part of the inner circle, talking to Casey's steady girlfriend, Kim.

Like her, Bri was not the most popular girl in school

nor was she the most hated. They were both averages. Average body's average grades average looks average clothing average everything. She had a real boyfriend once, but he had moved on when she explained she was still a virgin and intended to stay that way. It taught her a lot about teenage boys, and how little she was missing out on.

Almost as soon as she sat down, Cooper appeared, sliding into the booth beside Brianna.

"Who is it this time?" Bri asked. She figured some girl must be chasing him again. She leaned back against his chest, giving anyone watching the impression that she had a perfect right to be there.

"No idea. She's here with a couple of friends. I think one goes to Hearthstone." He propped his chin atop Brianna's head, looking every bit the devoted boyfriend.

The disappointment on the young girl's face was clear for everyone to see, she felt kinda bad about it. Cooper is one of those boys every girl fell in love with the handsome blue-eyed boy next door. That would be great for Cooper- except Cooper didn't like girls. In a small town like Chickamauga, you didn't tell anyone you were gay. Since entering high school, she and Brianna had pretended to be his girlfriend at one time or another. He had come out to us in middle school. Cooper intended to stay under the radar for the next two years until he graduated. Then he planned to move to New

York. One day he hoped to be on Broadway. For now, he joined the cast of every play put on at school, sang in chorus, and pretended to be one of the good ol' boys.

"Where's Charley?"

"Filling his bottomless pit, of course. Diane marked everything down to half price so he headed for the snack bar."

Sure enough, Charley was heading their way with a loaded tray. As soon as he set his food down, Erika snatched a French fry and dunked it in the ketchup cup on his tray. It was crazy. She worked in a restaurant around food all day and was never hungry. But as soon as she got away from there, she was starving.

After the skating rink closed she would usually ride catch a ride with Brianna or Diane back to the house. They always made it a point to drive through the Krystal. There was something about greasy hamburgers, chili cheese fries and chocolate shakes at midnight. Nothing else compared to that combination. In the meanwhile, she would have to make do with Charley's fries and his coke.

She reached for the cup just as the ground started shaking the building. The cup fell over splashing coke over the table and Cooper.

"Damn, Erika. Clumsy much?" Cooper snapped.

"But."

That's when we heard the loud explosion. The tornado warning siren installed by the city commissioner began wailing. Screaming parents were running every-where trying to find their children. Panicked mothers were snatching skates off the bottoms of their feet and shoving them into tennis shoes. Some didn't bother removing the skates, just picked up the kids and ran for the door.

"Is it a tornado?"

"No, it can't be a tornado. That was an explosion."

"Maybe a house fell out of the sky. It happens in movies." Charley muttered around a mouthful of chili-dog.

"You are Kur shit crazy. This ain't Oz and you defi-nitely ain't no wizard." Brianna dumped Cooper out of her lap and began walking toward the front door. We all followed.

"Maybe China decided they were tired of reading our President's tweets."

"Cooper! Don't joke about something like that. It might really be China."

Joey skated by heading for the door and we decided to follow him. Eric was still outside. Maybe he knew what was going on. If not, he would be the one to find out.

There was another explosion, this one was much closer and strong enough to throw people around. Ceil-ing tiles were falling and the electricity went out. Diane left the snack bar unmanned and joined the rush for the exits, gathering several children whose parents were not around into a small group. It was no longer safe to be inside the building.

Brianna had fallen to the ground when the ground started shaking so Charley helped her back to her feet. Now we were running for the exit with everyone else.

She expected to see Eric standing by the exit of the parking lot directing traffic but he was nowhere in sight. That's when another vehicle exploded and Erika knew the first one must have been Eric's truck. Her stomach roiled when she saw the figure of a burning man through the smoke and realized that might be why Eric wasn't helping the cars get out of the lot. The big Dodge extended cab was fully engulfed in flames; the smoke too thick to see if anyone else was inside it.

People were running toward their vehicles, throwing their children inside and taking off. Someone had broken the back gate off its hinges and cars were using the broken fence as a secondary exit. Others were pulling out onto the main road, swerving in and around wrecked vehicles in an attempt to reach safety.

The noise was overwhelming. Power transformers were blowing up everywhere. Nearby buildings were burning. She could hear fire engines and sirens. Alarms were going off all over. There was a large explosion down the street followed by balls of flames lighting up the nighttime sky. A beam of light struck the motel next door and it exploded, scattering chunks of broken cement blocks. What was left of the structure was covered in flames. *Lasers? Do the Chinese have laser weapons?*

We stood huddling together under the awning, unsure what to do.

Brianna was trying to get her parents on the telephone but all the lines were busy. She lived out in the country about fifteen minutes outside town. By now her parents would have heard the explosions and started that way.

People were acting crazy driving like maniacs up and down the street. Erika had no idea what was going on but she figured it might be a good idea to start walking toward the restaurant. She turned to tell Brianna she could wait at the restaurant with her when she saw the beam of light come out of the sky lancing directly at the rink. The building exploded, throwing her like a dried out leaf onto the cement pad outside the door. Everything went dark.

When she came to, Brianna was lying on the ground nearby. Her right arm was missing and she was covered with blood. Her eyes were open wide and glassy. Erika knew without checking she was dead. Cooper was kneeling next to her crying. He didn't seem to notice the blood running down his face from a gaping wound on his head where the flying metal had hit him.. Diane staggered past calling for Joey. There were only four or five kids still alive. None of them were Joey.

"You kids go get in my van. Joey will drive you home. I'm gonna lock up. I'll be ready to go when you get back." She had to be in shock. The building behind the doors was gone. For some reason, the entrance was still standing, along with the two doors. Joey had never come outside.

"Erica, you need a ride?" Charley asked. I'm gonna take Diane's van and drive the kids home. If I can get her inside the Van, I will take her home, too"

"No. I'm gonna walk up to the restaurant. My mother will be frantic. I need to let her know I'm alright."

"What do we do about Cooper? He needs to go to the hospital."

"I don't know Charley. Just try and get everyone into the van."

Diane stood by the door repeating, "I don't know. I don't know. I don't know." Tears were running down her face. Erika was torn between helping with her and getting back to her parents. Eric was her oldest son, and Joey her youngest grandson. They were her life since her daughter had died in an accident when Joey was a baby. She couldn't be 100% sure it was Eric's body in the burning truck but she knew in her heart it was him. Eric would never leave his mother alone. Not when the world was falling apart around them. No one had any idea what was going on. Or what to do.

That same whistling noise came back and the flash of light came down from the sky, striking the gas station on the corner. The explosion rocked the service station, obliterating stone and metal in a great gout of smoke and flame. The flames rose high into the air, illuminating the midnight sky like fireworks on Independence Day. The shock of the blast threw debris high into the air. Red hot ash fell like rain, setting anything flammable afire. All the nearby houses began to burn.

Something or someone was destroying our town, and it shook Erika to the core. "Is it terrorists," she asked. "Are we at war?"

Diane's eyes went up to the sky, and for a moment her mind was clear. "I don't think so. I don't think China has ships like that. I've never seen anything like them." She paused and began herding the kids toward the van. "Erika, run! Go on! Run to the restaurant and check on your momma. Tell her to get out of the building. Don't wait. Run and hide. I don't think they're from Earth."

"What do you mean not from Earth? Where else is there?"

"I don't know. I don't know. I don't know." Diane sat down in the front seat of the van, put her hands to her eyes, and started crying. Charley took her keys and started the van.

As she was walking away Erika could hear Diane praying; asking God to give her some kind of answer about what was going on.

Erika ran. She didn't remember much about the two blocks she ran. Everything was on fire. That same high-pitched sound kept coming back. The shrill whistle would start then the beam of light would come down and something would blow up. Where houses, cars, and trucks and people once stood, were ashes, clumps of melted metal and charred bones.

She saw a little girl, maybe five or six years old covered in flames. She ran from a convenience store that had been destroyed and made it about twenty feet from the door before she fell prey to the fire. She hoped the child was dead. Her skin was black and cracking. The fire had destroyed her clothes though it was difficult to make out any portion of her body that wasn't covered because of the charring. There was nothing she could do to help her. Tears streamed down her face as she ran.

By the time she passed the Krystal, she could see her family's restaurant. What was left of it, anyway? The building was fully engulfed; flames shot high into the sky. There was no one standing outside. There was no way anyone was alive inside the inferno. All the vehicles in the parking lot were melted or burning. The heat from the fire was horrible.

Erika did everything she could to get close enough to call out, "Mama! Jose!" No one answered. She tried calling 911 but got busy circuits. Where was everyone? With this much destruction going on, there should be fire engines and police cars everywhere. And ambulances. Where were all the first responders?

Beyond the old fort parade grounds was a narrow access road that led up the ridge to the new county hospital. One a clear night like this you could see the brightly lit high rise building for miles. The top of the hill was dark.

Here and there a flickering light fire could be seen but there was no sign of the eight-story, stone, and steel building. If any of the building was left standing it was too dark to see it from a distance. She turned and stumbled back to the road, unsure where she should go, only knowing she had to go somewhere, anywhere, other than where she was.

Then she heard that strange high pierced whistle moving in her direction. Her heart started racing. Her legs trembled. She wondered if she had the strength to get out of the middle of the road or whether it was worth the bother. Her parents were most likely dead. Her brother's trucks were in the parking lot, so likely they were inside, too. There was no one left. All the surrounding buildings were on fire or utterly destroyed. Her instinctive impulse was to hide, but there was nothing left standing nearby large enough to hide behind.

Down near the end of the street, a sudden flash of light caught her attention. A minivan had exited the battlefield and was coming towards her. Somehow she knew it was Charley returning from dropping off the kids. He was headed back toward what was left of the skating rink. Or maybe he was going take Cooper to the hospital? The van was too far away for her to see who was driving but she didn't think Diane was capable of doing anything.

It was as though she was watching a bad science fiction movie. First, the whistle, followed by the beam of light, the look on Charley's as the van exploded around him. Erika saw one of the side doors fly by over her head, recognizing it was too high to hit her, just before it struck the remaining wall of the shoe store. She had enough time to scream before the brick wall came crumbling down… and the body of the burning Van stuck the side of a dumpster shoving it directly at her.

Chapter 2

Jake carefully pulled himself along the rope that had been slung over the jagged floor of the cavern. The silvery-white sand glistened under the halogen lights, offering a prism of color to the explorers while hiding the true danger of the access. One slip and shish-ka-bob. Not that he expected to have any problems. Eight of the men from his National Guard unit was participating in the project, along with about twenty seniors from the ROTC units of four local high schools.

His team leader was one of the premier spelunkers in the Tennessee Valley. He'd been wanting to work on his rescue certifications for months, and this was his first opportunity, When Payton had contacted him with news that his unit was coming down from Nashville to drill in the local cave system, he'd put off his trip to Las Vegas and signed up immediately. Santwan was certain it was a mistake, but then again he hated anything that took him beneath the ground for long periods of time. Payton's civilian job was to explore and map sections of the cave systems that wound throughout the mountains of eastern Tennessee. The project required his team to survey virgin caves in the system, recording distance, slope, and compass readings. He was also an expert cartographer, sketching maps as he progressed throughout the cave system. The US Government hoped to create a fairly accurate map that shows both the cave's profile (how the cave falls or rises with respect to the elevation) and the cave's plan (how the cave would appear if you could visualize it from above) diagramming the extent of the unmapped system and the depth to which it had previously been surveyed. Payton had made two earlier forays into the unmapped section of the topological area near Chattanooga and decided that the cave system could run the entire length of the piedmont section of the state. This was great since the military had petitioned for and received permission to develop a section of the cavern for government use.

After rappelling down the face of the rock, the team quickly set a base camp in the larger of the two mapped caverns. Two small-bore fissures lead off from the main cavern and they intended to start mapping from the right-handed one. Payton had set up an abseil rack with a rappelling harness supported by a metal support base that was too large to fit down the bore of the fissure. The group had a smaller version of the descender, its pieces shared out among the entire party but they would only use it if the rim were too wet to hold their pitons.

Jake watched Santwan hook up to the abseil rack, then start his descent, using pressure on the clamp to slow or speed the rate as he dropped into the darkness. Two sharp tugs on the rope meant he was on the ground and off the rig, so he attached his ring hook and double-checked his harness before following him down. He had descended into the fissure--or what Payton had called the bore Hole—for less than a hundred yards before his helmet flashlight showed the stone wall was getting closer. Mikey was last down; he used a slipknot on his harness that enabled him to keep control of the rope while dropping so that the hook remained on the bottom of the rappel line. This would enable the team to use the same harness to return to the top. The group had made good time, moving twenty-eight people to the jump-off point in less than an hour. Since it was still early in the day we chose to continue exploring. It meant some tough climbs and tedious belly crawls through narrowing fissures filled with small rocks, wet clay, and no wind; but the sooner we finished mapping, the sooner they could head for Las Vegas.

Everyone was elated when we discovered the unmapped fissure leading down into previously unexplored depths below Raccoon Mountain. We'd hoped to locate an area with sufficient headroom to use as a waypoint; instead, we found the passage blocked by debris. Sometime in the past, there must have been an earthquake strong enough to bring part of the tunnel down.

Digging is a slow and tedious process. Clearing a blocked tunnel is discouraging but you can't help feeling excited the further in you go. Airflow on your face increases with every rock you remove from the pile, bringing with it loose dirt and small particles of rock. But it is also dangerous; the area you are working in is already unstable. At any time, the ceiling could collapse again. Also, the passage behind you could become clogged with debris from the digging efforts, often making the exit equally as dangerous as the entrance had been.

Payton was an old hand at caving, but sometimes even the oldest and most experienced get a little sloppy and he was no exception. His hand slipped on one of the pitons and he fell forward striking his hip against the rock surface.

"Shit! Look out below!" He screamed, his voice echoing in the cavern. Mikey quickly pulled back against the wall, his body nearly gored by the hammer drill that came unclipped from Payton's. harness. It missed his head by inches, landing with a clatter on a boulder and shattering the bit into pieces.

"Sorry about that Mike I'll send you down a replacement."

"No hurry. The air feels different. I think we might be about through the blockage. Send Jake down. Between the two of us, our weight might just be enough to shake it loose. Feel like jumping up and down awhile?"

With the two men jumping up and down they managed to loosen the big rock enough that it slipped downward, landing with a crash at the bottom of the now open fissure.

Sant used a linking hook to add another section of rope to his drop line, and then he lowered himself slowly to the floor of the crevice. Once down he shouted back up to Jake, telling him that they needed a double-length line to make it to the bottom. Jake relayed the message on, and then added an additional line to his rappelling system before releasing the pressure that held him in the air. By alternating the pressure on his line he was able to control the rate of his descent and easily make his way to the bottom.

The narrow fissure in which they were standing branched off in three directions, all of which had a good airflow signifying the possibility of a larger chamber nearby. Payton walked a short way into each passage before deciding that the group would take the left fork which led downwards. A short walk brought them into a sizeable cavern complete with an underground stream of crystal clear water, a perfect site for them to take a break.

While everyone collapsed to eat lunch, Jake decided to check out a strange outcropping of rock toward the back of the cavern. At his feet was a crevice which went straight down as though it had been measured by a giant square. He got to his knees and looked over. Playing his light around he detected a few ledges like narrow steps far below. It was pitch-dark down there, and not even his strong light could reach the bottom. He tried tossing a few pebbles into it; listening he heard the faint rattle of their fall but could not be sure whether they had landed on one of the ledges or had reached the bottom.

He decided to mention the opening to Payton.

"That sounds like an interesting side trip. Might be a bit too much for the teenagers but maybe the two of us can come back and check it out later."

Payton spread out a map on the sand near the rocky area while the troop was eating, comparing the drawings that his team had completed, and comparing his measurements with those of his second, Tanner. Tanner was remarkably close in his figures, only one section caused a difference of opinion and it was quite possible that his measurements were correct and Payton's were off. Satisfied with his team's work on the project so far, Payton decided they would spend the remainder of the day working on rescue techniques; allowing the various teams to work without his supervision.

"There are three main offshoots leading from this cavern," he said amicably. "I'd like you to separate into teams and check out the smaller grottos. Jake, you can be one injury. Mikey, you got tunnel two, and Tanner will take three. Make it interesting but don't put any of the group in danger."

Tanner winked at Jake and the three men moved out into the tunnels.

Jake took the right fork off the main cavern following the stream as it made its way into the darkness of the virgin fissure. Two sections later he was thankful for his kneepads and heavy gloves as the crevice had narrowed sharply. A belly crawl through the water brought him to another set of very wet pitches that followed the river downward. He followed it downstream for a few hundred feet before the stream abruptly plummeted into a small crevice that did not appear passable. But luckily, there was an old fossil stream canyon leading off toward the left that looked to be a likely prospect for a rescue.

The fossil stream passage soon opened up; it was all "walking tunnel," a caving term that means there's little climbing, and no rope work, and you can walk standing upright. There were no vertical pitches, except for one narrow fissure that took about ten minutes to maneuver his way through. Beyond that first crawl, he worked his way quite a distance from the main cavern before he reached a section that required rope work.

He had brought a portable brake and piton cara-bineer system that allowed him to control his descent without having to resort to the old fashioned(and some-times painful)method of wrapping the rope around your body that so many of the older cavers still used. After a quick set up, he started lowering himself into the dark hole.

Since this was a military training rescue he had crammed his ammunition, food, and canteen into a knapsack and strapped his rifle to it. The floor of the shaft was about fifty feet down and covered with a thick layer of sand. Since he was supposed to be injured he used his backpack for a pillow, stretched out, and decided to take a nap.

It was warm down there, and as soon as his eyes closed he began to doze. The sound of laughter growing closer startled him awake. For a moment he forgot he was. He had turned his headlamp off, not thinking about how dark it was inside the cave. His old childhood terror of the darkness swept over him as he clutched this way and that and found nothing. Then he got a grip on himself and laughed at his fears--remembering that he had a spare flashlight in his pocket. It took him several tries to locate the headlamp in the dark. His hand brushed something soft and furry, a brown Kur that had left its upside-down perch and fluttered against his face, clicking its teeth in warning. He felt himself feeling infinite pity for all the men everywhere who spent their days working caves just as dark.

He sat there for a while, chewing at a bit of jerked beef, trying to wait patiently for the rescue to arrive, but after about fifteen minutes he began to wonder if they were coming. He checked the time on his watch, noticing that it had been three hours since he had closed his eyes. Clearly, something had happened to change the original plans and they were not coming. With a sigh and a curse or two, he began readying himself for the climb back to the top.

Climbing back up was a pain but nothing he couldn't easily handle. The ratchet on the rappelling rope took all the strain off his arms. He had tied a long catch rope to his pack, looping it through the trigger guard on his rifle to ensure it didn't come loose and fall to the bottom. He would hate to have to go back down and retrieve and then have to climb back up again. The interesting hike down was nowhere near as interesting as he worked his way back to the cavern where his team was waiting. Except when he reached the cavern the team was gone.

"About damn time you showed up," Mikey said. I was beginning to wonder if we needed to come and rescue you."

" Sorry. I dozed off and didn't realize how long I'd been gone. Where is everybody?"

"You must have been quite a way down into the cavern if you didn't feel it. Come on, we have to hurry. Something big is happening."

"Something big?

"Yeah man, we might be at war!"

Chapter 3

The first thing Erika noticed when she opened her eyes was the flies. They were everywhere. All she could hear was the buzzing of the insects. Everything else quiet. There was no whine of sirens, no shouting, no running, just an ominous and all-pervading silence. She had no idea how long she lay there unconscious between what was left of the shoe store and the green steel dumpster. She supposed the metal of that dumpster is what saved her life. Diane's van lay crumpled at the side of the big commercial dumpster like a discarded accordion. The remaining wall of the building was only a few feet tall and the dumpster had slid up against pushing her into a hollow between the two.

She wasn't sure if she could get out from between them. One of her eyes was swollen. Crusted blood fused the lashes of one eye shut but she could see light between the cracks. She was certain it was black and purple and didn't need a mirror to know there were similar marking all over her body. The dumpster must've slammed her against the wall.

Her legs and arms worked when she tried to move them, so she doubted anything was broken, but it hurt more than when she'd fallen off Goldie running barrels.

Somehow she had ended up on her side between

the wall and the dumpster. The slots where the arms of the trash truck fit had prevented her from being crushed by the force of the blow. The area wasn't much more than six or eight inches wide but she figured there was enough room to let her wiggle out from the between the wall and the dumpster. She began worming her body that way when she heard it again. That shrill annoying whistle.

Erika froze waiting for the explosion but this time there wasn't one. Just the sound of the whistle getting louder and then fading slowly away into the distance.

Suddenly she didn't want to leave her refuge, instinctively knowing that she was safe there. She had no idea why she was safe but whoever was in the ship had no idea she was there. The heat from all the fires burning down and the time she had spent unconscious after the attack had dried out her skin. Her lips were cracked and bleeding. Sometime during the night, she had peed all over herself. The ground underneath her stomach was still wet and smelled of ammonia. It embarrassed her but she had no idea why. It wasn't as if anyone were around to see what had happened. Even if anyone were nearby she doubted they would care what she did. From where she lay, she had a clear view of what remained of the restaurant. Most of the building was gone. The fire had left two walls of the shell but they looked like the first big wind would blow them over. Erika could see where the heat had blackened the paint on one of the coolers, but it seemed to have survived the flames. For a brief second or two, her mind allowed her to believe the possibility that her Mama had been close enough to duck inside one when the attacks began. Chances are if anyone had been inside the cooler it would have been Jose since it was his job to prep everything the restaurant would need the next day.

Or maybe everyone had run outside to see what was exploding and they had all found a safe place to hide. Her daddy's truck was not sitting in the parking lot, they could have all piled in and got away. She was certain that he would have come to check on her when she didn't come home. Or maybe he had and one of the melted blobs of metal was his truck?

Now that she thought about it, she didn't see anyone. There were no cars on the street. No people were walking around. Surely somebody had to be left alive beside her. Once again she began worming her way out from between the wall and dumpster. She had managed to get her head and shoulders clear when she saw them coming out of the park.

There was a small group of people, maybe a dozen or so, the men in one line and women in the other walking calmly down the middle of the street. No one was talking. No laughter. No one paid the destroyed building any attention. Truly bizarre behavior.

Behind them were several figures dressed in some kind of shiny material. Each had breathing tubes like scuba masks in their mouth. They were much taller and heavier than the people they were guarding. Even from the distance, she could see they weren't human.

Slowly she inched her way back to safety, staying as still as possible while hidden between the dumpster and the wall. They were carrying some kind of weapon but it didn't look like my father's gun. The metal was shinier and the barrel was skinnier. It didn't look like there's a place for bullets to come out. But it is definitely a weapon.

About the time they passed what was left of the Krystal one of the men decided to make a run for it. He made it five or six strides before the thing guarding him pointed its silver gun in his direction. The weapon didn't make any sound but when it struck him his body began jerking like electricity was running through him. Maybe that's what it, was some kind of fancy taser pulse. He lay on the ground jerking for five minutes or so before the alien thing came over and stood him up. Once he was on his feet it pushed him back into the line and everyone started walking.

Erika had no idea where they were going nor did she want to know. If they were going toward Chatta-nooga she was determined to go in the other direction. Once it got dark, she would be heading home. Her legs were not gonna take her anywhere right now. They were trembling so much she was scared she was having a seizure. It wasn't just fear, but that had a lot to do with it. She had no idea what she was gonna do once she reached the farm. Her house was about two miles outside the city on a dead-end road very few had reason to even notice. She intended to cut through the battlefield and take about half the distance off her hike. Not that she was looking forward to it. Her brothers had always warned her not to enter the park after dark because there were packs of coyotes hunting there.

Erika laughed. After seeing the aliens, a pack of coyotes didn't faze her. She needed to get home to her daddy and everything would be okay. He always told us that if anything ever happened we were supposed to come home. We all knew where the bug out bag was hidden. He made sure all his children knew how to load and shoot a gun. And clean it afterward. She was a decent shot with a rifle but she preferred her bow and arrow. With a compound bow, she could drop a dear at a hundred yards. Bobby was better with a gun than any of the boys.

Bobby! I can't believe I just now thought about Bobby. He had gone to Atlanta to serve his National Guard weekend down at Dobbins Air Force Base, near Macon. Bobby was a helicopter mechanic and a darn good one. Once he got out of the service he hoped to get a good job working on commercial equipment, freight airplanes, and helicopters for UPS. They had a repair shop at the Chattanooga airport and a friend of his had promised to put in a good word.

Was there even a Chattanooga airport left? Surely these funny, not funny at all, strange beings had destroyed it, too. Not beings that made her think of God, her God would never create something so evil. The word Aliens seemed to bland. *What should she call them?*

She tried to picture them in her mind. They had fur on their bodies but their face looked like a dried-up lizard. She didn't see a tail but maybe it was small and tucked inside their funny silver outfit. They walked on their back legs like humans but now that she thought about it she realized their legs were we're not shaped like hers. They had an extra joint or backward bend in their leg like a dog. Their feet were oversized and floppy, like a rabbit. No, not a rabbit. Rabbits were vegetarian and these things had big sharp teeth. Carnivores. Was that why they were here? Would they take all our cows? She didn't see any cows with them but that didn't mean anything. Maybe they preferred pigs or goats or horses.

It's crazy how your mind starts to wander when you're lying in the dirt and ashes of what used to be your hometown. She wondered what Brianna would think about it and then she remembered Bri was dead. She won't be thinking about anything. Eric. Dead. Cooper Dead. Charley was probably dead, too. Did she wish Diane were still sitting in front of the skating rink? Yes, waiting for her to wake up so she could tell her that a chunk of the ceiling had fallen when a truck hit a telephone pole and knocked her unconscious. That it was all a bad dream.

There wasn't even a skating ring to sit in front of…

Her mind was rambling and she might be having a nervous breakdown. Was anybody left alive? Logic told her there had to be other survivors. Hadn't a dozen or so trudged past her earlier that day?

What was our military doing? She hadn't seen an airplane all day. They were always flying big military transport helicopters down the valley. Not now. No fighter jets. Nothing.

The only police cars she'd seen were burning. Now that she thought about it, she hasn't seen any cars at all. She needed answers and she was not going to get any laying there. But no matter how hard she tried she could not force herself to leave the safety of her tiny space. Instead, she lay her head down on her arms and cried herself to sleep.

Chapter 4

Jake opened his eyes to a world drastically changed in forty-eight hours. Two days ago children played in the campground at the base of Grandfather Mountain. Boats towed skiers and fishermen cursed them for stirring up the fish. Now the campground was dull of melted slag that at one time had been a vacation camper. The blackened remains of trucks and cars sat scattered along the pavement cracked and rutted by the intense heat.

All through the day, they had waited for the aliens to settle down and move away from the area. Instead, the airships continued to fly over as they searched for any sign of human activity. Yesterday they had made the mistake of sending out a scouting team to assess the extent of the damage. Jake, Tanner Santwan, and Mikey had geared up and set out for Chattanooga in one of the four-wheeled utility vehicles that had survived the initial attack. The Gator could go places a car could not go and carry all four men easily.

They reached Point Park in less than an hour, hid the cart beneath a broken awning, and using binoculars took their first real look at Chattanooga. The change was heartbreaking. Every building had sustained damage with most of them being totally destroyed. The aliens' weapons had shattered the stonework and melted the steel frames like butter in the hot sun. Anything that could burn was left in ashes.

The aliens' mother ship had landed atop the National Cemetery, crushing the tiny monuments into gravel beneath the massive bulk. They could see movement around the ship, vehicles being loaded and equipment being set up. It was obvious the ship intended to remain for some time. Closer to their position was Finley stadium. The aliens had set up some type of staging station there. Many of the alien's airships were lined up in the parking lot of the stadium. They watched as a group of about thirty humans was brought in by a group of the aliens. They were moved into the stadium. After a few minutes, the guards returned, entered one the small airships, and flew away."

"At least we know we're not the only ones left alive." As always, Mikey was the optimist of the group, a glass half full person.

Tanner let loose a tight-lipped laugh, that sounded more like a deer snorted. "Don't make me feel any better about the ones inside the stadium. We have no idea why they are being rounded up."

"Shit," Santwan said, "for all we know, the damn aliens feel the same about us, as we feel about a cow. We got to get them out of there."

"How do you suggest we do this? There's a lot more of them than us. And we have no idea what kind of weapons they have." Jake wasn't sure rushing in to save the prisoners was the best tactic to utilize at this point. He had served a tour in Fallujah, two years in which his entire way of thought had been tested, destroyed, and rebuilt with an entirely new outlook. After finishing his active duty, he had joined the National Guard along with Santwan and two other men from his Army unit. He had no idea if Gary or Tyler had survived the initial assault. He doubted if any of his family had survived. His mother and father had lived in a high rise apartment building that was now nothing more than a hole in the ground surrounded by rubble. His sister worked at a local hospital, one of many buildings that were no longer there. She could have been at home, she lived in Hixson, but he had no way of contacting her to see if she were alive.

From the appearance of the city, the aliens were intent on destroying anything manmade. They had made a meticulous effort to follow each road, destroying every house and vehicle. It reminded Jake of the grid pattern the military favored in an assault. Tanner was right, they needed more data to make an educated decision. There was only one way to get it.

***

Sant was lying down under a block of stone that had landed on an angle against another chunk of stone, leaving a small aperture just big enough for him to shinny through. His body was concealed by shadows but any movement on his part could draw the attention of one of the many aliens who seemed to be guarding the equipment. For over an hour he had lain there without moving, his muscles twitching from being in the same position, watching the invaders move equipment from the mother ship onto aircars. Once the equipment was loaded, the flying transport vehicles took off, going in several directions. A few had returned empty. In his opinion, the mother ship was being used as a major base from which to stage operations in the area.

He had a clear view of the main ramp from the ship and could see the staging area. Mechanical lifts similar to a human's forklift would leave the ship with equip-ment, load an aircar, and return for a new load. Figuring one load every ten minutes, that was at least six an hour. Even his sad excuse for math could see that meant over a hundred possible satellite bases had been established since the ship landed. If they worked around the clock it could be closer to a thousand. That scared the hell out of him.

From the corner of his eye, he spotted an aircar skimming over the debris, its trajectory would bring it within a few feet of his location. He was sufficiently cam-ouflaged that he was not concerned about being seen however, he had no idea where the others had gone to ground. They seemed to be searching for something, go-ing slow, and studying the ground beneath the airship. This was as close to one of the aliens as anyone had come, without being one of the prisoners. He did his best to lock every detail in his mind.

The late evening sun was beginning to settle beyond the western horizon, causing shadows to lengthen, increasing the possible hiding spots. Once the aircar passed, he intended to return to the staging point Jake had established when the team had split up. Somewhere out there, the other three men were making their own decisions about when to move, where they were going and what route they would take to get there.

Something in the manner in which the aliens were acting gave him reason to believe they had located whatever it was they had been searching for. He shifted his eyes to the rubble near the airship. That's when he saw the girl. She was not fifty feet from the airship, moving stealthily along the base of a burned-out building. She was facing away from the approaching airship, intently watching a different pile of rubble. He was startled to see she was carrying a small child in her arms.

Suddenly she stopped moving and turned to look behind her. Spotting the approaching airship she began to run, moving in and out of the maze of rubble. It was clear to Santwan there was no way she could get away from the aliens. The airship moved close to the ground and two of the searchers jumped out and began moving in the girl's direction. The woman disappeared from his view for a few seconds before popping up again in a clearing about forty feet beyond the point where he had lost sight of her.

She dashed across the open area, running toward the burn out hulk of a bus. The aliens immediately changed direction, moving around a pile of twisted metal before cutting across the ground on an angle toward the young woman.

Sant fought his initial impulse to go to her assistance. The aliens did not appear to be interested in her death. It would have been simple to shoot her from a distance. Instead, the driver of the aircar hovered over her hiding spot until the two aliens on foot arrived. One tried to grab her arm and she kicked it in the face. The second alien seemed to think that was funny. There was a short verbal exchange between them, then the first alien shot her with what Sant could only describe as a taser. The alien slung her over his shoulder and they walked back toward the aircar.

That should have been the end of it, except Tanner decided he needed to rescue the girl. Shots rang out from behind the wall of what used to be a donut shop. Sant could see Tanner clearly as he fired shot after shot at the two aliens. None of the bullets got close. Sant could see them ricochet off an invisible barrier before embedding in something nearby. The alien carrying the girl placed her in the aircar, then he turned toward the building from which Tanner was firing. The weapon he was holding was not the same as the weapon he used on the girl. A beam of light was discharged, striking the wall before him. It disappeared in a burst of bright light, along with most of Tanners' lower body.

Sant knew he would bever forget the stunned look on Tanner's face. He reached his hand toward him as if he could catch him as he fell, fully knowing his friend was dead before his body hit the ground. He watched in shock as the alien climbed back into the aircar and flew back toward the stadium.

Santwan continued to stare at the spot where tanner died long after the sun had set. Around him was absolute silence. Then he heard it. The distant sound of a baby crying.

The child. He had forgotten about the child. She had been carrying the child when she disappeared. He could not remember seeing it after she came back into sight. She must have hidden the child in the rubble somewhere. He needed to find the baby now. There were too many things that might consider an unpro-tected infant an easy target. Taking a firm grasp on the rock to either side of his hiding spot he pulled his body forward. The time he had spent in the cramped space had slowed the circulation in his legs and turned them numb. As the blood returned to the hungry tissue, he was overcome by a series of sharp pains and cramps. He struggled to his feet and fell as the tortured muscles re-fused to support his weight. He would have to wait until the tingling stopped and his body got back to normal. After a few minutes, he was able to climb back to his feet and hobble in the direction of the cries. The darkness added to his confusion making it difficult to locate the area where the woman had vanished. The baby had to be hidden in that area. Time and again he slipped on the uneven surface, scraping his shin against loose rocks. His fingers were raw and bloody by the time he could clearly hear the child's cries. Finally, after what had felt like hours, he found what he sought.

In a small bowl-shaped indention between a group of fallen bricks, he found the child. She was scared and wet and wanted her mother. Sant felt his heart breaking. The chance of successfully saving her mother or any of the prisoners had become much harder after witness-ing the way their bullets had been deflected. Finding a weapon that could hurt, much less kill one of the invaders would take time. More than likely many more of his friends would die before they found a way to help the prisoners. A bar of chocolate he carried in his pocket brought some comfort to the little girl as Santwan made his way back to the mustering point.

"Was gonna ask what kept you, but I think I have a good idea of why you are so late." Jake handed Sant a cup of hot coffee. The little girl was sleeping, her head against Sant's shoulder, one thumb in her mouth. He had a lot of questions but they could wait.

Mikey was arranging the back of the gator to give the child a place to sleep during the trip back to camp. "Tanner is the one that usually shows up with a stray. Of course, his are usually the four-legged kind. Wonder what's keeping him?"

"Tanner won't be coming," Sant said quietly.

'You're sure of that," Jake asked. His face was set and any emotion he might have been feeling was hidden.

Sant passed him Tanner's dog tags.

"He went down fighting to save the little girl's mother. I was too far away to stop him. The aliens have force fields. Our bullets never reach them. They hit him with the same kind of phaser they used to destroy the buildings. It took out the wall he was hiding behind and most of his body. He didn't feel anything."

Jake nodded. He had a feeling he would be reporting the loss of more men in the near future. "They don't seem to like being out after dark. I haven't seen an aircar since the sun went down. We need to leave now or we won't make it back to camp before sunrise."

He climbed into the front next to Mikey. Sant climbed in the back, lying the child in the seat next to him. She never wakened.

Chapter 5

Erika winced as she tried to sit up and banged her head on the metal bracket above her head. For a few seconds, she had no idea where she was. Then it all came flooding back. Everyone was dead. Why was she still alive? Was it some kind of sign from God or was she being punished for something she had said or done?

The first thing she noticed was how dark it was. It's amazing what you get used to seeing and never notice until they were gone; streetlights and brightly lit businesses, even traffic going up and down the street. Now there were only the stars and the moon, no artificial light at all. Although the late summer night was a bit chilly, the moon was bright so she should not have any trouble seeing well enough to travel. Her eyes had easily adjusted to the meager light.

Erika guessed the power station had been one of the first things they hit. Now she wondered if the smaller explosions she had heard were transformers blowing when the power surged back against them.

Here and there she could see the faint glow of hot coals scattered around the rubble of destroyed buildings. Most of the fires had burnt out but most were still too hot to investigate. One of the buildings still burning was our family restaurant. I tried to get to my knees but realized there was no room. By turning on her side and wiggling like a snake she was able to inch her way out from between the dumpster in the wall. Her body ached in places she didn't realize could hurt. The extra rest had given her body time to recover some, she could almost open her eye. Now that the swelling was going down she knew she wasn't going to be blind, and that helped. The bottoms of her hands were all scratched up. She had no idea how that happened. Maybe in her panic, she had tried to claw her way out. Her watch said it was Monday night. She didn't remember a whole lot about what happened over the last few days. Unfortunately, the things she did remember she wished she could forget.

Her knees hurt when she stood upright but got better when she began moving. She stopped at the corner of the building, and crouched down behind the broken wall, ears open and listening to every sound, especially the shrill whistle that she had learned meant one of their airships were nearby. Other than the normal insects she couldn't hear a sound. She kept her eyes moving constantly, looking both ways up and down the street but it was too dark to see if anything or anyone were moving in the shadows.

Maybe if I can't see them they can't see me.

She was compelled to walk over to the burnt-out rubble that was all that remained of her family business. It was still too hot for her to try to get inside and look inside the freezer. Her heart had grasped at the possibility that someone might have tried to escape the inferno by sheltering inside the old cooler. But her head knew they were only used for storage. They always had to prop the door open to make sure no one got trapped inside. The fire would have sucked up all the oxygen in minutes. Hopefully, once the fire was completely out, she would be able to do a better search for her family. At least she could bury their bones.

She needed to concentrate on getting home. She glanced at her roller skates and thought about putting them on and skating towards the house. At first, it sounded like a good idea but then she remembered she would have to follow the streets and that left her out in the open. There was no way she was the only one who survived. The prisoners walking through town had proven that. All bets were off and not everyone she met would be concerned with her wellbeing. Her father was a vet. He remembered Viet Nam and all the horrors he had seen. From the time she was old enough to listen, he had drilled all the bad things that could happen during war, into her head. And made sure she knew enough to prevent them from happening.

Tears welled in her eyes as she remembered the times her brothers had surprised her, pretending to be a man intent on rape or murder. She had learned the way to disable an assailant, and then two or more at a time. No one had ever envisaged it being an alien.

It would be much safer to cut across the battlefield. A hundred and sixty years earlier our country had fought a war over civil rights. One of the biggest battles of the war had been fought in a small Georgia town called Chickamauga. The valley where so many died was now a Federal park, full of monuments, plaques, and statues dedicated to both sides.

She had ridden her horse though out the park for many years and was comfortable finding her way even in the dark. There was a wide horse path that ran from the front of the park on an angle, ending next to the railroad tracks that lead towards her house. She started walking then stopped and picked up a heavy rock and a thick stick.

Two sets of red eyes shining in the darkness showed her she was not alone. She gripped the stick tightly in her right hand and began jogging towards the backside of the park. Hunting was illegal inside the battlefield so herds of deer ran freely. Late in the after-noon, you could see them grazing in the fields. Several packs of coyotes had moved into the area. Normally they would avoid humans but a single girl walking alone through the park at night was a tempting target. The stick would not help much if it were a large pack but it might discourage two or three long enough for her to getaway. Hopefully, sufficient time had not passed since the invasion for the coyotes to realize they were now the dominant species in the park. It was about a quarter of a mile to the railroad tracks she intended to follow to her neighborhood.

At one time the railroad carried freight from Chattanooga to Atlanta. Now the tracks that ran through the park made a loop in Rome and circled back alone side Lookout Mountain. It was occasionally used to move some local freight but primarily it was a tourist attraction. The City of Chickamauga owned this section of railroad tracks and maintained it well enough that she could follow alongside the tracks almost to her family farm. If she could reach them.

She caught a glimpse of movement and quickly turned her head, spotting at least three shadowy figures in the tree line. If she spotted three, there had to be at least twice that many she had not seen. There was no way they would allow her to reach the tracks. Too many people lived nearby.

She looked at the trees that bordered the path. The park maintenance team kept them neatly trimmed. The lowest limbs were at least five feet above her head. It was highly unlikely she could straddle and climb the trunk without a harness. She tried to picture the grounds of the battlefield, searching for anything she might possibly use as cover. The nearest possible protection was the old watchtower. There was a branch on the path ahead; left took her to the railroad, right took her to the tower. She increased her pace a little, hoping to reach the junction before she needed to decide. The shadows stayed with her. The junction was less than a hundred feet ahead. She knew they would attack soon.

When she reached the Y in the path she did not hesitate. Breaking into a run she raced for the tentative safety of the old tower. The coyotes began barking and howling as they followed. The pack could travel at a similar speed but they had been on her left when she took off. The extra fifty feet was her only advantage.

The first hundred feet passed quickly but she found her pace slowing about a third of the way through the second two hundred. She had run further many times but not while carrying an awkward wooden stick and a rock. She had slung her roller skates over her shoulder by the laces and every step ended with the skates slamming against her ribs. Her heart was pounding in her chest and it was difficult to take a deep breath. The time needed to stop and remove the skates would remove the razor-thin margin of distance she maintained on the pack. She began to mumble a childhood prayer under her breath, not wanting to give up any advantage she might have. She had no idea if her prayer was answered, but she did seem to feel better. Her brothers would have called it getting a second wind.

She could see the stone tower in the distance. So could the coyotes. They split into two groups, moving to either side in hopes of cutting her off before she reached the granite sanctuary. One of the wild dogs was a little faster than the rest. She could see him closing the distance between them. He put on a burst of speed and leaped for her back.

Erika did the only thing she could do. She stopped, set her feet, and swing the wooden limb like a baseball Kur. The crack of the wood as the limb struck the coyotes head was loud in the silence of the forest. He yelped once, and hit the ground, rolling to a stop at the side of the path. She wasted no time verifying he was hurt, racing for the tower.

Someone had locked the gate.

With no other available options, Erika placed her back against the stone wall. At least none of the pack could get behind her. The first coyote, a skinny female that looked like she was nursing pups dashed in, snapping as she came. Erika slammed the rock in her left hand down atop the bitch's head. She yelped once, then fell and lay still, unconscious or dead. The rock had cracked her skull behind one eye, blood flowed for a moment and then stopped.

The remaining pack was more cautious. She counted seven sets of red eyes gleaming in the darkness. Every so often one would move closer, staying just beyond her reach for a moment before moving back into the shadows.

Then one ran out and snapped at her. She swung the oak limb, striking it along its spine, then wincing as she noticed the crack in the wood was spreading. Now she was worried, the wood would not hold up much longer. Once the stick broke, it would be really difficult to keep the snapping maws away.

Just as she expected the coyotes began inching closer, stopping just outside her reach. She set her feet apart and lay the limb across her shoulder, then removed it and slid her skates off, dropping them to the ground at her feet. It would be bad if she'd tried to swing the branch and got it caught in the skates' laces. Keeping her eyes moving from side to side she looked for any hint that the pack was about to attack.

When it came it happened all at once. A big grey male ran forward. Instead of attacking her, he locked his teeth on the branch and jerked it out of her hand. Before she reacted, two more of the pack leaped for her. Swinging wildly with the rock she landed a blow alongside one's face, but the second latched into her arm, ravaging her wrist until she dropped the rock. When a trio of the mongrels moved closer, she panicked and began fighting with her fists and feet, jabbing her fingers into the eyes of the coyote biting her arm and landing a solid kick to the side of the one that she had hit with the rock. It threw her off balance and she fell to one knee. Her hand landed on the roller skates.

Without really thinking about it she swung a skate at the coyote, hitting it with the metal wheel frame over and over. The coyote whined and limped away. With one hand entwined in the laces of a skate, and the other holding the long laces like a whip, she began laying blows about her body, striking any animal within reach. She had no idea how many times she swung her makeshift weapon, all she knew is that if she stopped, the pack would pull her down.

Her hands were slick with blood by the time the adrenaline rush wore off and she realized she was alone.

Chapter 6

"Looks like a different place." Mikey sniffed and smiled as the scent of freshly baked bread wafted through the access tunnel when they opened the door.

Jake was surprised by the amount of progress made during the twenty-four hours the scouts were in the field. Somehow they had managed to get electricity and rigged up strings of lights around the cave. Looking around he could see that the interior of the cavern had drastically changed.

Santwan shifted the little girl in his arms and looked around for someone to take her while he reported in. Spotting one of the older women who had been camping when the attack began, he began walking her way. The woman was sorting clothing, something the girl desperately needed. He had tossed her diaper hours earlier. "Think there's anything there that would make a diaper?" he asked.

The woman looked up, Curious about Sant's question. "Lands sake. Where did you find her? The poor dear. Let me take her and clean her up. She looks like she hungry. When was the last time she ate?"

"I gave her a candy bar but she didn't want the jerky. That's all I had with me. She lost her mama to the Kurs. No idea what her name is." He paused. "Would you mind taking her while I report to Captain Jeffers?"

No. Of course not. You go ahead. We will take care of Hope"

"Hope?".

"It's a good name. And right now we need all the hope we can get." She walked away as Santwan rejoined the others. He watched as the baby was surrounded by women, most of which had not been around when they left to spy on the aliens.

"Hope is in good hands. Let's go." Jake turned to walk toward the area that had been designated for the military's use. Mikey and Sant followed.

It took them longer than they expected to locate Captain Jeffers. During their absence, he had ordered the old bomb shelter to be opened up. After the men removed the heavy lock they had discovered the storage area they expected to find was actually a warren of rooms connected by tunnels. A map of the tunnel system was located on the wall of a small room Captain Jeffers immediately claimed as his office. Using garden hose, they had scavenged gasoline from an underground tank and after some minor tweaks, now had several generators working. The tunnels were lit by electric lights.

Captain Jeffers's expression darkened as he listened to their report. "There was no question of his death?"

"No doubt. His body was missing from his lower chest down. I piled rocks over his body to keep animals away from the remains. It didn't take many rocks."

'May he rest in peace. Sadly, he will have a lot of company. " He stood and walked over to the map on the wall. I want you to study this map. Then I want you to check out every inch to ensure there is no back door left unattended. This tunnel," he pointed to a long stretch that ran under the river toward Chattanooga, "is already verified and open. We have placed golf carts at each end to cut down on the travel time. It opens up at Ruby Falls. I have men working on making the emergency stairs stable. The elevator shaft was damaged beyond repair when the elevator crashed."

Jake read between the lines. More lives lost. " That's great. It will give us a safe way to reach the top of the mountain. We should have a clear view of the mothership from point park. Any idea who they are or what they want?"

" We were blindsided. No one thought it could happen. Any idea of invasion from space was considered science fiction propaganda. The higher-ups laughed at the idea and called it 'fake news'. Everybody knew it was code for black ops money. Something to get Congress to increase the amount of money marked for the military's use."

"Were they wrong. It took less than three days to wipe us out. It's hard to fight an enemy you can't hit."

"What about Nukes?" Mikey was ready to wipe them out. Tanner had been a cousin and the only relative he had left.

"Tried them. Lost the plane, and the island of Oahu will be uninhabitable for fifty years, maybe more. Zero damage to the Spaceship. Made them mad though, they increased attacks on our military bases. Most have been reduced to piles of burning scrap. No type of long-range communication is working now so we have no idea what happened next."

"So you're saying humanity has been forced back to the middle ages?"

"We still have bare-bones essentials but without technology, they will not last long."

Sant cleared his throat. "I have a question. There seem to be a lot more people inside the main cavern. But I did not see any of the Unit."

"The unit is not occupying rooms along this hall. I prefer that we maintain separate quarters. The large room you enter from the cavern is being set up as a company kitchen and dining area. It seems this entire area was developed for military use in the case of an atomic war. It's surprisingly well-stocked. We have also designated two rooms for medical and two for deten-tion. I hope we never need to use them."

He returned to his desk and poured himself a glass of water. "Your rooms are on the left down the hall. Your name is on the door. Jake, if you can stay, I need to clear up a few things."

Santwan and Mikey knew they were being dismissed. Both men saluted and left, pulling the door closed behind them.

Jake remained standing until Captain Jeffers offered him a chair. He removed a bottle of Jack Daniels from his desk and poured them both a shot, sliding it over to Jake before taking his in hand.

"Tanner," he said as he downed the shot.

Jake downed his shot, too.

"So tell me what happened. Not the report. What happened."

"It was a clusterfuck. We went out armed with the best we have and we might as well have been shooting rubber bands. Nothing got through the force shield. If they had wanted to, they could have wiped us all out. The only thing that's saved out ass was it got dark."

"You think they don't like fighting in the dark?"

"I don't know if they can't see or if it's some kind of cultural taboo. But when the sun goes down they all head back inside the ship. The ones that guard the stadium keep it lit up like is noon on a hot summer day."

"You said they chased the woman down? Any idea why?"

Jake shook his head no. " We were able to slip into the stadium through a but in the fence around back. They have about a hundred captives inside an electric pen in the middle of the AstroTurf. Mostly women, some young men. Could be slavers."

"I don't want to ask, but what about food?"

"I don't know. It's possible. They may be taking breeding stock. Could explain why they kill off all the old or unhealthy. No young children either."

"Speaking of children, how is the little girl doing?"

"She's scared. Wants her mommy. She clings to Santwan like he's the second coming."

"Poor Sant. He looks like he's about to cut and run at any moment. He was really happy when some of the women took her off his hands. I take it you noticed a few changes when you got back."

"I was hoping you might fill us in on where they all came from."

"It was the damnedest thing. I sent out a few teams of salvagers, telling them to check out Tiftonia. Figured they could search through some of the houses that were still standing. While they were looking through what was left of the town for anything that might use, they began to run across groups of survivors. Most of them had been at the same wedding, once of the local girls. The parents had rented some man's barn, in the middle of a cattle field. They had to park on the street and walk to the barn. The aliens missed it or didn't figure it was worth bothering with. They destroyed all the vehicles. They chipped in with what they had gathered. Most of the Tarps came from Walmart, only part of it burnt. The bedding, too. Some of the sheets came from a motel. Same for a lot of the furniture." He grinned. "I saw that they had hung some from ropes to form sleeping areas.

Guess they wanted a little more privacy than one big communal bedroom area."

Jake nodded, worrying about the sudden increase in population. Sooner or later there was going to be some head butting. The sudden increase of testosterone in a confined space was bound to cause trouble. None were going to be happy about the no going outside in the daytime rule.

Captain Jeffers seemed about to say something more but dismissed him for the night instead.

Jake wasn't complaining. He decided to detour through the main cavern and pick up something to eat before finding his room. That soup had smelled great.

The refugees had done a lot to make things comfortable in the cave. Furniture that had escaped the flames formed public seating areas around firepits. There was now a makeshift kitchen providing meals for everyone. Scavengers had spent one day digging through the rubble for usable can food. Meat was scarce, but one of the men had brought down a deer which was cut into small pieces and went into the communal soup pot. He was pleasantly surprised to see there was even some of the wedding cake left. The young woman serving the cake looked pretty sweet, too. Maybe he could satisfy more than one craving. He grinned and she smiled. Things were looking up.

Chapter 7

The eastern sky was beginning to change from blues and purples to reds and golds as Erika trudged up the final hill before the turnoff to her family farm. The neighborhood looked like a war zone. There were no lights and all of the houses on the road that fronted the tracks had been destroyed. She wondered where everyone was, surely not everyone died in the fires? Have they all been rounded up by the aliens? That's what the people walking through town were, prisoners. She had no idea where they were being taken and had no idea why. She just knew she didn't want to be one of them.

There was an old overgrown mobile on the hill below her father's farm. The people who lived inside them we're little better than animals. They had generators to provide electricity since the trailer was too old to be hooked to the power grid. She didn't see any lights through the trees but that didn't mean anything. They had heavy blankets nailed over the windows to keep people from knowing anyone was living there. On warm nights you could smell burning plastic or rubber for miles as they burnt the cover off the wire they had salvaged. Scrap metal didn't bring a lot but it didn't cost them a lot to live. She didn't smell burning wire. Trailers burn fast and there's very little left when the fire was through. She prayed they had not been inside.

Unlike most of the houses in the subdivision below their property, their house was not easily seen from the road. Her father like privacy and he kept a thick growth of trees around the house. Her grandfather had built our house back in the 1930s, just before the Great Depression and the War. A brick mason by trade, he had built the house of cinder blocks. All of the ceiling rafters were gone, burnt away but the fire. She was surprised to find most of the walls still standing. Even some of the floors were still there.

Unfortunately, it had not stopped the smoke. She was certain that was what had killed her daddy. He was lying on the kitchen floor, curled up like a sleeping puppy. His body wasn't burnt but his face was blackened from suet and his clothes were covered in smoke residue.

She sat down next to him pulled his head into her lap and held him, talking to him as if he were still alive. "I'm scared, daddy. I don't know what to do. These things I don't know what they want, but they're killing everybody. Well not everybody, some of the people they're taking prisoner. I think they are taking them to Chattanooga. There's a big spaceship sitting in the middle of town but they fly around in aircars about the size of your old truck,…or maybe your old convertible because they don't have roofs on it. They destroyed everything. We can't stop them. I saw a man shoot a gun at one. The bullets just bounced off. It's some kind of force shield like they have on Star Trek." She stopped talking and wiped the tears from her face with the end of her tee-shirt. The sun was up outside so she could see much better. Her father needed to be buried soon. His body was swollen and turning colors. But she could not force herself to get up until she finished saying what needed to be said.

"I don't know what I'm going to do without you. Mama is dead but I guess you know that already. The restaurant's gone. I don't know where the boys are. The last time I saw them they were at the restaurant with mama. And Michael… I guess he's still in Atlanta. If I find Mama's body, I'll try to bring it back and bury it beside you. I guess that means I need to bury you now." She began shaking as the idea of burying her father took hold in her mind. She would need to dig a grave. Maybe down near the big apple tree would be good. The ground would not be hard there.

"Daddy, I don't want to be alone. I'm scared. I'm hungry. I don't know what to do. I know you taught us to take care of ourselves. But you were talking about human wars with guns not furry lizard people from space. Why didn't you teach me how to fight space aliens? Maybe none of this is real. Perhaps I got hit in the head with that piece of shrapnel I thought I dodged when Erics truck exploded. I could be unconscious and dreaming. If this is real I don't want to wake up. I'd be better off dead."

She stood up looked around. First things first. She opened the refrigerator and took out a bottle of water. Without electricity it was warm but it was water and that was something she needed. She drank the entire bottle. Then she started thinking about food. Almost everything in the refrigerator was spoiled. There were a few apples on one shelf so she ate one and felt better. Thanks to the block walls a lot of the cabinets had survived. That meant the food in the pantry should be alright. She was surprised how much was still frozen solid inside the deep freezer. She could smoke most of the meat, and it would last longer. What couldn't be smoked she would cook and eat.

First, she needed to take care of her daddy. His soul was gone, she needed to get his body in the ground That meant a shovel since it was too dangerous to use a tractor during the day.

The garage was made of cinder block too. Like the house, the roof it burned but quite a few things inside were still usable. With a shovel in one hand and a pick in the other, she headed to the side yard beyond the house. The ground in this area was always soft because the septic lines ran that way. It would be easier to dig there, and it wasn't like she was going to be doing laundry or taking any showers. She found a reasonably flat area and started digging.

The sun was directly overhead when she finally decided the grave was deep enough. It wasn't six feet deep, more like four, but it would have to do. She wanted to get her daddy in the ground before the aliens decided to fly over the area.

Now she had to figure out how to get him there.

Back in the garage, she remembered seeing a stack of tarps her father used to cover up the lawn equipment during the winter. She grabbed one of the heavier ones and put it in the wheelbarrow. Then she pushed the wheelbarrow around by the kitchen door. There was enough room to spread out the tarp next to his body and roll him on top of it. She hadn't noticed before but he had soiled his clothes when he died. Burying him with all that over him seemed wrong, but she had no intention of undressing her father and seeing him naked. His clothing would deteriorate long before his body did. She sighed and rolled the tarp around him, using duct tape to seal the openings.

Growing up on a farm she was familiar with death. Even though she hadn't seen any flies around him she knew they had been there. In a week or two, the maggots would start the process of returning her father to the soil. Other insects would join in.

Dragging his body across the kitchen floor was not easy. He weighed about 200 pounds. She'd heard people use the expression dead weight before but until today she had no idea what it meant. Getting him from the porch to the wheelbarrow was not going to be easy. She had parked the wheelbarrow as close as possible to the side of the porch.

Sorry about this daddy.

There was no way to get him down the steps, so she rolled him off. His body landed with a thump, causing the wheelbarrow to wobble from side to side. Then the weight settled to one side and the barrel fell over. His body rolled out.

That had been a waste of time.

She rolled the tarp back around him and drug the tarp across the grass to the hole and rolled him into the grave. One of his legs sprawled outside the tarp and she felt bad about it, but there was not a lot she could do. He was wearing the new Harley-Davidson boots mama had got him for his birthday. Daddy had spent the winter restoring an old Panhead that had belonged to his father. He painted it Candy Apple red, his favorite color. It was gorgeous. But when he set it out the sun to dry after he washed it, it had blushed and turned the prettiest shade of cotton candy pink. Without the money to repaint it, he did the only thing he could. He got his paints out and added the Pink Panther smoking a joint on the side of the tanks.

Her daddy was never anyone to mess with. One or two cocky young guys had commented about the old fart on the pink motorcycle but it had not taken long for word to get around that the old fart would whoop their asses. Daddy had been a Golden Gloves boxer in his younger days, both at home and during his two tours in

Viet Nam. No one messed with him more than once.

Since she couldn't get his body back out of the grave, she covered his body with the second tarp so she couldn't see him as she shoveled dirt into the hole. It took a lot less time to fill it back in. One day she would gather stones and make it look like a real grave.

She tried to remember the words to one of the prayers he always liked, but all she could remember was the Lord's prayer. So she asked God to look over him and Mama and Marcus and Martin.

It's crazy the thoughts that go through your head when you're burying your daddy.

It suddenly hit her that all her brother's names started with an M. That was weird. Now that she thought about it, her fathers' name was Matthew and her mom's name was Marissa. Her other brother and sister were Maddie and Michael. So why had they named her Erica?

The low mooing of the milk cow brought her attention back to the present. Carrying the shovel and hoe to the wheel barrel she rolled it back toward the barn. The old barn had collapsed on one side but like the cows, Goldie, her horse was still in the stable yard. So were mom's three goats. The fence was down and she had expected to find them missing. The barn and pasture was their safe spot, maybe they needed to feel a sense of security.

Her father had used the cab of an old box truck to hold hay and grain. It was still in pretty good shape.

So I tossed out a bale of fescue and dumped a bucket of mixed grain out for the horse and goats. Rosie the cow had her bucket and refused to share. Hopefully, they would stick around if I fed them. There was no way to lock the pasture and she wouldn't want them to be locked inside the way things were anyway. They needed a fighting chance if something happened and she did not come back.

The sun was going down so she needed to start looking for a place to hide out and get some rest. During the two days she had lain beside the dumpster, she had noticed the aliens didn't come around at night. She would smoke the meat while it was dark so the smoke would hard to locate.

The metal locker that they stored their camping equipment in was still standing against the far wall of the garage. The bug out bags contained everything she would need to survive. For now, it could wait. The old desk chair in front of daddy's worktable had a faded cushion he used to support his back. She grabbed it, along with a pair of coveralls hanging off a peg. The coveralls were too big but they were cleaner than what she had on. She stripped off her jeans and shoved them into one of the big buckets of water next to the barn. Her tee-shirt and her underwear went in next. Then she put on her daddy's coveralls. Without soap, she could not get the material clean, but she was able to get most of the blood and dirt out. Then spread them over the fence to dry in the sun.

Once she had settled everyone for the night, she picked up her tarp and cushion and headed back to what remained of the house. Her first instinct had been to go lay in the kitchen but she could hear the ghost of her father screaming *No!*

If anyone had survived they would be looking for food. Among other things. Her house would not be one of the first ones searched but she didn't want to take any chances. Opening the door to the crawlspace under the burnt house, she tossed in the pillow and two tarps, then crawled inside.

Chapter 8

The sun was just going down when Erika crawled out of the basement. There was still enough light for her to make her way into the kitchen to search for something to eat.

Maddie had not shown up. She hoped she was with Ryan in Subligna, about twenty miles south of the family farm. The valley where his family lived was so secluded cell phones didn't work and the only way you could get Internet was through a satellite system. If they had been out together when the attack occurred, Ryan would have made a run for his family. Without a way to verify she was alive; she had to keep an open mind and assume she was safe. She turned the strips of meat over she was smoking. The tough dried out meat would last much longer than fresh meat and was easier to carry.

One thing she was certain of she knew she could not stay where she was. Anyone that survived would be scavenging. Any grocery store left standing would be the first target. People looking for food and supplies would go building to building -hunting through burnouts for anything worth keeping. She needed a place that she could defend, a place off the main grid where no one would expect to find her. One thing Daddy had taught us was to always think ahead. The logical place for looters would be where food was grown. It may take a few weeks but eventually, someone would find the farm.

Inside the chest in the garage were six bug out kits. Each kit contained enough freeze-dried food to feed a person for a month. Since Maddie hadn't taken her pack she could only assume she was not coming to get it.

Goldie could easily carry the six packs. In the ravine that ran behind her house, her dad had buried several military ammo boxes. Inside each box were enough supplies to keep her alive for a week. She would leave them buried exactly where they were. She would come for them if she needed them. Instead, she concentrated on what she could use from the garage.

Hand tools were a priority. She filled the canvas bag with tools and metal cutlery, drug it the barn, and buried it, applying a liberal coating of manure filled hay scattered ashes over the dirt. No one would be able to tell it had even been touched. In the animal graveyard, she buried two ammo boxes containing anything of value that had not been destroyed by the flames.

All of the smoked meat went in the packs. Two sleeping bags and extra blanket went on the saddle skirt. After removing anything from the packs she couldn't use she had it down to four; two laced to the back of the saddle and two hooked over the saddle horn, hanging to either side of Goldie's whithers.

While waiting for the meat to smoke, she had searched through the pantry, making up an ice chest full of staples, then buried the ice chest behind the hay and grain locker in the edge of the woods. A few of her favorite canned foods were now in a pillowcase on Goldie. At the last minute, she had added a can opener.

Her brother's slingshot and ball bearings, and her extra bow and a quiver of arrows were in the bottom of the metal locker in the garage. She had no idea when her dad had put them inside. She added a collapsible animal trap to the pile and hid the other two in the rubble of the burnt-out bedroom.

The hours she spent sorting and working had given her time to think about where she was going. Her refuge needed to be convenient to the city so she could do her salvaging but in an area where no one would suspect her of hiding. It also had to be near a place where she could leave Goldie during the day. It took most of the day but she finally realized there was only one place that met all her needs.

Years ago, before the bypass was built the main road had run through the battlefield. Once the bypass was open the government had closed off the road that runs through the eastern side of the park and removed the concrete paving, allowing the scrub brush to grow back. She headed that way.

If you did not know about the old road it would be easy to miss it. As a child, she had explored every inch of the battlefield with her brothers. We all loved to fish and the creek was a favorite spot. But even better than that, when the government had removed the paving they had not bothered the two drainpipes that went beneath the road. The pipes were about six feet square. A storm had broken off a section of a tree, dumping it into the creek. It had wedged itself inside the mouth of the right side pipe. Over the years sand had built up around the tree, blocking the flow of water but the other side was still open.

Recent rains had ensured the briar thicket was too heavy for casual exploration, and unless you knew about the hidden trail, it would be easy to miss it. The new bridge was only a couple of hundred feet away and it offered better access for fishing. The curve in the creek hid the drainpipes from view.

She dropped the packs on top and took Goldie to her new home.

About a block beyond the bridge was a small pasture area beside a mobile home that had burnt last year. Someone was pasturing a bay horse there, the grass was deep and the creek edged the field, proving fresh water. Goldie would have company. By shaking the bucket of sweet feed she had brought, Erika enticed the bay close enough for her to ensure there would no problem between them. Satisfied that Goldie was as safe as possible, she headed back to her sanctuary.

At first glance, it looked like the entire pipe was full of debris. When she was twelve she had discovered that the sand on one side did not fill the drainpipe. There was a gap about a foot from the top that you could shimmy across. Five feet back it opened up, dropping the floor level four feet lower. The lower area was long enough for a person to stretch out and sleep. She had napped there several times when her brother refused to stop fishing or while a rain burst passed over. It would not stop a flood but unless the area suffered a direct hit by a tornado it would be a perfect place to hide out. One of the bug out packs, her pillowcase of comfort foods, and the sleeping bags went inside.

Now to find a place to leave the other two packs.

One was easy. Mike was a history freak and years earlier he had discovered a secret hiding spot in the stone foundation of the old covered bridge. Even if the aliens burnt the bridge they would have no reason to move the stone that covered the hidden compartment. He always figured it had been used to hide runaway slaves during the war since it was just big enough for a person to squeeze inside. It wouldn't have the most comfortable place to stay, but she doubted any of them would have complained.

She hid the final two in a stand of cedars growing beside the bypass. After picking one of the center trees she threw a rope over a limb, then used the rope to pull the backpack up into the higher boughs. A hundred feet away she hid the other. The packs olive color was so close to the evergreen color no one would know it was there. It would be hard to run across it by accident.

By now the sun was beginning to come up. Erika

knew she needed to get under cover before daylight. The aliens liked to follow the main roads but occasionally they would fly over some of the less inhabited areas like the park. Somehow they could find anyone hiding despite how well the spot was camouflaged. With any luck at all, the cement, sand, and dirt would prevent the machine they used from getting a good reading. As the sun began to rise over the treetops she slid into her new home.

Chapter 9

Erika wrapped a strip of a blanket around the collar of the old military pea coat. Just a week earlier she had been wearing long sleeve but no coat was needed. Today she had on three pairs of socks, and the wool coat she had taken off the dummy in the basement of the Military Surplus store. October had turned cold overnight, and by the look of the dark grey clouds, it could snow before the week was out.

The sharp whistle rup-rup sound froze Erika in her tracks. It was moving fast; the whistle was getting louder.

With no idea which way they were heading she did the only logical thing, drop down in a gutter and pull a space blanket over her. If they had not spotted her moving around, they would have no reason to stop and do a ground search.

She had discovered the space blanket's ability to disrupt their search equipment by accident. She had been searching through the basement underneath the ruins of the old military supply store by the park when she heard the sound of footsteps. In a panic she had shimmied a table and pressed her body up against the wall, making herself as small as possible. Several of the aliens came down the stairs. They had a square metal box in their hands and were moving it around the room as if they were looking for something…or someone. She was certain they would find her.

Instead, they had passed by the table she was hiding beneath and began moving things away from the opposite corner. Cowering behind a stack of newspapers and boxes was an old man. How long he had been there she didn't know. Despite being in bad shape, he fought with his assailants, kicking, punching, and cursing them as they drug him from his hiding spot. As the aliens pulled him toward the stairs he shouted aloud, "Stay hidden. They can't find you. Something near you is blocking their machine. They hunt by body heat. Their vision is weak! If you don't move they won't find you. Stay hidden!" He continued to shout random things as they marched him out to the airship. She could hear him shouting warnings for some time until it faded in the distance.

Erika remained where she was for over an hour thinking about what the old man had said. What had blocked the signal? Maybe it was something in the boxes? One was open so she checked the contents. Inside were cheap Chinese 'Space-blankets', the kind of infomercial product they advertised on late-night television that no one paid any attention to. She had one in her bug out bag. There had to be twenty unopened boxes beside the three on the table. On a nearby shelf was a stack of disposable weight loss suits made of the same metallic material. Was it possible? She knew the chemical coating kept body heat in. It was like a portable mini, the kind rich people paid a lot of money for. If they were tracking people by body heat as the old man said, that would make sense.

She had already noticed the aliens often missed you if you stayed very still. They were attracted to movement. Their hearing was better than their vision which made sense. Humans who wore glasses could often hear better than those with perfect eyesight.

She put one of the sauna suits on under her clothes, grabbed a couple of space blankets, and went out to test her theory. Being out in daylight made her nervous, so she had her escape plan mapped out just in case. There was a manhole in the middle of Chickamauga Avenue that had a ladder inside. Heavy metal pipes ran in four directions from the base of the concrete barrel, and all four were more than big enough for her to crawl through. She had discovered them by accident while hiding from the aliens during the weeks after the attack. There was a locking bar on the metal cover that she would use if she had the time, if not she doubted the Kurs could land the aircar and climb down the manhole before she could escape through one of the pipes.

Traffic over the area was regular, so she didn't have to wait long before she got to test her theory. She stood on the top rung of the ladder in plain view and waited to see if they spotted her. No human could miss the shiny metallic space blanket, but the aliens did not see things the way humans did. Her hands were shaking, fear made it difficult to remain standing in the open as the Kurs drew closer.

They didn't even slow down.

In the next few weeks, she tested several variants of the outfit and none of them failed to provide the necessary protection. The space blankets had given her hope.

Chapter 10

Scattered flurries of snow drifted across the heat fractured floor of the building. It was cold enough to stick, so she needed to hurry. Erika finished digging through unburnt boxes in the back of Tractor Supply. Luck had been with her for a change. One a shelf back in a corner, untouched by the fire, she had found an unopened box of assorted vegetable seeds. Inside were several hundred packages, enough to supply everyone she knew with seed.

Since the initial attack, her priorities had shifted. She'd rethought everything she originally believed was necessary to survive and cut it back to real essentials. Her needs were simple and easily met. Most of the extras she passed on to the survivors she met. She had also set up multiple food caches inside safe houses scattered around the area in case she found someone that needed help. There were still people scattered around. Most alone or in small family groups. I had run across several down in the Cove living in the basement of a burnt building. Another group lived at the bottom of the ravine at Cloudland Canyon. There was a small cave there that the aliens had not located. It was only big enough for two or three people but they squeezed in two adults and two kids whenever they heard the whistle.

Today had been hard.

After delivering a load of supplies to the small community being built down in the Cove, she had been riding back toward her home when anguished screams caught her attention.

She stopped and strung her bow, took the safety off his gun then rode slowly in the direction of the woman's screams. She could have been galloping, no one would have noticed.

At the back of a burnt-out drug store, a small group of men was standing near a fire they had built in a dumpster. Edging Goldie closer, she winced as a burly dark-haired man backhanded a young woman, sending her to the ground. The woman struggled back to her feet and ran toward him, screaming "stop!".

It was too dark to see what happened. The woman's screams were suddenly cut off.

Holding her bow ready, Erika walked Goldie toward the back of the building. So far, she had counted four people, three men, and the woman. As she moved closer to the fire, she was able to see the woman better. Despite it being cold enough to snow, she was naked, lying on the ground near the dumpster. As she got closer to the flickering light she was to see the glisten of liquid along the base of her throat. The woman was no longer a concern. The child was.

A little girl, maybe six years old was crying and begging for someone to stop hurting her. The three men were passing a bottle of whiskey between them as they took turns. No one was listening to her pathetic cries. Except for Erika.

Nocking an arrow, she sent it through the neck of the man on the ground by the child. His head flew back, and he collapsed forward, choking and coughing as bright red blood bubbled into his mouth, running in scarlet trickles down each side of his chin into his blonde beard. He tried to pull the arrow out, but the barbed head would not come through the muscle.

The skinny, bald-headed drunkard seemed surprised when he saw her. "Now why you gonna go and shoot ol Mark? We could've had a little fun. Now I got to kill you." He began shuffling her way, taking short wobbly steps while trying to remain upright.

Her second arrow struck his breastbone, cutting a narrow furrow across his chest, before striking the metal bin behind him. The force of the ricochet threw him to the ground, but he was already scrambling to his feet. He wasn't moving fast but soon adrenaline would kick in, overcome the alcohol haze and he would become a problem.

Erika decided the remaining man was a bigger threat.

"Crazy bitch, I'm gonna slit you open like a pig." The third man, clearly the alpha of the group, was much heavier, bearded, and covered with tattoos. He ran toward her, brandishing a heavy hunting knife. With no time to reload an arrow, she drew her pistol, putting two slugs in his chest. He managed a few wavering steps before falling. He wasn't dead but it would not be long. He could wait.

The injured man began backing away, muttering slurry pleas for mercy.

Erika's gaze went to the mother and the child, and her eyes darkened.

The injured man saw his death in her eyes. Realizing his knife was not going to help in a gunfight, he turned to run. She carefully lined up the barrel and shot him…twice. He fell face-first into the muddy slush.

Erika was shaking as she slid off Goldie and moved to help the little girl. Kneeling beside her battered body, she saw there was nothing she could do to save her. The ground below her was soaked in blood, way too much for such a tiny child to lose. Tears streamed down Erika's face as she held her close and rocked her until she faded away to join her mother.

She could see vultures flying above. Before long coyotes and other scavengers would begin to gather. They could have the men, but not the mother and daughter. She threw everything that would burn into the dumpster, breaking the sofa and a few wooden pallets that the men had been using as furniture into smaller pieces. She figured it was about half full. It would have to do.

"God. They didn't deserve this. Keep them with

you. Amen." She didn't know any real prayers, so it would have to be enough. She felt bad as the woman's head hit the side of the dumpster as she was pushing her body through the door. She was more careful with the little girl. The child lay in her mother's arms atop the debris. To make sure they burned well, she poured the rest of the whiskey over their bodies, smiling as the fire flared up around them. Once she was sure it was burning well she shut the side door, leaving a small slot for air to funnel through. She cracked open the top, propping it open with an old tire rim. The fire was burning well, and smoke began to drift upward. It was time to move on, the Kurs would be there to investigate soon.

She mounted Goldie and headed for the farm.

***

Three months had passed since the invasion and Erika was nothing like the scared teenage girl that stumbled away from the skating rink. There was not much of the area she had not explored. Occasionally she came across scattered groups of survivors. Most were the same, skinny, scared, and desperate, digging through the burnt-out hulks of their former suburban neighborhoods in hopes of locating anything still safe to eat.

One day she had chased chickens, gathering a dozen or so to release in the pasture near her family home. No one had ever come into the hidden valley, and there had been no survivors in any of the homes nearby. The goats and the cow roamed free around the valley but she had dropped a tree across the access road. The small herd had grown by a few more goats and another cow. Her guess was they had followed her animals when they returned home at night. She had discovered several places barns with bags of grain and made a regular run to pick up feed, at every opportunity. The animals had food and they happily supplied her with milk and eggs.

An old copy of Mother Earth News had provided instructions for making butter and she had rigged up a churn. It would be a few weeks before she would know if the cheese press worked. It had also had directions for making a water wheel for power and other interesting tidbits of information that had not seemed important to her before the invasion.

The possible snowstorm meant extra hay in all the racks since any grass remaining would be covered. The goats would eat things the cow couldn't, so she gave them all extra grain. She had closed the burnt section with canvas from a tent she had found in a basement. There were no poles, so she wondered why they had kept it, as she drug it outside and sliced it into sections. It wasn't perfect but it kept the wind off the animals. The door was left open enough for the two horses and the cow to get in and out. Even if the water froze in the buckets, there were several creeks around the valley that they could reach. They would be okay.

The roller skates lying in the corner made her smile

and she decided what the hell. It would take a little longer to skate down the roads but it would be fun. Five minutes later she was skating along, smiling for the first time since she had found the mother and daughter. As she approached the old railroad trestle she realized this would be the first time she had traveled down this road since the invasion.

She was surprised to see several buildings still standing. The road wound its way through a heavily wooded area, and ancient oaks shielding the road from view. Since it was not near one of the main highways, the aliens might have missed the area completely. She had certainly forgotten about it.

Making a mental note to come back and search through the houses, she continued skating toward the park. Just before the street she was following merged with the road that passed through the park she heard the whistle. She could see it approaching the road ahead, moving back and forth in a grid pattern. They had to be looking for someone. She wondered who they had locked in on. After two months she didn't bother hiding when she heard the whistle, instead, she simply sat down and waited for them to pass by. She sat down on the side of the road and pulled off her skates, replacing them with the tennis shoes she had tied around her neck. The house nearby had a covered porch so she left the skates under a ceramic urn. It was doubtful they would bother burning anything nearby, it had been over a month since the last time she recalled an explosion. She sat down in a rocking chair on the porch to wait until they had finished their search.

That's when she saw him. He was creeping along the side of Mr. Patterson's' tire shop. The building on the corner had been partially destroyed during the original days of destruction when they first landed. One side of the burnt-out buildings was still standing and he was crouching against what was left of the wall. He was wearing camouflage clothing similar to what the military wore, which stood out against the white paint, making it easy for her to watch what happened. Seeing armed men in camos gave her hope that more of humanity had survived. Unfortunately, the Kurs had picked him up on their sensors and were not going to stop the hunt until he was found. The small transport had landed and two of the creatures were searching on foot. It was only a matter of time before he was found.

Before she could decide to try and help him, the Kurs blew up what was left of the building. They must have hit the inground tanks because it set off a fiery inferno. One of the Kurs was knocked backward by the blast concussion, causing him to drop the scanner. He was helped back to the aircar by his partner. He must have been hurt because they stopped searching for the man and flew away.

As soon as they had moved out of sight, she rushed toward the burning building, only to fall back as a blast of intense heat hit her smack in the face. Whoever he was, he was not going to be moving away from that inferno on his own. The blocks had protected him from most of the blast, but there was nothing to protect him from the heat.

She began working her way closer to his body, crouching low to keep her face protected from any sparks that might fly off the burning building. She was almost crawling by the time she reached his foot. He was lying face down in the dirt. She checked his neck, ensuring a pulse before she moved him.

"This is going to suck but it's the only way I can do it." Grasping his foot with both hands she began backing away from the flames, dragging his inert body behind her. He began to mumble after a few tugs but did not regain awareness of his surroundings. This was good since she wasn't ready to fight with him and drag him at the same time. Once the temperature dropped enough that she could take a break, she dropped down on the ground beside him.

He lay in the same position as when she dropped him, only the regular lift and fall of his chest showed he was still alive. His face was filthy, his hair and beard covered in smoke and grey ashes, making him look much older than she had thought he was. From the way he had been moving, she had guessed him to be a few years older than her, in his late teens or early twenties.

There was still enough water in her canteen to

wipe away some on the soot and still have enough for him when he woke.

Her attempt to clean his face must have broken through the fog in his brain. His eyes cracked open. Her appearance must have startled him because he swung his gun her way.

"Whoa. I'm not the enemy. They are gone. We have a few minutes before we need to move. They could come back."

He didn't seem convinced, but even in my mismatched get up it was still obvious I was human so he took the barrel off me, but he kept it in his hand.

I handed him the canteen. "Drink some water. You lost a little blood."

"Do you think they will come back?"

I'm certain they will be back. The only reason they left is one of the Kurs got hurt. They had to get him to their version of a doctor."

"Kurs?"

"Kurs, aliens, whatever you want to call them. They have been gone long enough to reach the mothership and start back this way. If you think you can walk, we need to move."

He groaned as he pushed his body off the ground, but he was able to get to his feet.

"Follow me. I know a safe spot not far from here". She handed him her space blanket. Wrap this around you. It blocks body heat. They won't be able to track you. It won't stop it completely but it might trick the machine long enough to reach safety. Hurry."

For once she had found a man who did not argue. He wrapped the blanket around his body and followed her. He was limping on his left side, and she could see fresh blood on his thigh. One of their lasers must have caught him a glancing blow. He was lucky; if it had hit him full on he would have lost his leg. One of her safe houses was nearby but with him hurt it was going to take longer than she liked to reach it. She decided to head for the old Burger King instead. It had been built during the 1980s, back when they would put a basement under the building for storage. There was nothing left of the building but heat warped metal. She had covered the basement entrance with charred scrap and so far no one had discovered it. It was only a few streets over but she could already hear the whistle.

"Damn! There is no way we can make it before the Kurs arrive." Instead, she headed for an overgrown evergreen bush. It was going to be close. "Quick. We need to crawl under here. There is a drainage ditch under the bush. Lay down, Pull the blanket over you."

"What about you."

"My body is covered but you will have to share a bit for my head." She gave him a little shove so he would move faster.

He slid into the ditch. She made sure his body was covered and lay down in front of him, facing his way.

"What about my feet?" he asked.

"Just stay still. I've done this hundreds of times. If they spot the heat from out feet it must register as a small animal, like a cat or a dog. They never bother checking them." Usually, they didn't. Once she had seen them burn a wild dog but it had been growling at the Kur. She could see the doubt reflected in his expression but she knew he was not in any position to argue the point. The aliens were getting smarter, adapting their techniques for hunting, just as we did as we learned more about them. Leaving two in the air and two on the ground was now standard operating procedure. So was the grid pattern they were flying.

We stopped talking as the aircar landed and the pair on the ground walked in the direction of our tentative hiding spot. I could feel him tense as they approached the thicket. He stayed silent, only flinch-ing as one of the aliens shot at a cat running across an open stretch of ground. He missed, and the second alien made a hissing sound that she had come to believe was what passed as laughter among them. Satisfied the cat had been the shadow on the machine, the aliens returned to the aircar and continued the hunting pat-tern without giving the bushes a second glance. We remained silent for quite some time after they flew off.

Erika could feel the tension leaving his body the further they flew from the area. It was only after they finally gave up the hunt and returned to the transport ship that we broke the silence.

"I thought you were crazy," he said. "I'm glad I was wrong."

"That's nice to know. Someone goes out of their way to save your ass and you thank them by calling them crazy."

"Look. It's not personal. This invasion has changed a lot of people and not always in the way you expect. Some get stronger. Some go stone-cold killers. Others lose any part of sanity they may have started with. For all I knew, you were loony as the rest of them." He smiled and she suddenly realized how close their faces were.

"We should head for cover. That won't be the only team out searching." She rose to her hands and knees and began crawling out of the bush. He was right behind her.

"My unit is probably wondering what happened to me. The standing orders are to return to base before daybreak. I need to let them know I am okay."

"You need to shut up and follow me. That burn on your leg needs to be treated before it gets infected. You can let them know you are safe once the sun goes down." She stood up and began to make her way through the brambles.

After a few seconds, he followed her, holding the space blanket overhead to prevent it from tearing on the branches.

She didn't wait to see if he followed. If he wanted to head off in the other direction at least he had some idea of how to stay hidden now. She looked carefully around before moving to the next pile of rubble. Over the past six months, she had found the best possible way to travel around what remained of the town. She had three secure hideouts that she was relatively sure no one knew about. Two others were good in emergencies but they had been discovered and cleared of anything of value. She had set up over a hundred similar hiding spots with caches within a day's walk of the battlefield. Most of the supplies had come from houses and garages that had not been completely destroyed by the invaders. Some she buried. Some were in trees. Others were established in underground bunkers located in the basements of burnt outs. It irked her to share the Burger King location but if there were military still around she wanted to know more. Keeping him alive was worth the gamble. The only nearby location with a med kit was too far for him to walk. He was losing to much blood.

When she reached the old Burger King she looked around once more to ensure no one was watching. Most humans had switched to sleeping during the day and moved about at night. She could spot one of the aliens' transports long before it got near enough to see her. But they were adapting and it would only take minutes for help to arrive if one spotted them moving around above ground.

"Help me with this," she said as she shifted what remained of a huge commercial range hood to the side. The opening was only a few feet wide, but by sliding on her backside she could wiggle inside. She indicated for him to go in first. The hood was balanced against a piece of metal. Once she started into the opening she let it down behind her. Other than a tiny sliver of light leaking through the cracks, it was pitch black inside. That didn't bother her.

"Don't move around. Give me a second to get a light." She folded a thick piece of rubber down to block out any light from outside.

Jake shuffled across the dark room. Despite her warning, he tripped in the darkness, falling forward onto his hands.

"I take it your mother didn't name you Grace," she snapped, irritated that he hadn't waited as she asked.

"Let me take you into one of our compounds and let you try to maneuver in the dark. I doubt you would do any better."

She didn't answer, but from out of the darkness surrounding him came a sound that resembled a pig's snort more than a laugh. Seconds later he felt her hand on his arm. She helped him back to his feet and guided him to a box she knew was sitting a few feet away.

"Sit still."

She made her way across the room, picked up a lighter, and used it to light a candle. It was an exceptionally cold day, but inside the basement room, it was almost comfortable.

Erika pointed to an office chair next to a small prep table. " Sit there. Take off your pants."

"Shouldn't I buy you dinner first?" As his eyes adjusted to the light Jake got his first real look at the girl who had come to his rescue. She was probably about average in height and maybe a little on the slender side, but that could have something to do with the way she had been living. Food wasn't easily found in the dark. A long lean body that curved in exactly the right places, a really cute face, and wavy red hair that reached her shoulders.

Erika caught the change in his tone and stared at him. "Ha-ha. Funny man. Just take them off so I can clean that burn." She moved a half-filled box of ketchup packets and pulled a plastic medicine kit the box was hiding from beneath the shelving unit. Then she opened a can labeled rat poison and pulled out one of those battery-operated emergency lights.

He arched an eyebrow.

"I don't like using these unless I need a lot of light. No idea where I can find more batter-ies."

He didn't comment, removing his pants by sliding them down toward his ankles.

She was surprised to see the black boxer

briefs, expecting regulation tightie-whities. He sat down on top of the table leaving the chair for her.

She did her best to ignore the obvious bulge in his boxers. The burn looked painful. The edges were blackened and the skin was bubbling and wet. This was not going to be a good experience for him. The second day after she settled into the drainage tunnel she had hunted through the wreckage of the hospital. While searching the remains of the repair shop she stumbled upon a clear passage from the into the basement into the lower level of the main building. She had been looking for food. Instead, she found the main pharmacy storage room. Getting in wasn't easy, she had to chop her way through the door keypad with an ax and lever it open with a crowbar. Inside was a treasure trove of basic supplies. The hospital dispensary was in shambles, shelves were overturned and broken, glass shattered, plastic containers smashed, their precious contents spilled across the floor. A lot of medications were still intact, vials still whole, still usable and she concentrated on packing those first. Surgical kits and lacerations equipment were among her next choices. Thanks to a pill identifier paperback she found in a desk drawer, she was able to identify antibiotics and pain meds. She also gathered any anesthetic's she could find, both spray and injectables. She easily filled two backpacks. Every kind of bandage available went into the packs. Over the next few months, she returned several times to collect anything usable. She figured other survivors must have discovered the entrance as the pickings grew slimmer each time she returned. The last time she tried, she discovered that the invaders had destroyed the remaining section of the building and the repair shop.

He appeared surprised when she opened the surgical pack and removed the spray analgesic. He visibly relaxed as the spray-coated the burnt area, taking the edge off the immediate pain.

The sedative she gave him had to help. She had no idea how he had handled the pain while running from the aliens. Maybe adrenaline? He watched as she filed a syringe.

"Once I get this local injected it will be even better."

Instead of answering he picked up the empty bottle and read the label before allowing her to inject his hip.

"So much for trust."

He grinned. "As you said, I have trust issues, but I trust you as much as I trust anyone I've only known for an hour. Not that I trust anyone." He did his best to ignore the waspish sarcasm in her voice, blaming it on pain, fatigue, and her red hair. She didn't comment on his answer. That surprised him, most women would have felt the need to defend themselves, taking it as personal instead of a direct reference to his feelings.

"I am going to need to cut away the dead edges. That's blackened skin will not heal. Before I start, do you have any allergies?"

"None that I know of."

He watched as I filled the syringe with 2 more ccs of the analgesic and ensured there was no air before beginning. She injected a small amount in several locations, making sure she got the area adjutant to the worse burns. She waited for the usual 30 seconds and tested by making a small snip. He didn't notice it. Satisfied that the tissue was as numb as possible under the circumstances she began to abrade the burn. Most of the dead tissue came off while she was cleaning the wound. That meant she only needed four additional cuts to take away the heavily charred areas. She was happy to see most of the damage was surface burns. Deep tissue damage was harder to heal

and often left scar tissue that restricted movement. With proper care, he would not face
that. That's when it clicked into my mind she
had no idea who he was.

She glanced at his uniform. *Williams.
Hmm.* " Well, Williams. I think that's got it. I'm
going to add an antibiotic spray and cover it
up. She tossed him a 4 pack of pills. This is for
pain. Don't take them until you need them. I
will get you antibiotics to take. She passed him
some burn cream and a few gauze pads. "Use
these when you can't leave it uncovered." She
paused. " I feel strange calling you Williams."

"Jacob," he said. "Well, Jake is what most
call me."

"Erika."

"You are not like most of the girls I know.
You scare me, Ericka."

"Good. It shows you're not the typical
jarhead soldier."

"What makes you think I'm a soldier. I could have
found this outfit at a surplus store."

"You could have. But you locate, log, and classify
everything you see. It reminds me of my brother. He was
the same way."

"Was? The Kurs get him"

"No idea. He was at Dobbins the night they attacked. I believe if there was a way he could get home

he would have made it by now."

"Have you been alone the entire time?"

"I have my dog. He's good company. He doesn't talk much but he's a great listener." There was no way she was going to tell him about the other survivors. Chances are he was exactly what he seemed to be, a soldier who survived the initial attack. But risking her own life was one thing, risking everyone else was out of the question.

If you say so. "We have a small community, mostly the men in my unit and a few others that survived the initial attack. We were having a company camp out down near Raccoon Mountain. We got everyone inside the caves. Luckily, they don't seem to be able to read our language. They blew up the gift shop but didn't collapse the cave."

"That's good." Still wasn't going to give anyone up. She watched as he yawned, his eyes beginning to close. The pills were kicking in. He should be out for a while. She needed to get some sleep. She managed to get him off the table over to an exercise pad she found in the karate studio. Once he stretched out he was sound asleep.

Chapter 11

Jake awoke to a monster of a headache while lying on a pallet in a candlelit room he did not recognize. The cute redhead looked vaguely familiar but he was certain he had not slept there for the usual reasons. Gradually, the events of the previous day began to crystalize and he realized he owed the woman his life. Stretching for a moment, he began to get up, then stopped as a sharp pain made him wince and sit back down. He rubbed his temples, noticing that one hand came away smeared with blood. Now curious, he began examining the bandage above his ear.

"Leave it alone," Erika snapped, slapping his hand away from the laceration above his ear. "You will get it bleeding again. It's just butterflied shut."

"Don't remember getting that one. Come to think about it, I don't remember much after the laser hit the building. Some vague images about lying in a ditch, and you saving my ass from the aliens. Then it fades out."

"That was the idea, you would not stay still until I knocked you out. I got tired of arguing with you." She could see a range of expressions passing over his face, frustration, doubt, pain. Then he gritted his teeth and scrambled to his feet. The muscles in his forehead twitched, and she could see him trying not to show how much it hurt.

"I could use one of those red pills now." He was breathing heavily and favoring his leg as he walked over to the table, but she could tell he felt much better than he felt before he fell asleep. He sat down in the chair he refused to use the day before. He had watched without comment as she put together a camp stove from parts hidden around the room and a propane cylinder, poured water from a bottle into a pot, and set it on the flame to boil. "Is that coffee?"

"Instant, but I have sugar and creamer. It's not too bad." She lifted the pot off the camp stove, pouring the water into two oversized mugs she had found while digging through one of the burnt-out stores. She added a liberal amount of instant creamer and sugar to her mug and stirred it well. Then she offered the spoon to Jake.

He shook his head. "I drink it black. Do you know what you could get in trade for this? It's like gold back at the compound."

"I guess I'm rich then. I found a case of the stuff and rarely drink it. What I would really like is a coke. I tried to stretch mine but it's hard to give up an addiction you love. They were gone before a month had passed."

"We might be able to hook you up if you would consider giving up some coffee."

"Well, I can't offer you eggs and bacon, but I do have some muffins and jerky. The cooking facilities here are rather limited."

"Don't tell me, you found a bakery too?"

"Nope. Just some of the store brand prepacked mix bags and milk cooked in a frying pan. More like thick pancakes than anything."

"Milk?"

"Cow and goats. A small herd. Nothing special." She passed him a thick slice and a chunk of jerky.

"Woman you are rich. Wanna get married?" His grin lit up his face and it made her furious that he would consider her a source of amusement. She was tempted to see if he would keep smiling if she said yes.

"I think I need to keep my options open. Now that I know there are others around, I might get lucky and find out Chris Helmsworth is available. No, wait, make that Jason Momoa."

"You like tall, dark, and handsome, huh? I got that covered, you know. Forget the washed-up actors."

She grinned. "I'll keep it in mind if the other two are not available." Things got quiet for a moment as they both tried to decide what to say. It had been a long time since she had been alone with a man that was not one of her brothers. She wasn't afraid of him, just unsure. That was unusual enough. She fought to keep the smile from her face as Jake wolfed down the last two slices of the skillet muffin.

Finally jake broke the silence. "Thanks for breakfast. What do we do now?"

"We wait," she said calmly.

Wait? Trying not to sound exasperated, he asked, "For what?"

"Until the sun goes down of course. The Kurs are blind as Kurs in the dark." She was surprised none of the soldiers in his unit had noticed the vision issues. Like most of their ilk, he was a typical by the books recruit, not willing to look too far outside the standard operating procedure guidelines.

"They can't see at night? Dang, that's why they never seem to come around after dark. We thought it might be a religious stricture or something cultural."

"I have no idea if they even believe in religion. Now that you bring it up, the Kurs may be mindwiping the prisoners and turning them into perfect little zombie workers. Humans are obedient up to a point, and then all loyalty and discipline fail and they become radical rebels. I can't imagine the Kurs want someone around that dreams of fifty ways to kill your owner every night."

Jake broke out laughing. "Kurs, lol. You called them that before. Why not Bats if they are blind?"

"No wings. No ears. They look like some mad scientist took three of four different animals and mixed them into one beast. My dad would drown them at birth. He never liked mongrels and called them Kurs."

"Kurs is as good a name for them as any we have come up with. So, if we have to wait for sundown, what should we do?"

She could hear the slight hint of suggestion in his

tone but choose to ignore it. "We are gonna be here a while. Wanna play cards. I get tired of playing solitaire." She pulled a card carousel complete with chips from a shelf near her hand. "You deal first."

"Before we start, you are not going to take advantage of me, are you?" He grinned, wiggling his eyebrows suggestively.

She rolled her eyes. "Only in your dreams soldier. Pretend I'm just one of the guys."

He looked doubtful but shuffled the cards and dealt out seven apiece. "Should we use the chips."

"No need. There's just two of us." She picked up her card and arranged them by suit, before drawing a card. It didn't play with anything in her hand so she discarded it. "You are military. Are you going to get in trouble for being away so long?"

"No. I'm a scout. It's my job to check the situation out and find out as much about the aliens as I can. No one will miss me for a few days."

"A scout, huh. That means you know a lot about our new neighbors. Do you know what the Kurs are? Or why they are here?"

"Not really. They surprised us just like everyone else. By the time we identified the approaching spacecraft as dangerous, it was too late. We had communication with other units for the first few days. Then we lost that."

"Lost it?" She understood the surprise part. They

were all surprised. Somehow she had managed to shove all the painful recollections of her friends and family down below her conscious memory. It was not acceptance; it was a conscious refusal to deal with their deaths. One day she might let down her walls enough to grieve. But not until the Kurs were gone.

"Our commander believes they targeted the bases first. Radio towers, satellites, anything that looked like a business went next."

"So why didn't we fight back?" She couldn't imagine her brother standing back and watching everything he cared about being destroyed without making some effort to stop it.

"We did. We hit them with every weapon we had. Nothing could get through the force field. We even tried a nuke. Not here, in Hawaii. They waited until the fallout ended, and then flew away as if nothing had happened."

"All those people dead. That's so sad."

"They were dead already. Or at least most of the were. All for nothing."

"Nothing about it makes sense. They killed so many people. Then suddenly stopped and began rounding up all the survivors. Why? It crazy."

His eyes darkened. "They are not taking all the survivors. Just the healthy young women and a few young men. No older men or women, no children, those overweight, or with some type of disability… they kill them all."

For a second she felt the reflexive lump in her throat, along with the impulse to scream and cry out before she shoved it all back and waited with bated breath for him to say something. When he didn't, she took a deep breath and asked the first thing that popped into her head. "So what are they? Slavers?"

Jake had noticed her brief blanking out and wondered if she suffered from seizures. She seemed to have it under control but it was something he needed to keep in mind in case he needed to help. "We don't know. We have tried every method of communication available. They do not respond to any of the attempts."

"It should be dark soon and we can take off. Just promise to keep this place a secret," she said. "It's hard to find supplies to restock after they get raided."

"You seem to have it all under control. Something I wanted to ask you. You did not cover anything but your head when the Kurs flew over. Why did they miss you?"

She stood up and began to unbutton her jeans. Jake wasn't sure what he was supposed to do, so he sat quietly and waited. She removed her shirt and pants, exposing a silvery metallic top and bottom, made of a similar material to the space blankets. "These were designed to make you sweat. They keep heat in, so I figured they would work the same way as a space blanket. They are not as good, but they don't tear as easily. I sewed a layer of the blanket on the front and back of the shirt and the front and back of the pants. I also lined a balaclava with the blanket. I roll it down over my face. It's in my pack, I didn't have time to get it out earlier."

"That's smart. There is a base inside Chattanooga, next to Findley ballfield. That's where they keep most of the prisoners before they load them into the ships. We tried to save a few but none of our weapons hurts them. Whatever they use for protection, it prevents weapons from touching them. A flame thrower works but you have to get close enough to use it and their lasers cut us down before we get into range. With suits like that, we could get close enough to the mother ship to see if there are any weaknesses we could exploit. I'm sure the Captain will tell everyone to be looking for them once I tell him what you discovered."

"What about grenades or rocket launchers?"

"Can't breach their force field. Nothing we have worked. Our pilots tried shooting them out of the sky. I watched the planes destroyed one by one. Nothing stops them. Unless we figure out a way to destroy the ships, humanity doesn't have much of a chance."

She decided to change the subject. " I'm hungry. What about you."

"He grinned. "Starving. I didn't want to mention it because you have done so much already. Breakfast was great but it's been a while and I am really hungry."

She shook her head, muttering something about men and bottomless stomachs. Then she moved to a different section of the room and pushed a deep fryer to one side. Underneath it was a food cache. Twenty minutes later he was digging into canned roast beef and gravy over rice and canned peaches. You would have thought he hadn't eaten in months. We split a second bottle of water with lemonade mix with our meal. It was almost normal. Almost.

Chapter 12

"So you are telling me a teenage girl discovered a way to avoid the ALF 21739 searches when all our best came up with nothing?" Captain Jeffers tried to keep the excitement off of face as he listened to what Jake had to say. This was the first positive thing he had heard since the alien invasion had begun. If it proved to be true, it could be the tipping point he had hoped for.

"Yes sir. She is a very unusual young woman. You would not believe what she has done. Since watching her family business burn she set up a series of safe houses all over the county. All are fully stocked with food, medical supplies, clothing, extra space blankets. She even wears a set of reflective clothing under her regular clothes. She made them out of sweat-suits and the space blankets. She is virtually invisible to the aliens. As long as she stays still they fly right past her."

"So… this space blanket. It's the same emergency blanket we pass out by the thousands during disasters. Don't we have some of them?"

"Yes sir. There is a case of a thousand in stores. Maybe two."

"Then have someone drag out a sewing machine. Sew up a few suits and let's try them out. Full coverage. Make hoods to go under a balaclava. Make socks to wear inside the boots. I want the heat leakage down to as close to zero as possible. If there is a way to move about without being seen, I want it implemented immediately. Ask for volunteers and test the limits before we send out the info around the country."

"Yes sir." Jake walked across the room to address the young attaché working at a nearby table. "Corporal Thomas."

The young man jumped up and stood at attention. "Sir."

"Take two men and find me a sewing machine. Surely one or two survived the destruction. Captain wants three suits made by daybreak. Go door to door through the rubble if you have to. Surely, there has to be one that still works somewhere."

"What if there are none?"

" Then we have to improvise. If you don't find a machine, the men are going to hand sew them. Use super glue to make sure they don't fall apart. I expect you to use the brain God gave you and find me a machine or everyone in the unit will be sewing instead of sleeping."

"Yes sir. At once sir. He walked across the break room and addressed four men playing cards. You four! Drop those cards and help me find a sewing machine. Take all the Gators. This is a top priority. The captain wants three men suited up and ready by sunup."

No one argued. Time was already running down.

***

"Jake. What was this girl *really* like? Smokin?" Trey

made a quick hip thrust before Jenkins threw a pillow at him and destroyed the image he was trying to portray.

"Cute, nice body. Not a model, but nothing you would be ashamed of being seen with." He thought about Ericka and realized he had enjoyed his time with her. He wouldn't mind having another chance to see her again. True, she wasn't his usual type, most of them were barely able to read a menu. Her age might be a problem, she said she was only sixteen, but then again, she seemed more mature than most of the women in the cave. It wasn't as if he was that much older than her, he was about to turn twenty, only three years difference. His father had been five years older than his mother. Besides, all the dating rules were forgotten after the invasion.

He thought about what Trey had asked. Erika was not the typical definition of hot. She was pretty but not beautiful, still, there was something about the way she smiled that lit up the room. Definitely lighter-skinned than any of the women he usually dated. Most of the women in the cave were Latino or mixed black and white, though there were two older black women among the nurses. The three white women were all dark-haired, late twenties, and married to men in the unit. They had been camping in the park by the lake. When the attack happened, they grabbed the kids and ran for the cave. The three nurses had been taking the tour. It was an eclectic mix, but everyone got along well.

It was easy for him to picture Erika; she had that fiery auburn hair and freckles. Her eyes were green, bright green like clover in the spring, and sprinkled with flecks of gold. Not dark enough to be called emerald, or light like moss or lettuce. His mama had green eyes and freckles like her. He had always wondered if that was what had drawn his father to his mother. Thinking about his father always made him sad. He was only seven when his father was shot by a member of a rival street gang in the projects. Rico had been a banger. Most of his friends hadn't had a father in the home so it had not bothered him once the initial pain had stopped. It had not been easy growing up mixed in Chattanooga but things had calmed down after the race riots ended. He had enlisted at eighteen, spent two years active duty, then registered for college, and was looking forward to starting UT Chattanooga that fall. Then the invasion changed everything.

He wondered if anyone would ever care about race again. There were so few humans left alive, worrying about what race you were, seemed petty. It was the human race against the Kurs. Nothing else mattered.

Erika made him think there might be a future to look forward to. His lips quirked, remembering how surprised he was when he opened his pack after he got back to the compound and found two of the sweat-suits and a dozen space blankets inside. She had no way of knowing they had boxes of the space blankets, so it was a real gesture of kindness. He liked that.

He considered grabbing a few hours of sleep when Trey knocked on the door and interrupted that thought. The Captain had called a meeting and most of his unit was already there. Everyone had assumed someone else had told Jake, so he was the last one to arrive.

Jake blanked his expression as he felt the weight of his captain's eyes boring into him. He was explaining Jake's discovery, explaining the Space Blankets could be a major breakthrough and asking for volunteers to test the limits.

He asked Jake to join him at the front of the room and continue the conversation talking.

Jake gathered his thoughts before beginning. "Erika wasn't a hundred percent certain the outfit would work for everyone. She was convinced that when she wore the outfit the Kurs could not find her. She would lie down on the ground in plain sight and they would miss her completely. The cheap metal-coated plastic disrupted their sensors. Erika had a sensible approach to dealing with the Kurs, as she called the aliens. She had discovered the aliens were like bats but instead of sonar, they used heat thermography to see. She suggested the Kurs had been on Earth before and were possibly the source of the fairy tales about demons. Any questions?"

Is Kur the official name now?"

"No. Since it is easier to say Kurs than Alien Life Form 21739, I have adopted the habit for expediency."

"To bad ALF was already taken," Sant added. Everyone laughed.

"What was that she said about the transports?," Captain Jeffers asked.

"She called them flying convertibles without wheels. They reminded her of an old ford Fairlane convertible complete to the back fins," Jake said.

"They might be open-topped, but it ain't a top that keeps anything we shoot at them from hitting the target. There's some type of force field protecting the passengers." Trey tended to grow angrier the longer he thought about the aliens. He had lost his entire family to the invasion.

Jake was ready to end the conversation before it got tense. "Another thing Erika noticed, the airships do great up in the air where there is nothing to avoid. But once they got down close to the ground, the operator seemed to have trouble controlling them. She said when they were patrolling the river, they kept skimming across the water like when you skin a cat with a rock. That's what made me think they were not used to our atmosphere. And they didn't seem to be going very fast when they do a search pattern."

"I don't understand what you are saying," Captain Jeffers looked puzzled.

"Ever see little boy skipping stones across the water?" His hand shot out and described a series of violent ricocheting motions. "Like that?"

"I see what you are getting at but I don't see the connection."

"The Kurs may come from a low gravity planet. The transports may not fly that way at home but the pilots may be having trouble adjusting to a heavier atmosphere than they were used to flying in. This could be to our advantage."

Captain Jeffers tapped the tabletop with his fingers. "Interesting. All right, so the objective is to find out if we can get closer to the base without being seen. One of you will have to be the target. Who wants to volunteer to test the suit first?

Jake shifted his feet. "I guess it should be me. I'm the one who brought the info in. If it's not good info, I should be the one who takes the biggest risk."

He nodded. "Agreed. Any disagreements? No. Then Jake is our guinea pig."

"The rest of you can get started sewing your suits. Make sure you give yourself room to move without tearing the material. It doesn't stretch." He turned to Jake. "Come to my office after the others leave. I want to have a few words."

Captain Jeffers opened the door himself to Jakes's knock and then waved him to a chair. He opened a drawer in his desk and pulled out a half-empty bottle of Jack Daniels, poured them both a shot, and pushed one his way.

Jake wasn't much of a drinker but he realized this

might be his last opportunity to taste good whiskey. He took a sip, coughed a bit as the burn his chest, and then drank the rest in one shot. It sat heavy in his stomach, but the warmth was beginning to spread through his limbs.

"Got any idea how you are going to handle it? I'm not sure what would be the best way to test it."

Jake shrugged his shoulders. "Not really. Erika said she was scared the first time she tested her theory. I expect it gonna scare me, too.

"A man would have to be damn near crazy not to be afraid. We have all seen what was left after the Kurs got through with someone. Not even enough to bury. But I expect if they see you they are going to want to capture you. You have already caught their attention."

"True. I think I'd rather be dead."

"Figured you would say that. I'm gonna send Thomas to keep an eye out. He's a damn good sniper."

Jake nodded. He understood what the Captain meant without him saying the words.

"Try and get some rest. They should have the prototype ready for you in the morning. You might want to stop by and ensure they have your measurements. Wouldn't do for it to pull apart."

Jake nodded and the Captain waved him away.

As he walked back toward the area of the cavern where most of the men were sewing, he realized he wasn't afraid. Erika had risked everything for him. He needed to trust her.

***

As he expected Jake didn't get much sleep. He tossed a bit on his bedroll unable to get comfortable on his leg, despite knowing most of the pain was in his mind. The medic had examined it and declared there was nothing more he could do. Erika had done an excellent job and it was healing well. Not that it didn't hurt when he rolled onto it. After an hour had passed he gave up trying and decided to head for the access point and choose where he would set up. To add an extra layer of protection, the survivors never exited the cave near the campground. The extensive cave system ran under most of the area between Signal and Lookout Mountain, and multiple access points had been marked well away from the primary cavern entrance. During the civil war, the southern army used the cave tunnels to move about without the Yankees knowing they were around. The Cherokee considered them a spiritual place and often held religious ceremonies and meetings between tribal leaders inside. During the Cold War, the US Government established the National Cave System, setting up fallout shelters throughout the United States in anticipation of Russian or Chinese aggression. Most were still stocked with supplies. At the end of the Viet Nam War, the US Corp of Engineers had opened up a service tunnel to connect Signal, Raccoon and Lookout mountains in case of National emergency. Now the service tunnels provided the resistance a way to reach Lookout Point atop the Mountain without the need to travel on the surface. The tunnels pass under the Tennessee River, yet only a small portion was ever damp, mostly in the rainy season between March and July. The rest of the granite tunnels remained dry year-round, providing the perfect way to avoid Kur surveillance.

Jake grabbed an oil lamp from the stores' area and headed to transport where a golf cart carried him down an access tunnel to the emergency exit near Ruby Falls. With the elevator no longer an option, he would have needed to climb the metal staircase to the top of the mountain. Normally that would not bother him but with his injury, the half-hour climb would have been hell. He didn't dare take anything for the pain before his test, there was always the possibility the Kurs would see him and he would need all his facilities to escape capture.

He passed one of the twins on his way up. Both the girls had served in Iraq during the last war, but he had no idea which one was which. They had both lost husbands to the Kurs, leaving them with an intense urge to kill as many as possible. So far that wish had been nothing but wishful thinking. If Erika's outfit worked, it would allow the twins, and a whole lot of others, the opportunity to get up close and personal with the invaders. So far, because of the shields, the only weapon they had that worked was flame throwers at close range. Barry had killed the Kur, and then was killed by one in the airship, just before two others fired their weapons. None of the aliens missed their target.

Arriving at the top of the stairs, Jake looked around, hoping to see one or two of the men from his National Guard unit. Other than the civilian guard stationed inside what remained of the gift shop, the area was empty. Dawn was still a couple of hours away, so he decided to walk out to the point. The enormous flat rock there was a perfect spot to observe the Kurs ship in Chattanooga, as well as a good place to think. He had a set of binoculars equipped with night vision lenses that allowed him to see the ramp area adjutant to the ship. There was very little activity at night, they never left the ship after dark. There was a pair of alien guards outside the entrance to the stadium, but they didn't look like the Kurs. Most of the humans the aliens had captured were kept inside the arena until they were loaded on ships and taken off Earth. One of his friends was inside Findley Stadium, Tony had been captured last week, the same day he had been injured. Jake had been search-ing for Tony when he drew the aliens' attention, and Erika had to come to his rescue. A few blocks away from the spaceship were the remains of the National Guard Armory. One of the unit's primary objectives was finding a way to get inside that building without alerting the Kurs to their presence. Erika's discovery could make all the difference.

If he didn't bug out at the last moment.

If he didn't piss his pants while waiting.

If it worked.

If he survived.

That's a lot of *ifs* for man to deal with.

The first hints of pinkish-grey were showing in the eastern sky as the sun began to rise above the distant mountains of North Georgia. Dawn came fast in the Appalachians. One minute it was pitch black with only the quarter moons light to break the darkness, the next he could see movement around the Kurs ship without the night vision glasses. He hadn't realized how much time had passed while he was sitting on the rock. Already the Kurs were doing their morning routine, checking out the flying aircars they used for transport. He watched as the first one took off heading west toward Nashville. That was a regular trip they made daily. At first, the survivors had not realized the transport was going anywhere specific. After a few times, they noticed more aircars would return than had left that morning. He had decided the area at the base of Lookout Mountain would work as a testing field. The Kurs made regular runs down the valley passing over what remained of Saint Elmo. It was close enough that his superiors could watch the experiment with binoculars. And close enough for the sniper if things went south in a hurry.

He stretched and rose to his feet. If he hurried, he had just enough time to slip into his new reflective suit and rappel down the old streetcar track before the aircars began their daily runs south toward Atlanta.

***

At one time the railway that pulled a train car up the steep incline of the mountain had been a big tourist attraction to the area. Over the years, rides had become much wilder and scarier but there was something about being inside a train car going straight up the side of a mountain that made us all feel like little kids. Now, sitting alone at what remained of the garden area at the base of the lift, he realized how much he missed that feeling.

The current rash of emotions he was experiencing left a lot to be desired. His hands were sweaty and cold one minute, and hot and shaking the next. He didn't have asthma but he was having trouble taking a deep breath. But none of it was as bad as his roiling stomach. It felt like he had just eaten Tex-Mex at sea in a storm and the motor on the boat was dead. Basically, Hell on Earth.

And he had volunteered to be the pigeon in this hunt.

At least he wasn't cold. Despite the early morning frost and the mid-thirties temperatures, the space blanket suit was keeping him warm. If the invaders would just come by and take the bait he would be satisfied. Of course, today would be the one day they were running off schedule. Usually, by an hour after daybreak, the transport heading south would have passed overhead.

Not today.

Jake had opted to skip breakfast, choosing to head down through the side exit and follow the road around the base of the mountain to Saint Elmo instead of rappelling. The owner of Ruby Falls had closed up the cave with a heavy metal gate and built a lean-to against the side of the mountain to discourage explorers back in the 1980s. Not that it wasn't broken into, stubborn spelunkers were not hindered by locks and it was only meant as a deterrent, not a guarantee. No one was sure who owned the land it opened onto, but everyone assumed it was the state of Tennessee. Now it allowed him to cut off a couple of miles of hiking while preventing the Kurs from discovering where we were hiding out.

After one of the longest hours he could imagine, Jake finally heard the whistle-whap noise he associated with the transports. And it was transports; three aircars, not the usual one heading down the valley. He immediately began walking toward what was left of the street. In seconds he could see one of the transports slow and he knew his movement had their attention. The question was if the space blanket clothes would hide him from view if he were not moving. He turned and ran.

Once he was out of their sight, he moved right, creeping toward a drainage ditch he had spotted earlier. There was no cover, it was an open ditch with nothing to prevent him from being seen. If Erika were right, and they saw by heat signatures they would not be able to spot him as long as he stayed still. He did his best not to move, even holding his breath as the transports passed directly overhead. He knew that Morris had him in his sights at all times. His friends would not let him be taken.

The three transports spent several minutes tracking back and forth across the area, crossing several times looking for his heat signature. Every time one passed overhead he was certain they had spotted him. His muscles were trembling as his body fought against his need to remain motionless.

When the final transport gave up the search and joined the other two ships, Jake collapsed. Erika had been right.

Chapter 13

The steel grey Neapolitan Mastiff charged across the light dusting of snow, his oversized paws leaving deep prints in the soft white blanket as he barreled toward the rabbit cowering in the metal trap. Once he arrived, he bounced around the wire box, a two hundred pound puppy gamboling in the snow as he waited for Erika to catch up and fetch his dinner.

At one time eating a bunny would have broken Erika's heart. Now she only saw enough food to keep her alive another day. Not that she was in any danger of starving. She had food cached everywhere. But she preferred to leave her emergency stashes for future emergencies.

Over the last few months, she had built a small smoker in a burned-out building and smoked enough deer and beef jerky to last most of the winter. A chance encounter had provided a good size pig, too. She had meat covered. Chance had his own opinion on smoked meat and preferred his dinner rare if not still alive. His heart was set on fresh rabbit, and now that he had seen it, there was no way she could release it without him knowing. That didn't mean she couldn't give it a fighting chance. She reached for the lever and the trap opened. The rabbit bolted and Chance was right beside it. It had a fifty/fifty chance. That's how he got his name.

Lately, she had been eating less meat and more fresh vegetables. About half a day's ride south of the battlefield she had met a farmer who grew and canned a large variety of vegetables and some fruits. She traded luxury items, like chocolate pudding or Pringles chips, for vegetables she could not find growing in abandoned gardens. He now had her goats in with his herd. His cheese was much better than what she made and he ensured she had a wide variety. They had a good working arrangement. There wasn't a lot of survivors, maybe twenty in the area, but everyone was determined to outlast the invaders. At one time she had believed they were possibly the only humans to survive the attack. Since they were all married with small children, she had always felt the odd one, even though they did their best to make her feel a part of the community.

Now that she had met Jake and discovered there was a bigger resistance than she'd imagined, she was no longer wracked by depression over the idea of being alone. Humanity was not going quietly into the great darkness beyond. The future was still open to possibilities.

Erika was feeling pretty good about life in general when she headed back to where she had left Goldie, carrying what was left of the rabbit carcass in one hand and her bow in the other. Suddenly Chance stiffened, the fur on his back standing straight up as he released a low growl. The last time that had happened it had been a wild boar who decided we were trespassing in his woods.

From the corner of her eye, she could see the Cypress trees limbs moving. Then then the ferns along the base of the trees bent to one side as something big tried to force its way through the underbrush. Whatever it was, it was bigger than a wild pig. Her first thought was a bear. Usually, when they stumbled upon a bear, Chance would be barking loudly and trying to move closer. Instead, he was backing slowly away. She had never seen him acting this way, standing and shaking, and growling so quietly. Whatever it was, that was coming through the trees, it was enough to scare a two hundred pound Mastiff. There was no way she was going to let it get close to her.

She looked around, trying to spot a way out of the clearing that did not require her to move toward the cypress grove. She always set her trap in this area because there was only one clear way in and out of the gully. There were plenty of places for the rabbits to hide but not so many for a human. Or a mastiff. And there was no way she was leaving without Chance. Resigned to the possibility of a fight, Erika put her back up against the rock and pulled an arrow tight against her ear. Her hands were shaking making it difficult to get her range correct. She did not want to release the arrow too soon; she might not get a second shot. There had been a cougar spotted near the high school a few years ago. This ravine not so distant it could not be part of the big cats' normal territory. At the back of her mind, she was hoping it was simply a buck in rut trying to show off in front of a disinterested doe. But the weather had been warm enough for hibernating bears to wake up and seek out a midwinter snack. All she needed was to piss off a hungry bear, leaving him annoyed enough to consider her part of the menu. She blanked her mind, concentrating on what she could remember of bear anatomy, hoping a sensitive spot would pop into her mind. Then he stepped out of the tree line and every bit of her concentration went to hell. She released the arrow and fell to her knees knowing she was about to die.

Chance was whining but for some reason, he wasn't running away. This surprised her because if she could have run she would be gone. Her eyes were squeezed tightly together. She was praying to Jesus and God while crying for her momma If she could have remembered some of the other religious leaders she would have prayed to them, too. It was only after she had lost every sense of control including her bladder that she realized she was still alive. She was certain it had seen her but it hadn't killed her. She cracked open one eye and looked but she could not see it. Then she spotted a foot sticking out of the deep grass. It wasn't moving.

Chance was growing braver as he moved closer

without getting any type of response.

She waited, watching the foot, waiting for it to move for at least fifteen minutes before she felt brave enough to get to her feet. Slowly she crept toward it, wondering if it was playing some kind of sadistic mind trick to lure her close enough to grab. Did they do that? She knew that they were omnivores, eating both fruit and meat. But she had never heard of them playing dead to lure their victims in close. Damn thing sure looked dead.

Erika inched closer and touched its foot. It was cold but there was snow on the ground so everything was cold. She nocked another arrow, giving her some imagined sense of security. As if an arrow could take one down.

Yet somehow it had. She stood looking at it a few moments before she picked up the shiny metal weapon it had been carrying. It was remarkably similar to a rifle, with a barrel and a trigger. Clutching the Kur's weapon in her left hand, she moved a branch out of the way so she could examine the body. Her arrow had somehow struck its breathing apparatus, slicing into the supply line. The flint arrowhead was buried in the side of its neck and the wooden shaft was broken off beside its head. She had no idea why its force shield had not been functioning at the exact second she had fired, but she was taking the win anyway. Maybe God had answered her panicked prayer. She wasn't going to hang around and push her luck.

Somewhere in the woods nearby were his partners and its transport. She intended to be as far away as possible when they came looking for him. The rabbit was still lying in the snow where she dropped it. She ran past a lone coyote heading toward the ravine. He could have it. Goldie would turn up in a day or two, she wasn't tied and would make her way back to her paddock. After a glance at the trail leading toward the battlefield, she hit the creek in full stride, Chance running beside her. Tracking her south through the water would be harder for the aliens. She figured she could make Trion in a few hours. She'd been missing her goats anyway.

Chapter 14

Royce Jeffers had served his county through three wars. Until recently, he had thought nothing could be worse than his memories of his two years in Iraq. He was wrong. Looking around at the devastation wrought by the invading forces, he realized the battle in Fallujah had been a simple child's conflict in comparison to what Earth was experiencing.

He had not always been so pessimistic.

For a long time, his greatest ambition had been to become a bank president. He wanted more than the title, he wanted to be in control of operations, to show the world that the poor kid from the projects could make it to the top without being an athlete or in movies. A simple ambition perhaps, but realistically, something that rarely happened without having someone inside helping you climb the ladder. He had done it the hard way, joining the military to earn the education credits needed to attend a decent college. For most of his twenties, he had no time of his own. His days belonged to the Army and his nights belonged to the University of Georgia.

Nature had conspired against Royce by bequeathing him a taller than normal but muscular body along with a pair of large but uncoordinated hands. Add hopelessly myopic eyes and astigmatism and you ended up with a man who literally couldn't see his hand in front of his face.

For a while, when he was very young, his teachers had thought him unteachable. When they realized it was his eyes, they got glasses for him but he was already a year behind in his studies. Then no child left behind came along and he was never quite able to catch up. Teachers cared more about pushing a student through the system than teaching them the basics needed to function in society. Black kids were passed because no one wanted to be considered bigoted or biased. So what if he could barely read, he was not expected to succeed anyway.

The Army changed all that. For once in his life, he was given the necessary training he needed to succeed. He devoured every bit of training the military offered, often taking additional classes when others in his unit were hitting the beaches and nightclubs. He rose quickly through the ranks, becoming a Sargent withing his first tour of duty. People looked up to him and listened when he spoke.

While serving in Fallujah his luck had taken a bad turn. The rocket that destroyed his transport had taken more than his leg. It had changed his career path. No longer qualified to lead in the field, he had moved to Chattanooga, becoming a recruiter, working with ROTC units in the local high schools and colleges.

He had been holding a weekend training camp for ROTC, covering some of the darker aspects of military life when the invasion began. The attack had interrupted his discussion of spelunking, a hobby he enjoyed even without one leg when the sound of multiple explosions crashed upon his ear-drums. The stone of the cave carried the vibrations through the rock, making it seem as if the inside of him and outside of him were coming apart all at one time. The rough stone floor of the cavern rose upward toward him as several sections of the limestone ceiling broke away, crashing down around the students and the National Guard reserves that had been assisting him over the weekend. For a fleeting second Captain Jeffers's mind flashed back to a story he had started to read once called "The Pit and The Pendulum". He regretted in that insane moment that he had never had time to finish the story to see how it came out. Then all was darkness and quiet and unconsciousness.

When Royce came to, he was overcome by DeJa'Vu and knew that something was desperately wrong. He gingerly got to his feet, moving arms and legs experimentally. Assured that nothing was broken, he immediately began searching for his glasses that had fallen from his face. His glasses were intact, thank God! He would never have been able to find his way out of the dark cavern without them. He made a mental note to have a spare pair made to keep in his pack when on field trips. His prescription was on file locally, but it took time to grind and polish the thick lenses into his complicated prescription.

Something momentous had happened, something worse than an electric transformer blowing up, or a gas main Exploding. His gut told him it was something worse than anything that had ever happened in the area before. Had China invaded? There had been rumors of their intent for years. The country had been experiencing an economic upturn that showed no signs of slowing. Imports from China had fallen off as more US manufacturing companies had reopened. People had more money and "Made in America" was once more the ideal. China had not been happy.

"Call out, anyone need help?" Royce waited but no one appeared to be injured. Flashlights began coming on, relieving his fear of an EMP burst disrupting the city. His next fear had been of an attack on the power station upriver. Nuclear waste from fallout was not a problem as the air currents would push them north and east but people up the coast would need to be warned. It would play hell on the fish in the river, too.

Once he assured himself no one was seriously injured they began working their way out of the cave to the main entrance. The gift shop was gone, replaced by a pile of rubble and pieces of charred wood that blocked the exit. They had to wait almost a day before the rocks cooled enough to be moved. By then, most of the city

had been destroyed. The fifty-odd recruits were an unlikely army but it was all he had. Over the next few days
over a hundred survivors had been located and brought
to safety. Other than a few minor skirmishes between
the alpha males vying for power, the adjustment to life
in the cavern had been relatively smooth.

Once they located the old fallout shelter morale
had improved. The addition of simple things like the
weekly movie and the library had offered the possibility
of things going back to normal in the future.

The discovery of the tunnel system had added a
layer of security, allowing them to move about the area
without risking exposure. The unit had immediately
set out to open up the closed off access to Ruby Falls.
He could still picture the first time they had entered
the chamber at the base of the elevator. The car lay
crumpled at the foot of the shaft like a discarded accordion. There was something inside of it that most of
the soldiers could not look at, something that had once
been a family, or perhaps two couples, it was impossible
to tell now. The flesh that remained after the car hit the
ground was deteriorated, swollen and distorted. Maggots were working it over. That vision would haunt him
for a long time.

"Burn them where they are. Use gas to make sure it
burns." Feeling nauseous after he had ordered the bodies burned Royce had staggered toward the main room
of the falls. The old metal steps were still there, but over

the years the wood on the treads had rotted. The weight of the metal frame had caused twisting without the treads to brace it, pulling the empty sections back upon one another so that it was more like climbing the side of a mountain than mounting a typical stairway. One of the men was a welder and he had been able to repair the damaged sections. It was one hell of a climb to the top of the mountain, but it offered protected views of the aliens' ships in Chattanooga.

During the initial days, he had lost several people as they went out into the neighborhoods and salvaged anything of possible use. The Kurs preferred to take prisoners but felt no reluctance against destroying anyone interfering with their objectives. Humans were treated little better than animals, culling out the very young, old or disabled and destroying them. The healthy adults were loaded into spaceships and taken away. While no one had any idea why they were taking them; his imagination easily filled in the blanks.

Erika's suit was the first glint of hope they had experienced in six months. As soon as Jake had verified the reflective material worked, they had sent word to Nashville, Knoxville, and Atlanta. The survivors in each area had formed a loose confederacy of freedom fighters willing to take advantage of anything that helped them to combat the invaders. Together they had come up with a plan. A lot depended on being able to move around the city without being seen. If it worked, they might have a chance. A small one. But any chance was better then what they had now.

***

Erika crouched behind an outcropping of rocks watching the Kur soldier come closer. It had a funny walk, with a bouncy jerk in its step. She figured that might be because its knee bent the wrong way, kind of like a dog would.

With all that fur you would think they would prefer a colder planet. They had to be miserable. She could not think of a more inhospitable environment for a furred being then Chattanooga in the summertime. In the spring it was a comfortable 72 degrees with cool mountain breezes. By the Dog Days of August it hovered around 100 degrees and often went above it. The early morning rain had ended but the evaporating water was making it feel like a steam room. They had to wear the heavy breathing apparatus whenever they left the controlled environment around their mothership. For a brief few seconds she felt a bit guilty about utilizing their weakness.

Then she released the arrow. There was no chance of the Kur sounding an alarm. The wooden arrow and stone arrowhead was not affected by the invisible barrier. The long wooden shaft slipped through the force field like a hot knife through butter, the chipped stone head lodging itself in the air intake hose around the neck of the alien on guard. The hissing sound of his air escaping alerted the Kur to his imminent death. He managed to take two steps before his eyes rolled up in his head and he collapsed to the ground. Erika immediately ran up and collected his gun. Then she pulled the arrow from his air hose, placed it point down in the quiver, and disappeared back into the forest.

Chapter 15

The keypad still worked but Jake had to use the manual override to open the heavy metal door.

He sighed as he dropped his equipment inside the entrance and slid to the cement floor beside it. The last mile or so had been beneath the bright summer sun. At least three groups of the flying transports had passed directly over the nervous unit crouched against whatever cover they had found. By the third flyover, a few of the men had simply laid down in the road, using the rubble from the damaged streets to help disguise their presence, the only sound their pounding hearts and their relieved exhalations. The psychological strain was hell. It may not be as deadly as the lasers, but it had to be hard on the heart. His felt like it was going to explode in his chest. Gradually the pounding decreased as his heart went back to its normal rhythm.

So much was riding on the ten men scattered around the hall. Some were sitting, others had lain back against their packs. The stress was showing on every face. So was the sense of pride, something he had not seen on anyone's face since the invasion began.

The entire plan centered on the success or failure of this first attempt to operate within the city without the Kurs knowing they are there. Erika's discovery had decreased the dangle level exponentially. It would not win the war, but it helped.

Captain Jeffers had called all available fighters in for the briefing. The packed room was buzzing with rumors with most speculation centering on what each believed was going to happen. Whatever the mission was, it was going to be dangerous.

They all respected the man who had come to be their leader. Jeffers was not really a division commander but he was a military professional who had served in a war zone, giving him a perspective none of the survivors had. He had not let his injury destroy his life. A tall slim man that had probably been considered handsome at one time, Royce Jeffers now walked with a distinctive limp, often favoring his right leg. One side of his face was severely scarred from burns he had received during his last tour in Fallujah. He survived the rocket blast that had blown up the troop carrier but he had lost one eye. Expecting to be red stamped out of the military completely, he had been surprised when the government had offered him a supervisory position working with instructors training inner-city youth in ROTC programs and a desk at the local recruitment center. Until the invasion he had been living the perfect life, a job he liked, a home that was paid in full, and a family he loved. In one day he lost it all. A lesser man would have crumbled.

He stood by a table, shuffling through papers until

the last man had arrived. Once everyone was seated, he walked to the front of the room and signaled for quiet. Every eye was on him as he began to talk. Suddenly nervous, he reached up and adjusted the black patch he now wore over the hollow socket. This was unusual. Whether he was crawling through a tunnel or standing at the front of the room giving a speech his camo fatigues always managed to look crisp and sharply creased. To always look your best was a quality he tried to instill in every man under his command.

"Thank you all for coming. I won't to thank those of you who are not under my command for volunteering. This is an unusual situation, but one that can have far reaching benefits if we are able to pull it off. With that being said, this is what we have in mind…"

He explained his plan, ensuring that everyone understood the operation had a limited chance of working. He stressed that it might be the only possibility they had to save the human race. It was going to be a daring raid that would put every man involved in danger. If they could pull it off while working under the noses of the aliens, it would be worth it. Then he asked for volunteers. Every hand in the room went up.

Two hours later he had his dirty dozen. The team consisted of twelve of the most qualified men available. The idea of losing them all in a failed attempt scared him. The idea of not trying scared him more. As he watched them saying what might be their final goodbyes to their friends and families, he was overcome by a wave of indecision. He pasted a fake smile on his face and pretended he was a hundred percent confident in their success. The Devil must be laughing so hard he's rolling on the floor.

***

The exhausted group had started out just after the sun had set beyond the western horizon. The scouts had carefully mapped out the best route, cutting cross country through what little remained of Alton Park and up Rossville Blvd. to Holtzclaw instead of following the much shorter route through the ruins of Chattanooga. Knowing the Kurs rarely traveled away from their mother ship during the night should have relieved the worry Jake was experiencing. Unfortunately, there was always that one exception, and no one wanted to risk discovery and come face to face with that one atypical alien.

The hike had been uneventful until they reached Rossville Boulevard.

Trey had been scouting ahead, watching for any sign of an outpost. Something had changed the way the invading force was behaving. The Kurs had recently begun to set up small satellite posts instead of returning to the ship every night. Finding one this close to the mother ship would be unusual, but they had discovered one in Lookout Valley earlier that week. For the next few days, they had remained inside the cave, afraid to go outside in case the aliens were watching for signs of the sanctuary. Once we were certain the cave had not been discovered we had continued using the underground passage to move back and forth between the base and the Ruby Falls access.

They were chatting amongst the pairs as they walked, reasonably confident there were no Kurs in the area, when the first shot rang out. Everyone immediately went of full alert, moving in the direction of the shot, while maintaining strict standard operating procedure. SOP didn't cover it.

The ravenous dog pack had attacked without warning. The sound of rapid-fire alerted us that something was wrong. Trey knew bullets could not get through the force shield so we knew whatever threat he faced it was not the aliens. The entire unit took off running.

We were too late.

There must have been twenty dogs in the pack. Most looked like Pit bulls, but there were several smaller hounds, two German Shepherds, and one very large Rottie. Jakes stomach lurched as one of the Pits trotted by, carrying Trey's arm in his mouth. The rest were busy eating. You could hear the crunch of bones along with growls and barks as the pack fought over his body. Lonnie the youngest of the Dirty Dozen was standing on top of the cab of a pickup truck crushed by a fallen tree. He was using his rifle as a club to batter any dog that tried to jump up from the truck bed.

"Hold your fire," Mikey said as two of his men pulled out their pistols. "There's nothing we can do to help him. Wasting ammo won't bring him back."

"Fuck bullets. I'm gonna kill every one of the bastards," Santwan said as he raised his hand, totally ignoring Mikey's words as he began firing at the animals. He managed to hit three of the dogs before the rest of the pack ran off. Now he was driving his bayonet into the final quivering mass of blood and fur to ensure they were all dead. Mikey put his hand on the distraught man's shoulder and he dropped the barrel of the gun and began crying. Trey was his oldest friend. They had been in kindergarten together. When the invasion started the two ex-marines had been smoking a blunt, sprawled out on a big rock atop Lookout Mountain. At first, they had thought someone had laced the pot with PCP causing a hallucination. Now Sant wished it were a nightmare and he could wake up.

"I need two volunteers to take Trey's body back to camp." Not that there was a lot of his body left to return for burial. Jake hated to send anyone back. Twelve men had started the mission an hour earlier. Now there were eleven. If things continued at this rate there might not be anyone left to complete the mission.

"No. Trey would not want that. We burn him." Sant's shoulders slumped together, aging him in seconds. He looked around, spotting a wooden pallet lying against a burnt-out shell of a building. There was a car crushed beside the truck, the body inside already too deteriorated to guess a man or a woman. That would do. "Put the body inside that car. "He began breaking up the pallet.

Mikey knocked a hole in the gas tank of another crushed car and motioned for the others to help. The remaining men used anything they could find to hold the gas. One man found a donation bin full of old clothes. He gathered an armful, soaking several pieces in the gas that had spilled across the ground by the car. Cloth burned fast. It would ensure the fire stayed burning.

Sant said a short prayer before tossing in the flaming shirt. The fire immediately blazed upward, lighting up the area nearby.

Jake frowned, knowing his words were not going to sit easily with Santwan. "We need to go now. The Kurs may not like coming out after dark but there's no way they will miss the heat signature of the fire. They will be looking for us." He shouldered his pack and began walking toward the road that paralleled the one they were on. The other men followed.

Sant looked torn but after a few seconds, he joined the rest of the group. Trey would understand.

The first time the enemy flew over the group everyone hunkered down behind any solid barrier they could find. The second time they had less warning and the men had looked for anything plausible to use. The aircars had not even slowed down. By the third flyover, they had merely dropped where they were and remained still. Several were laying in the open atop the concrete. The aircars had passed within ten feet of the men without noticing them. Erika's suits were a success. They were hot as hell in the late summer heat, but what was a little discomfort when it kept you alive.

The sun was high overhead as the team approached the Veterans Cemetery next to our target, the old National Guard Armory. Most of the equipment had been relocated to the new Armory on the northside of the airport years earlier. That building had been destroyed, along with everything in the yard during the initial attack. The equipment in the old armory was outdated but it was kept in working condition just in case it was needed. If there was ever a need it was now. There was no way to enter through the old front door, that part of the building was rubble, however, there was an equipment hatch inside the old garage and they were able to clear it. The crowbars everyone had complained about carrying came in handy. There was no way they could have opened the hatch without them. Once we had it open, it was a short drop into the access tunnel.

"Let's take a break and get some rest. Harley, you got first watch. Webb, you go, too. Switch up in one hour."

No one argued.

The two guards picked up flamethrowers and headed out to find a spot about a block away from the armory. He watched them walk away, wondering if he had just gotten two more of his men killed. It wasn't the first time he'd been faced with a hard decision, but after losing Trey, this decision sucked more than he expected.

On his last deployment, Captain Jeffers had worked with a scientist who had been refining laser beam targeting technology to enable pinpoint control of the highly accelerated particles. He hoped to create a weapon that could be easily controlled yet strong enough to wipe out an entire city. The end result had been frightening. The prototype he constructed was limited by the power supply available. Nuclear fission allowed for unlimited power, yet there was always the danger of residual radiation. The scientist had died within a few weeks of creating what was possibly one of the most dangerous weapons ever developed. Captain Jeffers had struggled with his decision to tell Jake about the weapon plans. The backup copies of Doctor Li's work was in a safe located in the basement of the National Guard Armory. Jake had been instructed to get those backups and return them to command. Not because they wanted to make the weapon. To minimize the possibility of the aliens getting the plans.

No one but him was present when the order was given. No one knew what he was there to do.

He decided to check out the vault while the others rested. The emergency batteries were still working, the keypad was hot. His passcode was still active, there had not been anyone to remove the access. He punched in the nine digits, taking care to ensure he had not made a mistake. He would hate to get locked out for imputing the wrong number and have to hang around another twenty-four hours for it to reset. The keypad was lit but that didn't necessarily mean the backup generators would bring the lights online. He released a sigh of relief at the burst of cool air that flowed outward as the door opened. The climate-controlled room was operating as expected. Command had been certain the Kurs would not locate it since the temperature was well below the heat of the surface. Their only fear had been damage from the initial attack. The lights worked, too.

He let his eyes move around the room, taking in and categorizing the contents. Boxes of data backups were piled around the walls. This worried him. He could imagine countless years of scientific research being destroyed in a flash of light and flames. Working in the cold laboratory in their temperature-controlled form-fitting polymer suits had been no problem. The custom-fitted bodysuits made the room feel like a warm spring afternoon. The makeshift space blanket suits were made from rolled plastic covered in a thin layer of reflective aluminum, sewn and glued together by hand. They did a decent job of holding in body heat but they could not compare with the custom jobs. He would need to work fast and get out. By now the men would be gathering explosives. Besides grenades, C-4, RDX, and Semtex they had been ordered to pick up any flamethrowers and fuel they could find. It would not take long for them to scour the bins of equipment and locate anything that might be of use. He punched in the unlock code on the safe and found the correctly numbered plastic case. Less than five minutes had passed before he had packed up everything he needed and was on his way back to the others.

When he rejoined them, he was surprised to find that two of the men had located rocket launchers, complete with four rockets each. That was something he had not known about. Now he wondered what else might be hidden in the dark recesses of the basement.

The guards had changed shifts, allowing Harley and Webb a chance to grab some rest. Most of the others had broken out cards and were playing poker. He decided to join them. There would be no cooking. There were plenty of MRE's on the shelves. Cases of bottled water too. Dawn was breaking in the east and it was going to be a long day.

Chapter 16

The Kurs were getting smarter. Or running scared. Either way, I guess I'm going to have to change how I hunt.

Erika wiped a bead of sweat from her forehead with the side of her sleeve knowing it would be replaced by another in a matter of moments. It was so damned hot. She stretched the fingers of her left hand, and then released the string of her bow so she could stretch her right. That was the problem with bows, your fingers could cramp before you realized it. She glanced at the alien gun propped beside the rock she was sitting against. She had fired it twice and felt comfortable with the way it handled. It was too bad she had no idea how long the charge would last; it would make taking the Kurs out a lot faster. For now, she had to be happy with one at a time.

The Kurs had caught on to the idea that someone was hunting them. Whenever they traveled the area between Lookout Mountain and what was once Interstate 75, they stayed high above the trees. If they had to land and search, they now walked in pairs instead of alone. It was kinda funny, watching them jump every time a rabbit or a cat cut across their path. They had no idea how she was killing them, which made the hunt even more amusing.

The whistle that always announced their arrival alerted her to get ready. She always wondered why the Kurs never realized how the humans knew they were coming. Perhaps the sound was too high pitched for their ears? Dogs could hear sounds a human couldn't, so it made sense that a human could hear a whistle the Kurs missed.

Just as she expected the two aliens came down the path together, one walking right in front of the second. She waited until both had passed and pulled back her bowstring, holding the arrow tight against her face. The snap of a limb behind her made her pause and drop to the ground. She froze, staying as still as possible. Two more Kurs were walking through the brush about thirty feet behind her. Erika knew as long as she stayed still they could not see her, but they might notice the bow waving around in midair. She held her breath until they had passed beyond her hiding spot, then picked up the bow and gun before slipping through the brush back in the direction the Kurs had come.

In less than five minutes she had spotted the clearing where they had landed. Just as she expected there was an aircar on the ground. One Kur remained inside, sitting in the driver's seat. He was looking at something on the screen before him, not paying much attention to anything around him.

Her stony expression broke into a brief smile. *Big*

mistake.

Rising up from behind the granite stone she raised her bow and fired, hitting the square box on the back of his suit. The arrow struck the outside of the box with enough force to pass through the box into the Kurs back. There was a brief burst of sparks then the box caught on fire. The Kur did his best to put out the flames but whatever he was breathing was highly flammable. In seconds he had fallen over the side of the aircar and was burning on the ground nearby. For a short time, he cried out some kind of hissing squeal, before finally growing silent. The entire body was covered in flames, the stench of the burning fur growing stronger the longer he burnt.

Erika sighed and began to run. She had only a few seconds to snatch the arrow away from the burning body, grab the gun that was sitting beside the driver's seat, and run for cover. Luckily, she had located a safe spot to hide a few weeks earlier. She dove for the thicket about a hundred feet from the aircar and squirmed her way into the narrow space beneath the rock that was almost hidden from view by the heavy growth. The narrow burrow went back about five feet before opening into a slightly larger den. Earlier in the year, she had noticed a fox and her kits there but this late in August the den had become too small and they had moved on to better hunting grounds. The odor was horrible but better to stink than dying. She could always take a bath.

She had barely enough time to pull her bandana up over her nose when she heard the voices of the four Kurs. They were chattering away in their whiny squeal as they climbed aboard the aircar. They did not bother with the dead Kurs body, other than to notice his breathing apparatus had caught fire. The whistling sound of the aircar disappearing into the distance let her relax. Not that she had any intention of leaving the den anytime soon. It had only taken one near-death experience to show her the error of her ways. Now she never assumed all the Kurs were gone. The burnt tissue on her shoulder had kept her awake for weeks as it healed. Laying her head down atop her folded arms she slept.

***

The night was eerily quiet when Erika slid out of the burrow. The hair on her arms was standing on end. She shivered even though she wasn't cold. The silence bothered her. The forest should have been alive with the normal sounds and noises of the inhabitants. They were only a short distance from the creek, but nothing was heading toward the water. Deer were usually active at this time of the day. So were bullfrogs. Birds normally used this time to call out their final songs. Crickets quieted down in the evening, but it was a katydid year, and cicadas were always noisy. She heard nothing. No insects. No animals. No frogs. Nothing.

There were only a few things that could shut down the forest completely. After countless generations, most animals had learned to ignore humans. Even the deer knew they were only hunted in the late months of fall. A big cat or a bear might signal a brief hiatus, but after a moment or two, they would start back up.

No. Something was out there in the darkness. Something the forest inhabitants had never seen before. Something they feared. And if they feared it, she needed to fear it too. It located her scent and shrieked a challenge, but she could not decide where the sound had come from. She searched for a weapon, a rock or stick, or anything useful to beat back whatever it was. Then her hand fell on the alien laser she had dropped in her sleep. She had no idea how much of a charge it still held, but it had to be better than a bow if the animal got close. She could pull the trigger and it might do nothing. But she could slap it upside the head.

On impulse she picked up her bow in her left hand, carrying the alien's beam weapon in her right. The cold metal felt strangely comfortable in her hand. Erika told herself the shivers along her spine were from a cool breeze and not because she was afraid. She imagined dark shapes appearing from out of the shadows, unexpected apparitions that did little more than play tricks on her mind. The snap of a twig breaking to her right made her turn and look that way. She had barely enough time to raise the gun and fire before it was on her. Erika realized she was seconds from death. She was scared, too, but figured if she had to die, she was not going to go down without a fight. Adrenaline flooded her body as she jabbed the alien gun into its side, holding the trigger down as its beam ate into the creature's body. Her bow kept the maw of jagged teeth from closing on her neck as its vicious snaps grew slower and slower until stopped completely.

Her side burned from the gashes left by its claws. The double layer of material had helped prevent the claws from reaching anything lethal, but the slashes were bleeding. She needed to get to one of her medical caches. The chance of infection from foreign bacteria was always a possibility, and she had no way of knowing how her body would react.

The creature was nothing she had ever seen before. For one thing, it had six legs. It had reared back on four and used the razor-sharp claws on the front pair to tear into the soft flesh along her side. The head was about the size of a big dog's, with a thick muzzle like a pit but wider, and an oversize nose over a double row of teeth. The rest of it reminded her of a praying mantis. Short wiry fur covered its entire body, except for a thick leather band around its neck. A collar? *Damn. It was the Kurs version of a dog.*

Her eyes went to the remains of the tower atop Lookout Mountain. She thought about Jake a lot since meeting him last month but would never have tried to visit him without a good reason. Now she had no choice. They had to know about the strange creature. The aliens had brought them for a reason. She was willing to bet they were trackers. This one had found her. She was certain it could find the others. And it had no trouble seeing her. That put a lot of Jakes friends at risk.

First, she needed to slow the blood loss, or what she had discovered would not matter. She thought about things like lock-jaw and gangrene and her hand trembled. Earth science excelled in medicine but she doubted the tetanus shot had included alien Kur antigens.

Since she had not thought to bring a medical kit, she removed her shirt and ripped away both sleeves, using one to make a pad. Strips torn from the second were used to bind the pad tightly against her side. It did not stop the flow of blood completely, but it did slow it down. Tears of pain and helplessness welled in her eyes as she fought her way across the shallow creek and up through the rain-washed gulley to reach the flat land that ran through the middle of Lookout Valley. It was about two miles to the old Incline Railroad. Too bad it didn't work. Climbing the mountain was going to hurt like hell. Using the bow as a crutch she began walking toward Saint Elmo.

Chapter 17

The eastern sky had darkened into the comforting shadows of the night as the 'Dirty Dozen' began the long trek back to the home base.

"Sant, you and Cody take point. Head across the Art Park then north up Rossville Boulevard. When you reach the train tracks, stop. Don't cross them. Stay within a block of the unit." Jake shouldered his pack, a silent signal for the other men to do the same. Captain Jeffers had briefed him on the details of the plan but none of the others had been present. His orders might have surprised them but recognizing the rather daunting expression in his eyes, they realized he wasn't in the mood for a long explanation.

"North? That's going to take us awfully close to the Kurs. " Santwan knew Jake wasn't saying everything he knew, but he had learned to trust his CO's instincts. Not that he didn't occasionally question his commands. Losing Trey had shaken him more than he wanted to admit. They had been through so much together. Growing up in the projects, running with the same gang, then facing the choice between hard time and enlisting. They had immediately joined the Marines, going through boot camp and a tour in Iraq together. Trey had been the brother he never had. Jake was close, but not there yet.

"Yeah. We want to try to avoid them," Jake said. "There's lots of rubble on Rossville Blvd. We can cross the tracks at the end of the street, catch Main and then follow it through town."

Sant nodded and stayed silent, knowing Cody-would immediately furnish Jake with a crushing argument.

Cody was looking at Jake like he had lost his mind. "You forgetting the prisoners they have in Finley? There's bound to be several outposts around the area. The Kurs have that area lit up like midday."

"You got your orders. We take Main. Just keep following it west. If we run into any opposition, we detour and find a way around it." Jake's tone made it clear there was no room for debate. His eyes grew dark and hard as he studied the grey storm clouds gathering in the western sky. Rain was an everyday occurrence during the summer but the incoming front looked nasty. All they needed was the high and low pressure zones to collide over Chattanooga, leaving them to be caught in a tornado, with no cover available.

Sant signaled Cody with his eyes and the two men began walking up the street without another word. Everyone in the group had grown up in the city. They could all picture the route in their minds. Main ran east to west about a block north of Finley Stadium. The mothership had set down in one of the nearby parking lots. That was only a short walk from where they were now. Taking

Rossville Boulevard through what remained of the old train station would cut out a lot of the travel between their present location and Saint Elmo. There was plenty of debris to use for cover. He doubted an aircar could get through there without remaining at least fifty feet above the ground, making it almost impossible for their heat signatures to show on their equipment.

The remaining men waited until the two points passed out of view.

Jake debated setting a drag but decided it was not worth risking someone unnecessarily. The Kurs would open fire as soon as they came into range. He had never heard of them sneaking up behind their prey. And Mikey liked to walk at the end of the line, he would keep an eye on everything.

He signaled for the unit to move out.

***

Cody had fallen back to the railroad tracks to warn the others of the unexpected outpost while Sant kept watch. "They have the road blocked off. There's no way to follow Rossville north and get past that point. There's no way we can continue that direction. There has to be at least twenty of them. I counted five aircars."

Jake frowned. He had wanted to avoid following the railroad tracks. But now it looked as if they were the best option. As long as it was dark they would be fine. But it would suck if they had not found a safe house by daybreak. He tried to picture the area in his mind and nothing worked with the original scenario. Then he realized he had been overthinking the problem. "Get Sant. We will follow the tracks."

Peterman nodded but he did not look happy. He had been on patrol when their unit had been pinned down on the tracks by a Kur aircar. Out of twelve men, only four had survived. He had lost the lower part of his left arm and twisted his ankle in the attack. The only reason he was here today was due to Reese being trained to be a Corpsman. He had stumbled across Cody lying on the tracks in the darkness and bound his stump.

Reese had been blinded by the flash but Codyconsidered that a blessing. What remained of his face was covered in burnt skin and cracked seeping wounds. Two twisted holes allowed Cody to see where his mouth and nose had been. His eye sockets were empty. By working together, the two men had managed to stay alive long enough to reach one of the safe houses. When rescue arrived a week later, Reese was dead and Cody was in bad shape. It had been weeks before he regained strength enough to return to the field.

He grinned. At least it was his left arm. He could still kill the muthas.

Santwan was already making his way back to the unit when he caught up to him. "Change of orders, we are going to follow the tracks."

"What the hell is Jake thinking?"

"No idea. You know Jake is. He refuses to admit he's wrong. He's dead set on going through town. Can you talk to him?"

"I can try, but he ain't gonna listen. He's worse than a Pitbull when he gets his mind set on something. Nothing can shake him loose."

Jake met them as they approached. He glanced at his watch and calculated how long they had until daybreak. It was going to be close. "You need to switch out or can you keep going?"

Cody grinned, "That little bit of a walk didn't even bring up a sweat."

"Good. I need you to head south down the tracks. When you get to Chickamauga Creek, lay low and keep an eye out."

Sant raised an eyebrow; a quizzical look Jake was very familiar with. He decided to leave the conversation for later and get the rest of the unit moving again. It was going on midnight and they had a long night ahead of them. He dug into his pack and pulled out a chunk of cheese. There was no time to break for a meal.

No part of the mission had turned out like the Captain had expected. The situation they were facing was never a part of the planning. All of the scenarios had involved the unit moving north and west down main toward Moccasin Bend. Walking south down the tracks took longer than he'd expected. Instead of the clear passage he was used to seeing, the brush along the track was overgrown. Large sections of the metal rail were twisted. The burnt-out hulk of a small passenger plane lay wedged between the rubble of a fallen office building. In some areas, the ash from all the fires was ankle-deep. Once he set his teeth on edge to keep from retching after he stepped down into something that crunched and squished beneath his feet before tripping over a human skull.

It was an eerie feeling. Everywhere he looked there were strange, motionless lumps of fire-blackened ash that he could not bear to look at. They were not the worst. Jake felt a pang of real sorrow when he saw the rotting remains of a child's arm and shoulder extending out from under a huge fallen block of marble. Fire ants were busy cleaning away the last bits of flesh left on the bones. Once they heard the high pitched whistle of an aircar and hid until the sign faded away. It had been traveling south but it did not fly over them.

Occasionally they would pass the charred remains of smashed automobiles, some with their four wheels pointing skyward like the stiffened legs of dead animals. The destruction was horrible, but that didn't bother him. He felt uneasy because it was so quiet. There was no whine of sirens, no shouting, no running, just an ominous and all-pervading silence that ate into his subconscious mind, like a faucet that never stopped dripping.

The sight of Cody and Santwan reclining in the shade of a twisted water oak made him smile. They had reached the point he had designated and took advantage of the extra few minutes to rest and grab a bite to eat. His smile vanished when he noticed the bridge was gone.

"Son of a bit..." Hunk cut his comment as Jake dropped his pack next to the track and suggested everyone take ten. Like Peterman, Hunk was another one of the walking wounded. He'd taken major damage when one of the alien's laser blasts had struck a propane tank, sending a shard of metal into his chest, lodging it close to his heart and pulmonary artery. Only the density of his pectoral muscles from weight training had saved him from certain death. Years of weightlifting had developed his upper physique into something you only saw in health magazines or prisons. The corpsman who removed the shrapnel was only a year older than him. It had been the first time he'd performed real surgery. In a normal world, Ken would be recovering in a rehab center, enjoying spa baths and full-body therapeutic massages from petite nursing assistants eager to gain enough experience to pass their clinical training.

Captain Jeffers's idea of physical therapy was to ensure he could climb the stairs to the top of the mountain without passing out. Once he achieved that goal, he was assigned to a unit and sent back into the field. No one was surprised when he had volunteered for the Dirty Dozen.

Santwan waited and watched as Jake made

himself comfortable beneath the same group of trees they were resting under. His CO was usually on top of his game, he must have known the bridge was gone. What was he thinking? Chickamauga Creek was deep and almost thirty feet wide at this point. He wasn't looking forward to wading across. He was like the man in the song, he hated spiders and snakes and the area was prime landscape for both.

"So," Sant said as Jake flopped down on the grass behind him. "What now?"

"I'm gonna take a ten-minute break and eat."

"Okay, that covers the next ten minutes. Then what?"

"Guess you're going to have to wait and see. Hunk, pass me my backpack, would ya?"

Hunk picked up the pack, surprised at how heavy it was. It had to weigh at least eighty pounds. No wonder Jake needed those ten-minute breaks. He didn't remember seeing Jake packing anything inside it, so it had to be something he took out of the safe room while he was downstairs. He'd been carrying one of the rocket launchers along with his usual gear, so with the extra in the backpack he'd been carrying about twice as much as any of the other men.

Jake opened his pack and removed a plastic baggie full of trail mix and jerky. He bit off a large chunk of the leathery meat, washing it down with water from his canteen. He offered the trail mix around before finishing off what was left in the bag. The other men were using their break to grab a snack, use the bathroom, or relax. Everyone was curious what Jake had planned. They could follow the creek down-stream and look for another way across but walking cross country took a lot longer than following the streets. No one wanted to wade across the murky water. Both options sucked.

Then Jake pulled a plastic-wrapped package out of his pack and everything became clear.

"I'll be damned. A raft. That's the one thing I never expected to see. And it has an intact canister."

"Yep. So does this one." He pulled a second raft from his pack.

Hunk grinned. That explained the weight. Each of the rubber rafts weighed about thirty pounds. And those canisters added an additional ten pounds. It also explained why he wanted to head up Main Street, it was the shortest way to the river. And why he had changed his mind and moved the unit south. It would take longer to maneuver the rafts down the creek than traveling the entire way on the river but it was a whole lot faster than walking all the way back to home base.

Jake lay back against his almost empty pack. "Somebody wake me when we are ready to leave."

***

Shortly before dawn Hunk spotted a boat ramp with enough woods around it to provide camouflage for the rafts. Even in the dark, it looked thick enough to disguise the rafts from anyone flying overhead. He could just make out the burnt-out shell of a brick home on the hill above the ramp. With luck, there would be enough standing to give them shelter until night fell. Jake agreed and they paddled for the ramp. He could see the outline of the second raft following them toward shore. Traveling the creek had cut off almost a mile of walking but it had taken longer than they hoped. Once they reached the river , they had increased speed, using the current to propel the lightweight rafts downstream. They had passed Horseshoe bend and were moving along the section of the river that had once held million-dollar homes, all with their own private docks. Nothing salvageable remained. What hadn't been sunk had burned to the water line before sinking into the shallow water along the shore. Every building was destroyed. Fire finished destroying what little the alien's lasers had left standing.

"Looks like it might be our best spot. There's enough cover to hide the rafts. Once we land, Sant and Cody can scout out the best place for us to overnight while we make sure everything is secured."

Santwan nodded, signaling for Peterman to get ready to head inland as soon as they pulled the raft onto the boat launch ramp. They vanished into the overgrowth as the first raft was being pulled into a thicket. The two men made a careful survey of the ruined buildings, finding no signs of life. Nor were any tracks found on the cracked pavement or the ground around the remains. Satisfied that they had investigated and found nothing to prevent them from utilizing the area, they returned to the shore.

Both rafts had been moved to the thicket and additional brush was added to ensure they were was not easily seen from the air. There was almost no chance of them being located but they were leaving nothing to chance.

Sant was eager to get into shelter before the sun was completely up. "The house is gone but the basement garage still has a roof over it. Roll-up door but we can rig up something to keep out the light while we sleep."

"I'm surprised it survived."

"They did a poured floor throughout the house and carried it over the garage. Kept it from]]]burning."

"Find anything interesting?"

"Depends. How do you feel about Monopoly?"

Jake laughed. "I haven't played in years. But it will help the time pass. I'm burnt out on cards."

***

Hunk was the first one to spot her. He looked at her a moment as though to assure himself that he was not dreaming. "Mikey! Tell me that's not a girl out there."

"Out where?"

"There. On the river. See that big board? There's a girl lying on top. "

"Damn. It sure looks like one." Mikey suddenly felt an overwhelming urge to swim out and speak with her. There had to be a reason she was floating down the river. She could be bait in trap. Or she could be in trouble. "Hold my pack. I'm gonna swim out and check."

Hunk didn't argue. He wasn't much of a swimmer and Mike was like a fish in the water. They all liked to call him Mikey because he would try anything, but he could not think of a better person to have his back in a fight. If the girl were alive, he would know how to get her back to shore.

Finding an almost naked young woman clinging to a floating piece of plywood wreckage in the middle of the river was something out of a low budget Hollywood movie…one the Kurs might have seen. The survivors had lost a couple of people trying to salvage things from debris in the water before learning the Kurs like to rig the wreckage to explode. The good thing was that there was usually a slight delay, ten or fifteen seconds after they picked up the supplies before the explosion. This allowed most of the salvagers to escape into the water even though the landing was often harder than they would have preferred. The current often worked in their favor, moving the raft downstream away from the swimmers. However, the Kurs were always adapting the traps and this could be the latest version.

One minute he was standing on the shore, the next he was there beside the makeshift plywood boat.

Mikey studied the way the woman was laying on the wood. The sensor must not be activated by movement because there was no way she could remain motionless for long periods of time. So it was most likely set off by loss of the baits weight or heat signature. An idea had formed but he wasn't certain it would work. He needed to decide now. The water was moving fast, that would work in his favor but it also moved him farther from the landing than he liked. He grabbed her hand and slid her body toward the edge of the wood. The young woman made a slight sound but did not fight him. When he had her lying against the edge, he took a deep breath and pulled her towards him, swimming as hard as he could for shore. The suddenly lighter plywood picked up speed as the current carried it away downstream.

Mikey was still ten feet from the shore when the explosion hit them, rolling them over in the water. He fought to keep a grip on her wrist. The force of the blast had made his ears ring for a moment but they were already starting to clear up. He quickly drug her out of the water and carried up the hill, lying her under the bush near Hunk.

"Shit. That was close. There's no way the Kurs will miss that. We need to get her under a blanket now."

"She's not moving. You sure she's alive?" Hunk passed him one blanket and pulled a second from his pack. He relaxed a bit when he saw the rise and fall of her chest.

The woman didn't complain when they covered her with the two blankets, which made keeping her invisible to the Kurs technology much easier. He did a quick search over her body but he did not locate any type of tracking equipment. Not that he would find any if they had made her swallow it. He had no idea if the blankets blocked radio signals r whatever method of communication the Kurs used. They would have to do the best they could with the materials they had and hope it was enough.

Hunk lay on the ground beside her as Mikey pulled on his clothes and then lay on the other side. Between the two of them, he expected they could keep her covered long enough to evade the searchers. The last thing they did was pull the lined balaclava down to cover their faces. Wearing the lined clothes in the summer was hot, but it almost guaranteed the Kurs would not see them. Choosing to sweat for an hour or flaming out under one of their lasers is a no brainer.

The high pitched whistle of the Kur's airships announced their impending arrival seconds before they flew into sight. Without slowing they flew past the boat landing, heading west looking for any sign of the explosion. We figured we had about ten minutes before they returned since the Kurs had no idea what caused the raft to explode. For all they knew, the girl simply stepped off the debris into the water and drowned. Once the invaders located the debris they would begin a grid search of the area between the wreckage and their base, looking for the girl or her body.

Hunk raised his head covering, allowing his head to cool off in the late afternoon breeze. There was a hint of moisture in the air, just enough to make him wish he had been the one to jump in the river instead of Mikey. The thin reflective layer kept the temperature outside from warming him too much, but the occasional bead of sweat that rolled down his forehead into his eyes irritated him. The sleeve of his uniform removed the sweat but there was already a new bead forming.

The increasing whistle informed them the Kurs were coming back into range so the two men replaced their face covering and scooted their bodies tight against the girl's sides. It was important to stay as still as possible while the aircar was in range. They had no defense if the Kurs spotted movement and decided to burn out the entire area.

Hunk blanched when the aircar spotted the boat ramp and decided to check it out. He could have hit the aircar with a rock as it passed them on the way up the boat ramp. The thicket hiding them was about a hundred feet upstream from the paved driveway. The house was gone but the basement door was in clear view. The aircar floated along the drive to the burned-out hulk and landed. Two aliens got out and began searching through the remains. After what felt like an hour, they returned to the river and continued their search pattern. Neither man moved until the whistle could no longer be heard.

The sense of relief was palpable. The girl had awakened and was beginning to shift around beneath the thin space blanket. Both men rolled up their balaclavas into hats before removing the blankets.

The young woman was half-dead from exposure and badly sunburned. The few pieces of clothing she had left looked like she might have been caught in a fire. Her lips were parched and cracking, her skin red and blistered. The matting in her waist length blonde hair reminded Hunk of the old saying about a rat making a nest. Chopping it off might be the only way get the tangles out. When she moved, the twin bruises of a chain or collar showed against her pale white skin. Dark circles rimmed pale blue eyes, and a drop of blood trickled down from a tiny cut above one corner of her mouth.

Mikey held his canteen to her lips and helped her to drink. She tried to grab the canteen to get more but Mikey limited it to about half a cup. Anymore and she might get sick.

Hunk frowned. "The burns look bad. They might be infected."

"Not much we can do until we get back to camp. Sun will be down in a few moments." He worried about what Jake was going to say when he saw her. She hadn't said a word since regaining consciousness, so he had no idea who she was or where she had come from. Every time one of them brushed against her, she trembled like an abused animal.

The snap of a limb breaking behind them made both men turn. They would know the answer in a minute...

***

The woman struggled wildly against the two men that were trying to help her stand. Pale blue eyes rolled wildly as she kicked out at both men and bit down on Mikey's arm. "Someone get Peterman. Tell him to bring something to calm her down," he said firmly.

"Easy. We are not going to hurt you. You are safe." Something in the tone of his voice must have got through to her. She stopped screaming and dropped back to the ground, then wrapped her arms around her legs, rocking back and forth while humming under her breath. But she kept her eyes locked on Jake.

"Is she crazy?" Mikey wasn't certain she was salvageable. He was disappointed that the girl had latched onto Jake like he was the second coming and ignored the fact that he had been the one to save her life.

"No, I think she's been treated pretty badly. Looks like someone has beaten her. I'm sure she's been raped. She jumps back every time somebody walks within a few feet of her."

"Hell, any sane person would go crazy after going through that." Mikey was happy to see Cody arriving with a sedative. It took all three of them to hold her still while he jabbed the needle in her arm.

After a few minutes, the sedative kicked in and she began to quiet down. She stopped screaming. Every so often, out of nowhere, she would either start giggling or start crying.

At least she was calm enough to transport. They should have been on the river half-an-hour ago. They got her into the raft and began floating downstream. The current was steady, they should make it to the landing near camp within a couple of hours. Unfortunately, that landing was no longer an option.

The presence of the young woman had changed everything. Jake wasn't sure what to do with her. The compound had rules and one of them is no one would be brought to the Cave entrance until they were 100% sure there was no danger to the inhabitants. No one knew who this girl was or how she got there. She could have come from Hixson. Or she could have come from California via one of the mother ships. There's no telling how long she had been on the water. It could have been days or half an hour.

She had definitely been held somewhere, by some-one…survivors or aliens. Since Jake could not imagine any reason why either would release her, that left the possibility of her being a trap. They had equipment back in camp to look for electronic traces but nothing with them. He could not risk the people living in the cavern to save one shattered girl.

There was a small cave on the far side of the

mountain, overlooking the lake about a mile beyond the campground. It only went back about twenty feet. For now, that's where they would take her. He would leave Mikey to guard her. He was acting like a love-struck puppy anyway.

Chapter 18

The shattered remains of the sign pointing to the entrance to Ruby Falls brought on a fresh burst of adrenaline. Erika was walking as fast as possible, but each step sent intense bursts of pain throughout her body. One of the slashes had cut into the burn scar on her leg and the pain from that area was sharper as if the tissue were one giant nerve ending.

Struggling against complete exhaustion, Erika dropped to one knee, sweating and swearing but soon forced herself to her feet and kept walking. She knew if she gave up and stopped to rest, she would never start walking again. By the time she reached the top of the mountain and had the ruins of the building that housed the gift shop in view, she was almost crawling, her breath coming in sharp stabbing gasps. Her hands were torn and bleeding from multiple falls. Her tan jacket was sticky and dark red where the wound along her ribs had soaked through the makeshift bandage. The entire left side of her body was throbbing in time with her heartbeat but she knew that would be taken care of as soon as she reached her destination.

She fell again as she began walking across the parking lot. The sound of men's voices woke her.

"She's coming around," one voice said.

"Jake," she gasped softly.

"Soon," the voice answered. "Just lie still for now. I need to slow the blood flow. You wouldn't happen to know your type would you?"

She mumbled something but her throat was too dry to speak. It come out as a deep rasp.

Her mind vaguely noted seeing a pair of military-style boots, then someone lifted her head. "Water," the voice said as he held the flask to her lips. "Drink."

The water was lukewarm and tasted of minerals but Erika was thirsty and downed it greedily. She tried to raise her body to sit up but her muscles refused to obey. Gradually her vision cleared. She could have sworn that heap of rubble across the street hadn't been there when she fell, making her wonder how long she had laid on the broken pavement before someone found her.

"I need to see Jake," she whispered, surprised at how different her voice sounded. She pushed herself up on one arm. Then everything went dark.

Peterman called out for assistance, and two men came running with a litter. They transported her to the medical area, putting her in an old storeroom that had converted for treating injuries. Then Peterman sent for Jake.

***

When Erika opened her eyes, it hurt. Everything was white… and the light above her was very bright. In the background, she could hear a steady beep…beep…beep that was really starting to get on her nerves. She struggled to throw the lightweight cover off and felt a sharp sting as the I.V. needle in her arm was pulled out of position.

She could hear men's voices, so she knew she wasn't dead, or captured by the Kurs, but other than that, she was lost. As far as she knew, all the hospitals had been destroyed by the invading forces, but this room gave off the distinct hospital room vibe. She tried to focus her eyes but nothing worked..

She jumped, knocking a metal tray onto the floor when someone sprayed something cold on her side.

"She's waking up!" an excited male voice rose in pitch as Erika screamed and jerked away when he touched the cuts on her side. He called out to someone just outside her view. "Gonna need some hands, I still need to clean her wounds."

"Can't have that, can we?" He seemed to be moving away from her.

Erika was reasonably certain it was male talking…and human…but that's was all. The blur in her vision was gradually fading as her eyes adjusted to the artificially bright light. It was definitely a hospital room, no one in her family would ever paint a bedroom such a sickening pea green color. Plus, she was lying on an adjustable bed, on a real mattress, with sides that locked to prevent someone from rolling off. Somehow, someone had found a usable metal hospital bed with side rails. She wondered where all the nurses were. The last time she was in the hospital, they were everywhere. The two men in the room were wearing military uniforms, green camouflage, not the pristine white her mind insisted they should be wearing. She had no memory of how she got there.

"Where am I?" she whispered. Neither man answered. One was looking at something on the tray and the other was doing something on the counter behind him.

After a minute she began to get aggravated. Why wasn't anyone answering her? She was certain they had heard her question. The young man she could see walked over and pushed a button on the machine with the annoying beep and it finally stopped.

Too bad he had waited until the person using the jackhammer had busted open her skull.

Obviously, he had no intention of answering any of her questions. She could hear him talking to someone just outside her view, but she could not make out what they were saying. In frustration, she snatched the thin pillow from behind her head and tossed it in the direction of their voices.

They both laughed.

"You must be feeling better," the young man said as he raised her head and slipped the offending pillow back into its normal position.

"No. I'm not feeling better," she croaked. "My head is pounding and my side feels like someone is trying to turn my body inside out. Is Jake here? I really need to talk to Jake."

"That's going to have to wait," a new voice said. "Right now I need to finish closing your gashes before you bleed out." A good looking Latino man moved to the side of the bed and injected something into the IV running to her arm.

Almost instantly she felt a warm flush begin to spread across her body and relaxed. She tried to shift her body into a more defensive position on the narrow hospital bed. The side rails were up so she couldn't slide out, but she was certain she could roll forward faster than they could walk if it became necessary to make a quick escape. She thought she saw one man moving a rolling table toward the be...

***

Erika gasped sat up, blinking her eyes to adjust them to the dim light of the unknown room. She'd awaked in a sweat, heart pounding and unable to breaths. The pain radiating from the gashes across her ribs made it impossible to get comfortable. Lying back on the bed, she tried to get her turbulent emotions under control.

"Nightmare?" The speaker was wearing the same type of uniform Jake always wore. She had no memory of how she got there but knew she must be inside the compound.

"Um, yeah," Erika answered, trying to figure out what had happened after she passed out on the road. "Where am I?" The nightmare had been a bad one. She could not stop shaking. Her mouth was dry, her head was hurting, and she was certain something disastrous was about to occur.

"You are in a storeroom beneath Ruby Falls," the unknown man said, returning to his chair. "But I get the feeling you knew that already. You must be Erika."

"Yes. Who are you?"

"Cody Peterman. Nice to meet 'cha. I'm a medic. Jake is in my unit. He is also my friend, so I have an inside source."

Erika exhaled the breath she hadn't realized she'd been holding. If Cody knew Jake, he had to be with the resistance.

"I need to take a look at your wound to check for infection. The light is very bright. You might want to close your eyes." He flicked a switch and the overhead fixture, three oversize bulbs, harsh and unyielding in their intensity, made her narrow her eyes to shut out the glare as the room was flooded with light.

She closed her eyes, trying to give her eyes a chance to adjust, then she must have dozed off. The sound of a chair sliding across the floor nearby startled her.

"Can I sit here until she wakes."

Jake? Instantly wide awake, Erika sat up in bed, her long auburn hair falling in soft waves around her face. She hurriedly smoothed it back and rubbed the sleep out of her eyes. "How long have you been here?"

"Not long. I came as soon as I heard you were waking up." Something had changed the militant young woman he remembered. She had lost a little weight, not that she was skinny, but somehow she seemed delicate, almost waiflike lying in the hospital bed. The parts of her body he could see was in bad shape, it was impossible to pull his eyes away from her bruises and scratched skin. What had brought about such a chance is such a short time? Then Erika shifted position and the sheet that was covering her chest fell away, exposing a French cut bra that barely covered her breasts.

His pulse began to race. Immediately, he began to count backward from one hundred under his breath. By the time he reached forty-seven, he had his emotions and his lower extremities back under control. Luckily, she didn't seem to notice his discomfort. He picked a spot on the wall above her head, staring at the nail head, in an attempt to keep his eyes and everything else off the perfect pink globes.

"Yeah. About that. Where exactly is here? I must have passed out because my last memory was spotting the Ruby Falls sign at the entrance to the parking lot." She leaned back against the pillows, relaxing as her body registered the *everything's okay* signals her brain was sending out.

Jake shifted the pillows, adding another to give her more support. "You are in the supply room beneath the old souvenir shop. We use it as a holding cell."

"A holding cell. I'm a prisoner?"

"No. The soldier who found you, said you asked for me by name. That had never happened before. But I was not here to identify you so they treated your injuries and kept you here until I returned." He did his best to hide a thin smile. "Rumors abound in the barracks."

"I hope no one gets the wrong impression."

"No. They already think I'm a ho-dog. Now that your identity is going around your reputation should be safe. But I'm happy you came to see me."

"Sorry, this is not a social call. I guess you will have to find another way to proliferate stories of your prow-ess. I'm here to warn you about a new threat. The Kurs have brought in backups."

"Backups? I haven't seen another ship landing. And there doesn't seem to be any more of them in the area. If anything, there seems to be fewer."

Jake wondered if she was delusional. Clear think-ing was almost impossible while taking medication, and the medic had dosed her with enough sedative to put a man twice her size to sleep. He was surprised she could even sit up. She seemed a bit wobbly if nothing else.

"No. They brought their dogs. Well, it's not exactly a dog, more like someone bred a praying mantis to a wolverine. Lots of teeth. It found me, even with the suit. I think it hunts by scent."

"That's how you got hurt?"

"Yes, it's got teeth, two rows, and long sharp claws on its front feet." She seemed to shiver. "Scared the hell out of me."

"I bet. Is there anything about them that we can spot from a distance. I would hate to shoot a real dog by accident."

"Simple. Shoot anything with six legs."

"Six legs. Yeah, that might get my attention." He tried to imagine a six legged praying mantis with a wolverines attitude and it wasn't pretty.

There was a knock on the door. They could hear a man's voice talking to Cody and him answering back. Then the door opened and a tall, middle-aged man wearing fatigues came in.

Jake immediately snapped to attention.

"At ease. I'm here to have a talk with this young lady." He turned toward the bed, "Hello Erika, it's nice to finally meet you. I'm Captain Royce Jeffers."

Her eyes roved over the meticulous officer, noting the carefully ironed uniform, smooth shave and carefully manicured hair. He smiled, showing pearly white teeth and Erika noticed the crack in his glasses. That had to drive him crazy.

"Hello, Captain Jeffers. I've heard a lot about you." She wasn't sure how to address him. Was she supposed to salute too?

His eyes went to Jake for a second and then he smiled. "I'm sure you have."

Jake shifted uncomfortably but didn't say anything.

Captain Jeffers pulled up a chair and sat down. "So, tell me about this new threat."

Erika hesitated, wondering how he had found out about a threat. Then she realized someone had been listening to her conversations. She doubted it was Cody since she had no memory of telling him anything about the beast. But he might have been listening outside the door while she was talking to Jake. Her gut said it wasn't him.

Still she was pleased when Captain Jeffers offered an explanation.

"Since we use this room as a jail cell, we have monitors hooked up to keep an ear on the prisoners. No one thought to notify the recruit manning the technical console it would not be necessary, so I received the usual print out in my daily report. You talk in your sleep."

Erika blushed, wondering what other secrets she might have spilled . Then she explained what had happened, starting with her recent activities hunting Kurs and ending with the new creature. She lowered the blanket so he could see the length and depth of the claw marks. Then she pulled back the bandage on her shoulder so he could see the double row of teeth marks. Once she finished, he nodded.

"This is something we definitely need to take into consideration while on patrols. The men have become a bit lax about maintaining weapons at the ready since nothing we have could hurt the Kurs. Finding out about the arrows has greatly improved the death ratio. But I get the feeling a bow and arrow might not be enough to stop this new threat."

She nodded. "I hit it with two and it didn't slow down. The phaser was up against its chest and I kept my finger on the trigger. It still took a few minutes to die."

Captain Jeffers leaned back in his chair, stretching his legs out before him. His eyes went to the clock on the wall in the hall outside her room, and his face tensed for a second before relaxing again. "You know it's strange how things happen. Nature has many secrets. Six months ago, we were convinced humans were the only sentient beings in the universe. Now we know we were wrong. It is certainly within the realm of possibility that hundreds, maybe thousands of new species exist on a planet different from ours. We do not have a glimmer of hope of understanding them all. Whatever animal the Kurs evolved from, it was clearly several times bigger, and much stronger than the monkey most educated humans consider their ancestor. Now we have a new addition to the mix, and it seems as dangerous , if not more, as the Kurs."

Erika took advantage of the opening. "About the Kurs. Do we know anything about them? Like where they come from?"

"Not really. We think they travel through space by means of interdimensional gateways, a type of artificially created wormhole that allows the ship to cross great distances across the universe in a matter of seconds. Or maybe they slip sideways into an alternate dimension. No one really knows. Our every attempt to communicate with them fails. For all we know, they think we are nothing more than a new source of food."

"Don't tell me…we taste just like chicken."

Everyone laughed.

Captain Jeffers stood and shook her hand. "You have given me plenty of things too think about. I think it best I sleep on it. Please enjoy our hospitality tonight and we will continue our discussion in the morning." He turned his head and caught Jakes's eye, nodding toward the door, silently signaling he would like to talk to Jake outside the room. The two men walked out without another word.

They didn't talk much as Jake walked him back toward the golf cart. There really wasn't a lot to be said. Erika had provided them with important information but her fate was still up in the air.

Once he was seated in the golf cart he asked one

question, "Do you think her story rings true?"

"Yes, sir."

He nodded and pulled away.

But the time Jake made it back to the room Erika had turned over and had begun to snore softly. Jake made sure she was comfortable, the walked across the hall to a similar doorway.

Cody looked up as he entered the room, "How's she doing?"

"Out like a light." He gestured to the second cot in the room, "Mind if I bunk here tonight."

"No problem. I will check her again in a few hours, but she will probably sleep through the day." He turned over and fell asleep within minutes.

Jake lay awake for a considerably longer time, rehashing the conversation, and trying to come to grips with the possibility of falling in love with the independent young woman. Being open to it scared him more than facing the Kurs ever could. It also intrigued him. But it could wait for a better time. He was exhausted. He closed his eyes, and finally, he fell asleep.

Chapter 19

The erratic knock at the door startled her awake from her latest nightmare. This time, after the fire died down, she opened the cooler and found her parents inside. There was not a mark on them and somehow this made it worse. She sat up in bed, skin clammy with her heart pounding in her chest. Her head ached to the point she felt she was about to retch. Gradually she got her nausea under control and her heart slowed to a more normal rhythm. When the knock came again Erika checked her hair in the mirror above the small chest, straightened her clothes, and pasted what she hoped was a welcoming smile on her face before opening the door.

It wasn't Jake.

The young man standing at the door allowed his eyes to wander from her head to her toes before he let loose a short wolf whistle and grinned.

"Hi. You must be Erika. I'm Martin Davis but my friends call me Mace. I'm here to escort you to breakfast and then to the common area. Captain Jeffers has called a full meeting and everyone is supposed to attend. It's a bit of a walk down the stairs to transport, so if you need any help just ask."

"Uh...thanks." She hesitated. "Is there any chance

of a shower first?"

"If you can handle the cold water you can jump in the falls and rinse off. But the only real shower we have is over in the main cavern." He opened a pack he was carrying. "I almost forgot. Captain sent you a change of clothes. He mentioned yours were in bad shape."

What is left of them, she thought. The dried blood on her jeans felt stiff and sticky and her bra wasn't exactly covering much of her breasts. The medic had cut what was left of her shirt away before cleaning and stitching her wounds. A bath, even a cold one, sounded wonderful. As she followed Mace toward the waterfall, she wondered where Jake was but didn't put much consideration into his absence. He was an officer in the army, even though the number of soldiers was extremely small, they always seemed to be busy. Maybe he would be at the meeting.

She winced as a sharp pain hit her side. She could move but felt stiff and clumsy after lying in a bed for three days. The healing incisions on her side made each step painful, but nothing that she could not handle. She had faced worse during the initial weeks after the invasion, but somehow she had shoved that down below conscious memory, preferring to pretend the memories of her family were little more than an unwelcome dream. The hardest part of her recovery was the oppressive sense of imprisonment she developed after being inside all the time. With no windows, she could not see out, could not feel the sun on her skin, or hear the sounds of the crickets and frogs near the water or the birds welcoming the morning sun. After a few days, she adjusted to the monotonous grey environment but hated herself for it. The idea of seeing something, anything, except the four greenish-grey walls, was too exciting to resist.

After telling her he would be right back, Mace had left the room, returning in minutes with a towel, soap, and a small hotel size bottle of shampoo. The hall outside the room was lit by lights that must have been activated by motion. Within seconds of their passing, the light went out and the next one down the hall came on.

Taking a shower under the red-lit falls was more fun than she expected. She stripped down to her undies, unwilling to completely undress with Mace standing a few feet away. The cold water invigorated her, leaving her alert and feeling more like herself for the first time in three days. She could have spent an hour standing under the falling water but realized the amount of time she had available to eat breakfast was draining away like the water falling from above.

When she stepped from the water she realized Mace had exchanged the oversized tee-shirt for one that fit her body better. After adjusting the pants, she quickly slipped on clean socks and her boots, eager to head to breakfast.

As she started back toward her room, he stopped her. "Leave you dirty clothes here and I will get them washed."

He surprised her by walking the opposite way from the stairs they came down. Stopping before a locked door, he tapped a code in and led her down a set of stairs to what appeared to be an alcove by a service tunnel.

"Hop in," he said as he slid behind the wheel of a golf cart, one of two setting in the alcove. "The ride is not long. We will be there in a little over five minutes."

Erika wanted to ask questions but decided to hold her tongue and listen. Mace seemed eager to provide her with information about the compound. He mentioned that the US Government had set up the transport system to move men and supplies between their storage rooms below Ruby Falls and the Fallout shelter that had been built during the nineteen-sixties inside Possum Mountain. The cave system was commonly used for training by the Georgia, Alabama, and Tennessee National Guard.

"Our unit was training here when the attack occurred. We have been able to contact other active-duty survivors in similar situations. The known population isn't exactly large, but there is enough to guarantee the survival of humanity once we send the Kurs packing."

His comment brought a small smile to Erika's face. Mace reminded her of a small puppy; warm, cuddly, and overly eager to please. His idea of repopulating the world was so simplistic. It was gonna be easy. Kill Kurs, save Earth. No Problem.

There was an armed guard stationed at the end of the tunnel. He saluted Mace, then turned to Erika. " Happy to see you up and about miss. Your discovery has made life a lot better for all of us."

Erika was startled to realize he not only knew her name, he knew who she was. "Does everyone know who I am?"

Mace nodded. "There are about a hundred fifty people living in the cavern. I would say a hundred and forty of them do. So don't expect to slip in unnoticed." He held the door for her and followed her into the main military housing setup. "We will be coming back here after we eat. He opened the door at the end of the hall-way and announced, " This is the largest gathering area of the cavern."

Erika did her best to take it all in. The cavern they stood in was far larger than it had seemed from inside the military section. Erika had spent most of her youth exploring caves with her brothers. This was nothing like the caves she had crawled through. She was humbled by the enormous space. Many of the jutting stone for-mations were so ancient they had grown together into natural columns that reached from floor to ceiling.

She gasped in delight, as Mace held the high inten-sidy beam lantern overhead. Like jewels decorating the neck of a beautiful woman, the bright light illuminated veins of glowing minerals threaded throughout the vista of stalagmites and stalactites. It was beautiful.

Evidence of a prior occupation stood out amongst the modern furniture that had been salvaged from the destroyed homes and businesses around the main cavern. Fire pits burned around the outer perimeter. She noticed that the smoke was being drawn upward through small cracks in the ceiling of the cavern. Mace led her into a side tunnel that disappeared into the darkness in the distance. Every twenty feet or so, torches set in holders on the walls gave off a small amount of light. The tunnel opened up into a smaller cavern set up as a kitchen and cafeteria-style kitchen., set up with modern freezing and cooking equipment.

"We moved the buffet table down from the souvenir shop. The generator keeps the freezers cold and out food hot. Most of the people who survived were camping at the lake when the attack occurred. They were able to reach safety in the cave under the cover of darkness. The aliens concentrated on destroying the campers." His face fell and she realized that meant the majority of young people did not make it. Most had been asleep by the time of the invasion.

Mace gathered himself and continued his story. "About a hundred years earlier an enterprising young farmer had developed the mountain, lake, and cavern into a family campground. Over the years some of the original attractions had been declared too dangerous by modern standards, like the toboggan that ran on wheels down the side of the mountain. But the cave itself had been updated to current safety standards." He stopped talking and let Erika gather her thoughts. It was a lot to absorb at one time. "Okay. That's my tourist spiel. I'm hungry. Grab a tray and we can help ourselves."

She smiled and he showed her where to find the plates. Moving down the buffet he filled one plate for himself as she filled hers. Eggs did not agree with her but she was happy to see pancakes and syrup. There was even some artificial butter.

She followed him to an empty table nearby. As she settled at the table she could feel everyone's eyes on her. She made a mental note to thank Captain Jeffers for sending the fatigues. The pants were adjustable and once she took up all the available tabs they were a rea-sonably good fit. The tee shirt was a size too large but no big deal. It felt great to be clean and wearing freshly washed clothes again. The table gradually filled up as they ate.

The five men that joined them had no qualms about asking questions. Once they found out who she was, they acted like they had known her for years.

"You look nothing like I expected," one, a tall skinny teenager still dealing with acne said.

"What did you expect?" She was curious. Jake had been surprised when he met her, too.

"A middle-aged science teach with coke bottle glasses. Not…" He turned to a handsome blonde man missing part of one arm "Remind me to discuss a few things with Jake when he gets back."

"I'm Mikey" the blonde said. "Forgive Max, he has no manners. I'm really happy to meet you. Your space blanket trick has changed our lives. It makes it much safer when we have to go out on patrol."

"Glad I could help."

"Can we assume you being here is the reason Captain Jeffers is calling everyone in?"

"Possibly." She left it at that, choosing to enjoy the sweet taste of the fluffy pancakes and real maple syrup. Sweets of any kind were few and far between. She had no idea when she might get another chance.

"Well, we are glad to have you. Do you play cards? The cafeteria doubles as a breakroom between meals. Most of the time anyone not on duty is down here. We can always make room for one more."

"I will keep that in mind."

" You got any idea why the Captain is calling us together?"

Erika smiled. " I have an idea but I think it best he tells you himself." She was ready to get the meeting over with so she could discuss going home. Having Jake around made it easier but she was growing impatient. The medic wouldn't discuss anything with her. In her mind, she was more than healthy enough to return home. She had left Chance alone for a longer period of time, so she was reasonably certain he would remain near her hideaway until she returned. But Goldie wouldn't understand her absence and the animals that remained around the farm would be wondering why she had not come to visit. They were not locked in and roamed freely around the neighborhood, returning in the evening to sleep in the shelter of the old barn. She had dropped several bales of hay the day before she was hurt. Chances are there was still hay in the racks since there was so much grass available. But freshwater must be running low, and the nearest creek was often dry between rainfalls. It wasn't good for them to roam too far.

She was saved from answering by the clock on the wall.

"Five till. We need to head down to the meeting." Mace stood, taking her tray as well as his own. Erika waited by the door with the others and they all walked down together. Upon arrival, she was pleased to see several other women wearing similar clothing. They greeted the new arrivals by name so she felt it safe to assume they were also military.

The main cavern was already crowded when they arrived. The assembly area stank of too many bodies in too small a space. Babies cried, children laughed and played at the feet of their parents, or in the case of three young orphans, their guardians. She had been surprised to see so many children, she had assumed most had been inside campers sleeping when the invasion began. Then Mace explained that whenever a child was found they were brought back to the compound and placed in the care of a volunteer. Many had lost both parents in the initial attack. The raucous chatter of too many voices all talking at the same time grated on her nerves after living alone for so long.

"There's a lot of teenagers here," she said.

"Yes. Many of them are in the ROTC and were training in the caves when the invasion began. Others were rounded up during the first few days and were looking for a safe haven. Some were camping and lost everyone in their family. So we formed our own."

"Cool." It wasn't something that would interest her; however, she could understand why people who had lost everything would crave the support and security of an extended family. There was quite a few pairings happening already. One or two of the people were older than thirty, but most were high school or college-aged. The relationships may not last more than a few days but no one was thinking long term at this point anyway. There was no guarantees anyone would survive the Kur invasion.

She looked around, wanting to get a better idea of the people. There was a clear defining line between the civilians and the military. Several of the soldiers continued to work on projects as they waited. Erika watched a boy about her age field stripped a machine gun almost as long as he was tall. He cleaned each part, then reassembled the oversized artillery. Once he completed a weapon, he set it down near the door and picked up the next firearm to be cleaned. Some of the armaments he was working with she had only seen in videos during history class. She never expected to see one being made ready for use.

Despite her interest, she was happy to see Captain Jeffers walk in, accompanied by Jake and Santwan. He walked directly to the front of the area, stepped up on a platform and called for attention. Once everyone had quieted and was listening, he began explaining the new threat. He also took questions. This lasted about an hour during which Erika realized some people asked ridiculous questions, many of which were so far away from reality that there was no possible way he could answer them.

Finally, he ended the sessions with a general statement that made more sense. " In the pre-invasion military, officers do not mingle with enlisted men. There are not enough of us here to maintain any type of hierarchical separations. Our lives are more fluid. We eat with whoever we want to eat with. We sleep with whoever we want to sleep with. No one cares, or if they do, they are smart enough to keep their mouth shut and their opinions to themselves. As civilians, you have never experienced the rules and regulations that the military live by. That being said, it is important that anything that might affect your life should be explained. Before we take any actions that affect the citizens here in our sanctuary, you will be given an opportunity to speak. Then we will vote on what steps to take. We have no idea what the off-worlder's final plans are. We do know it's not in the best interests of humanity. Unfortunately, if we don't stop them soon, it won't matter. There won't be any humans left to care."

Murmuring broke out around the room at his words, some arguing for destroying the Kurs mothership even if it killed them all, others just wanting to remain in hiding until they decided to leave.

Erika felt that was an unattainable future. The Kurs showed no intention of leaving, and were instead, expanding their operations. The possibility of them simply packing up and leaving was too small to imagine. Now that aliens had discovered the planet, there would always be a need to be alert for other visitors. It was ridiculous to think the Kurs were the only intelligent race in the universe.

Captain Jeffers was winding up the question and answer session. "If there are no more questions you can all go. Talk about it among yourself. You know where my office is-- if you have any questions we may not have covered."

The silence at the end of his speech was broken by a single hiccup. Laughter broke out around the room.

The side of his lips quirked upward but was immediately brought back in line. "Units Alpha and Bravo remain. The rest are dismissed.

He turned to Erika. "If you can spare me the time, I would like to ask you a few more questions."

Erica nodded, her face flaming as she struggled to get her hiccups under control. She looked around for some water but no one nearby was drinking any. "I'm sorry," she said, in between hiccups. "I didn't mean to disturb your speech. I just can't stop hiccupping. Do you think I could go get some water first?"

Captain Jefferson nodded. "Of course. We all have things happen that are beyond our control. Corporal, would you please get our guest a bottle of water. While we wait, I'm going to… uh… allow a ten-minute break and ask everyone to meet back in the breakroom. I want all of you to start thinking about …hmm…I would love it if one of you has a brainstorm and come up with a way we could get inside the stadium. Time is running out and we need to rescue as many of the captives as possible. It has been several weeks since the last mothership arrived. We need to act soon if we hope to get some of our people out before the next transport arrives."

Mace hurried to get Erika a bottle of water. Three days after the initial attack, while scavenging the area, they found an intact truck crashed beneath one of the overpasses on Highway 24. The driver was not inside, so they had to break in. The truck had a full load of bottled water, and Coca Cola products. It had taken them several nights to completely transport the cargo to stores.

"Here," he said, "see if this won't help." He handed her small pack of peanut butter -cheese crackers to eat, along with the bottled water.

Erika hiccupped her thanks. The water made swallowing the crackers much easier. After a few minutes, she realized the crackers had worked. "Do you think he was serious about morning us to come up with ideas?"

"Jeffers's? Yes, he really believes that humanity has the best ideas when their back is against the wall. If you come up with something let me know. Better yet, raise your hand and tell him. He'll appreciate the initiative."

Erika laughed. "Right now, the only initiative I feel is my bladder clamoring for me to find a bathroom."

Anita, one of the female soldiers grinned. "I know that feeling. Come with me and we can talk on the way. I'm interested in knowing how you survived for so long by yourself."

"You ladies go on ahead to the breakroom. I'll catch up as soon as possible." The two young women were giggling as they walked away.

When Erika returned everyone was listening to Captain Jeffers's discussion on the power supply aliens we're using. They had identified two possible items of equipment that could be generating the force shield and were looking for opinions.

"… once we locate the source of the power, then

we worry about a way to destroy it."

"What if it's a wireless power source?" Sarah asked.

Erika had been surprised to find the young woman was part of Alpha Unit, the same unit Jake commanded. He had not mentioned a woman being in the group. Of course, the subject had never come up, so she didn't think it was an intentional oversite. Beside Sarah, there were twin girls in Beta Unit, Bess and Tess. The old fashioned names were a direct contradiction to the high and tight haircuts, tattoos and muscular physique of the three women.

"That's what Devonte is working on. If he can figure out their computer language, he may be able to hack in wirelessly even if its offline."

Erika had been surprised to recognize Devonte from school. He had been as much of an outsider as she had, spending all of his time online with his virtual friends instead of attempting to interact with real ones. His hair was longer and he had lost quite a bit of weight since she had last seen him, but he still wore the horn rim glasses , khaki's and golf shirts she remembered. Someone had spent a lot of time plaiting his locks into long thin braids that he had gathered into a tail running halfway down his back. He nodded as she entered the breakroom, the only sign of recognition he offered her.

Erika was surprised at the warm flush she felt at that simple nod. She returned the gesture with a smile, then directed her attention to the conversation between

Captain Jeffers and two of the men in Jakes unit.

"We have to do something. I believe Parker is still alive. If we can't figure out a way to stop them, then we need to make sure none of them make it to the transport."

"Let's leave termination as a final option. Our people are depending on us to rescue them."

Santwan cleared his throat. "I've been giving it a lot of thought and I don't think there are more than a hundred of the Kurs on the ship. We usually see them going out in groups of four. I've been counting and I've only seen about twenty of the small airships. It all the transports are out, that would leave about twenty Kurs on board at all times. Some of them will be in support positions; cooks, maintenance, techs… others will be officers."

"That's interesting info. How long have you been keeping tabs?"

"Since Parker got snatched up." Santwan had lost his best friend and family to the invaders. Any free time he had was spent devising ways to inflict damage on the Kurs in any possible manner. Helping the prisoners to escape would go a long way toward balancing the scales in his mind.

Jeffers nodded, and then made a few notations on a pad in front of him. " At this point in time, we have three objectives. First, we need transportation. The aircars give them the ability to move quickly between distant points. If anyone has any ideas on how we can get out hands on one, feel free to express those ideas. Crazy times call for crazy plans. Second, we need to understand their power source. Devonte is heading up that division. Third, we need to capture one of their weapons. That would provide the power we need and allow the techs an opportunity to examine and possibly duplicate it. He paused and drank some water, allowing what he had said to sink in. I'm not expecting miracles. Consider, if one objective is achieved, we have a foot in the door. Two would be great, three would be an ideal goal but an unrealistic scenario. I want you all to keep these objectives in the forefront of your mind while you are in the field."

Erica raised her hand. "What if someone was able to capture one of the flying cars? Wouldn't it take specialized training to be able to fly it?"

Captain Jeffers smiled. "Assuming a small strike force was able to overpower the crew of the aircar and bring one down without destroying it, it is possible one of our pilots could decipher the controls and fly it."

"What about the aliens. Could they find a ship … and then find us? Like a tracer on a lost phone?"

"Devonte?" He turned to look at the small group of techs.

"It is possible that the computer in the aircar would be able to communicate by signals to the home base. this would allow them to follow the signal sent out by the guidance system. It is equally feasible that they do not have the technology to know the position of the aircar at any time. Even if we assume the alien's minds work in the same manner as humans, there is no guarantee they would have developed the same technology as Terrans. They communicate differently. Their vision is different. They may not be able to see the aircars unless the motor is running. They always leave someone with the transport whenever they land."

"So they may not be able to trace them?" she asked.

Captain Jeffers smiled. "Humans like to know where our equipment is at all times--- the Kurs may not care. What makes you ask anyway? You plan on going out and capturing aircar next?"

"Well, I kinda already did."

Everyone started talking at the same time. Erika was surprised by the amount of questions she got bombarded with.

Captain Jeffers released the breath he had been holding in a silent whoosh. *Did the girl just say she had an aircar? He had to know but he was scared to hear the answer.* He rapped a small rock atop the table, getting everyone's attention. The room grew quiet. "Erica. Are you telling me you have an aircar... one of the aliens aircars?"

She nodded yes.

"Where is it? No... hell! Wait! You're gonna have

to give me a little more details. Is it wrecked? What happened… I mean, where is it? I wanna see it! When can we go see it?" Every bit of his usual restraint had vanished.

Jake had moved from his position by the door, up to stand next to Erika. He had never seen the Captain lose it. He wasn't sure what the protocol was.

He laid his hand on her shoulder.

Erika felt some of the tension overwhelming her fade away. She took a deep breath and let it out. Then began speaking. "It's about …uh… halfway between here and Lafayette. I've got it hidden under a bridge covered with space blankets. The Kurs flew over the area two or three times but they never found it. I figured they could find a general area where the aircar went down but couldn't locate their aircar. "

"Well hell, I just… I just… I'm floored. I don't suppose when you captured this air car you managed to get one of their particle beam accelerators?" Captain Jeffers was being facetious but figured what the hell, he might as well shoot for the moon.

"The ray guns? I have a few of them. Would you like a couple?"

Captain Jeffers's hand was shaking. He took a drink of water and gathered his composure. They had been trying to devise a plan to get one of the weapons for months, with no luck. Apparently, all they needed to do was ask. "If it wouldn't be any trouble. I'm sure that the tech wizards would enjoy looking at one up close."

"No. No problem. I've got one in my backpack. They can have it. I've got another one just like it at home."

Capt. Jeffers started coughing at her words. He took another swig of the water in the bottle, hoping to gain some control but could not stop the cough. Finally, he managed to squeeze out, "Dismissed."

Erika had removed the backpack and as the men began heading back to their duty posts, she began pulling items out of it. An unopened can of coffee caught his eye. Jake had mentioned her having coffee to trade. His pulse raced as she lay one of the shiny metal guns on the table before him. His hands were shaking as he picked up the weapon that had destroyed so much of his life.

He turned to the eager tech waiting to take possession of the gun. "Take it a long way from this base before you start testing it. Keep the tests under tight controls, no explosions that might draw the Kurs attention. An accidental explosion could have serious consequences. Make certain they only affect the opposition."

He turned to Erika. "Now, tell me how you managed to capture an aircar?"

Chapter 20

"Do you ever think about what life would be like today if the attack had never happened?"

Jake hesitated before answering. The way in which she'd asked the question, with sadness and a hint of longing, made him think about what he would be doing now if nothing had changed. He would probably be in the army full time. Maybe overseas, in Fallujah or Germany. The tiny military action that had seemed so important now seemed like a complete waste of time and resources. He remembered thinking that over a thousand dead was such a large number. That was a joke. There was probably not a thousand left alive within a hundred miles of Chattanooga now." Sure. I do it all the time. Then I pull myself together and get back to reality.

The sun was setting. Bursts of color lit up the evening skyline in shades of red, gold, and purple. Without the haze of pollution that had covered so much of the city, everything appeared brighter. It was as if nature had discovered new colors to paint the sky.

Earlier that day Erika had taken three of the men down to the barn to check out the aircar. Only one was a licensed pilot, but the other two had some hands-on experience in the air. She had stopped long enough to feed and water her livestock before returning to the compound. Now she was enjoying some hard to schedule time with Jake. "It's beautiful," she said. She turned her head and looked directly into his eyes.

Time seemed to stand still as he gazed back at her. "Yes you are," he echoed, and her face flamed. He leaned in, and lightly brushed her lips, then he pulled her closer against him and kissed her again. He could hear her heartbeat quicken. The high pitched whistle of an approaching aircar interrupted the moment.

Jake reacted on instinct. He grabbed Erika's wrists and threw them both off the rock. Their bodies tumbled to the ground into the dense undergrowth. Jake hit first, and somehow Erika managed to land on top of him. Their eyes locked. Jake had noticed that the bright green in her eyes followed her emotions, shifting them from winter evergreen to a softer shade of new grass in the spring. This color was a new one, an intense shade that reminded him of the back of his childhood parakeet. Before he knew it he was kissing her again. The feeling he got was not what he expected, pure and sweet almost innocent. Guilt overwhelmed him when he realized he had been expecting the same kind of reaction from her as he'd received from Destiny. She had practically climbed into his lap as she returned his kiss, throwing her arms around his neck and jamming her tongue deep into his mouth. The was no way he could miss the invitation.

"You don't like me?"

"No…Yes… yes, I like you. It's just…" She squirmed and Jake released her.

"What? My breath stink?" He sniffed the air and frowned as he caught a whiff of something rank that assaulted his senses. He raised an arm and winced. It was him. Gawd , he was rank. He needed to set up a hot date with a bar of soap and a thick wash rag as soon as possible. The signup sheet for the showers during convenient hours often included extra duties, so he tended to take a dip in the lake instead.

Erika was looking at him like he had just grown a second head. "No …it's not you. It's me."

"I've heard that one before, usually right before I get dumped. It a little early for that so, why not?" *Was it because of his race?* He hoped not. There was not a big gene pool to choose from and race discrimination should have died along with the vast majority of the human race. He crossed his arms defensively across his chest and locked eyes with her.

She sighed and resigned herself to the humiliation. "I'm still a virgin, okay? I've had a few boyfriends. Some of the boys I met in high school were nice, but me, well, I never found anyone I liked enough for that type of commitment." Her statement was accompanied by a defiant stare as if she were expecting him to break out in laughter at any moment.

Instead, Jake pulled her closer, wrapping his arms around her. It wasn't exactly the response he'd been expecting, but all the same… it was something he could build on. He wasn't sure where this relationship was heading, but he knew he wanted to see it through. It must have been difficult for her to be that honest, and he felt better for knowing she trusted him enough to reveal something so personal. In a weird kind of way, he liked the idea of her being untouched. It was rare even before the aliens arrived. Now it was almost unheard of. Girls like Erika didn't come around very often and he had no intention of letting her go. He would be satisfied with a kiss…the rest could wait. Besides, there was no sense in continuing a discussion about something that might happen in a future life no one was certain would ever come to pass. Families and relationships were dreams at this time. First, they had to get rid of the Kurs.

***

The raucous clamor of the old fashioned windup alarm clock startled him awake. Gaunt-faced and gray, Captain Jeffers, stretched his lean body and winced as the sharp pain in his lower back reminded him that sleeping in a chair at his desk was probably not the smarted thing for a middle-aged man to do on a regular basis.

He was exhausted. There were several important issues he needed to discuss with his two officers before they left that evening, but at the moment all memory had left him. Like a storm-tossed balloon, moving from place to place with no set destination, being directed by random bursts of wind his mind refused to co-operate. Somehow he had to develop an operating plan that would achieve the necessary objectives without costing the lives of the few remaining soldiers under his command. Jake and Santwan were two of his best and the thought of losing them both niggled at his conscious. He was still going to send them, but he felt bad about having to do it.

Private Pope, his aide for the week, set a cup before him and filled the cup with black coffee. Erika had provided a little heaven on earth when she traded two pounds of coffee for a case of cokes, with the promise of several more pounds in future. He may not eat for several hours but he expected the flow of fresh coffee to continue until he ordered Pope to stop serving.

A knock at the door drew his attention.

At a silent signal from the Captain, Pope opened the rubber flap, allowing Jake and Santwan into the room. "Anderson and Hutchins, sir," he announced.

Captain Jeffers fought back the grin that threatened to break free and waved them toward chairs, then offered both men coffee. Pope tried so hard, and that was a trait he didn't see so often in fourteen-year-olds.

"Thank you but I've had plenty. You want a cup Sant?"

"No thanks. My kidneys are floating now." He grinned, showing a set of almost perfect teeth.

Jake hid his smile. Santwan's mother had been

a dentist. He brushed his teeth more than anyone he had even met. The idea of being unable to maintain his teeth and possibly losing them was a fear they were all familiar with. Sant would neither eat nor drink anything except water until he was in a position to immediately brush them clean. Everyone knew this but they always offered anyway.

"In the past, I've had to ask you to do things that go far beyond the extremes of the oath you took when you enlisted. Today will be no different. But this could change the outlook of the conflict and if handled correctly, it might actually give us a slight edge for the first time since the invasion began."

The captain rubbed his gray stubble of beard, making a mental note to have Pope check his position on the shower and shave list. "Erika's aircar has been checked by the techs. They feel with your experience in light recon aircraft there is nothing there you can't handle." He nodded and Pope passed them both a simple diagram showing the controls of the aircar.

"Study this diagram. There will be horses ready at sundown. You should arrive at the barn in about an hour if you follow the ridge down Lula Lake and take Nick-a jack down to the valley. You will make yourself familiar with the operations of the aircar and then decide who will be piloting first. We estimate you can be in the Knoxville area in about an hour. Avoid the city but head for the area near the Guard Post. This should give you enough time to locate a secure hiding spot and then make your way to Resistance headquarters before daybreak."

Jake realized he was not expecting an answer. It was obvious he was not through speaking so both men waited.

"You will need to explain the use of the slingshot bows and the trebuchet. They must understand that only natural materials will work. Make sure you cover the threat of the tracking animal, making it clear that they can locate you in the suit. Get a force of men started this way. Then hurry back, I need you here tomorrow night."

The two friends locked eyes. On the surface, it seemed like a simple task. Fly up. Talk. Answer questions. Then fly back home. In truth, there were so many different things that could go wrong.

Captain Jeffers could see the doubt in their eyes. "I know I'm asking a lot of you. The people here are afraid. A pep talk isn't enough to keep them going any longer. They need something tangible; a win they can see. You know they look to our small troop for guidance. That's not your responsibility. It's mine. It's also on me to make the hard decisions. Like this one. I'm giving you a direct order. No one knows you are leaving or where you are going. No one."

He glanced at the clock. The sun would be setting soon. If they left now, by the time they reached the exit at the base of the mountain the horses should be waiting. He stood and walked around the table. Stopping to face the two young men, he snapped off a smart salute.

They responded with a salute of their own. Then they turned and headed directly to the Lookout Mountain access tunnel.

Captain Jeffers watched them leave before returning to the pile of papers on his desk. The decision to send then off in an aircar they knew nothing about was a difficult one. Humanity was losing the battle and this could be one of the final plays of the game. He was not a hero, able to stir intense feelings of strength and hope as the savior of the race should be. He was a paper pusher. What happened tonight could mean either life or death for the human race. That's why he picked Jake and Santwan. Neither man was willing to give up without a fight. The concept of self-sacrifice had been instilled in their DNA and honed since birth. They would challenge the Devil if it were needed. He wouldn't ask that, but the next 36 hours were going to Hell.

Chapter 21

Jake's hands shook as he loaded the hand-held crossbow, his eyes locked into a thousand-yard stare as the aircar moved closer to the aliens transport. Santwan's weapon was already loaded, lying next to him on the seat. It was moments like this that made him wonder why he had joined the military in the first place. Sweat beaded on his forehead, sliding down his face and into his eyes. His finger remained on his trigger, constantly rubbing it, never losing contact as he tracked the other transports speed and distance.

The pilot of the alien's aircar was pacing them, staying almost exactly the same distance away at all times, adapting his vehicle every time Sant made an adjustment to the controls.

Up until ten minutes ago everything had gone like clockwork. The ride to the barn had taken less than an hour. Once they'd arrived, the tech had ensured both men were familiar with the aircar's basic controls before announcing anything further would be a hands-on experience. He stood watching as Sant eased his lanky body into the driver's seat and inched the captured transport out way out of the old barn. His expression changed to panic as Santwan underestimated the acceleration rate of the machine, coming within a few feet of crashing

into the side of Lookout Mountain. When he overcor-
rected, the engine began to stall out…approximately a
thousand feet above the ground.

"Quick. Check Drew's notes and see if it says anything about parachutes," Sant snapped as he struggled
to get the aircar under control.

Jake lifted his hands, fingers out, and raised an
eyebrow, giving him in a puzzled expression. "What
notes?"

Both men cracked up, laughing hysterically as
they attempted to get their turbulent emotions under
control as the aircar leveled out once more. The rush
of adrenaline they experienced quickly dissipated and
they settled down to enjoy the ride. Sant was following
what used to be Interstate 75 heading north towards
Knoxville. The state had a large contingent of National
Guard in that area and hoped to make contact some of
the survivors.

Six months earlier, two young men who had been
training with the Chattanooga National Guard when
the attack occurred, had left riding bicycles. They were
heading home, hoping to find that somehow there
had been survivors among their friends and family in
the Knoxville area. With no way to contact them, there
had been no confirmation that they had made it home,
or if there were any survivors. However, the people of
the Smokey Mountains had long been known for their
resourcefulness, giving them reasons to feel optimistic.

Now, this had happened.

They had been in the Maryville area less than twenty miles from Knoxville when they first noticed the second aircar. It approached their path from the north-east, flying slowly but directly at the aircar. This was unusual in two ways. First, it was around midnight and they had never seen any of the off-worlders out after dark. Secondly, the driver was not a Kur. It appeared to be humanoid, but not human.

"Look at its eyes, how big they are" Santwan said. "They remind me of an owl. I wonder if it can see us?"

"Let's not take any chances. Turn west and see if we can lose them." Jake began loading weapons, set-ting backups within easy reach. On impulse, he added a machete, just in case it came down to hand to hand combat. He had no idea how to kill the new alien, but rarely did anything function without a head.

Sant gunned the motor and they took off, cutting cross-country in hopes the other airship would not fol-low.

It hadn't worked.

The pilot had no problem following their trans-port, even gaining on them until he was flying beside them. The pilot began pacing the aircar, staying about a hundred feet away, just beyond the limits of the hand bows. Within minutes it became evident he had more experience with the mechanics of the flying transport. It was also clear that they were not going to be able to lose them. The Kur had begun squeaking and chittering into a communication device. We were close enough to hear faint verbal responses.

That's when Jake began arming himself.

"Times up. We can't afford to wait for reinforcements to appear. We have to take them out now."

"What do you have in mind?" Sant kept one eye on the air before him and the other on the alien pilot.

"Whatever that is they got driving, can see at night. We have to assume that he can see us as well, if not better than we can see him. But the Kur can't, and that's their weakness"

"Agreed. But the driver doesn't need a breather. Not even sure where you would need to hit it to take it out."

"I don't know if the arrow will kill it, but I'm willing to bet it will slow it down. Just get me close enough to them and I will take care of it." Jake checked to make sure he had everything he could carry in every available pocket or pouch. The machete and aliens gun was hooked to his belt.

"10-4. Operation Indian Attack underway." Santwan began inching closer to the other airship. He could see the other pilot's eyes opening even wider and then he began chittering to the Kur. The Kur responded and the driver increased his speed. "Damn it, they are rabbiting. Get ready." Santwan pushed the lever up and turned the steering, moving the aircar as close as possible to the side of the other transport. Jake crouched by the edge of the airship, heart pounding in his chest. He expected to see Jake fire the crossbow at the driver but instead, he jumped, landing on the back of the other aircar.

Jake fired the crossbow seconds before he landed in the Kurs aircar. He saw the driver flinch as the arrow dug into its back but it was easy to see it was going to take a lot more to stop it. The Kur was looking around as if he had no idea where the bolt had come from.

Jake released the second bolt, grinning from ear to ear when he saw it slice through the air tube before coming to a stop in the side of the Kurs face. In seconds it had collapsed to the floor and was lying in a pool of fluid, twitching and gasping for whatever it breathed.

The pilot had abandoned the controls and pulled out a smaller version of the laser gun Erika had provided. As it turned to fire, Jake pressed the trigger on his weapon, and somehow managed to drop flat on the floor between the seats. The pilot had turned his body in the chair, leaving it with nowhere to go. The weapons laser clipped it across its upper back, burning a path through its shoulders and along the side of its face. It panicked and turned back to the controls, trying to increase the airships. speed as it made a sharp turn back toward Knoxville.

The laser had hurt but not stopped it. Jake thought about firing another blast, but the chances of striking something necessary to keep them in the air made him hesitate. He thought about the machete but instead, his hand dropped to the obsidian knife on his hip. Time seemed to slow as he dove for the pilot. The alien had him on height and weight, but it expected the force field to protect it from physical attacks. The crossbow bolt had surprised it, and it had recognized the laser in time to avoid a killing strike. It had no defense against the chipped stone blade. The worked obsidian held a glasslike edge, easily slicing through the forcefield into the fleshy area of its neck. Instead of boney tissue, Jake realized it was a type of thick cartilage that separated as the blade cut into the rubbery pads on the back of its neck.

Jake grunted and jerked his hand sideways, moving across and upward toward what he hoped was the creature's brain. Thick bluish-gray fluid flowed down its back, soaking his hand. The skin on his hand began to swell and sting, like battery acid when he got it on his skin.

The alien was still alive but now it wasn't interested in steering the ship. It let go of the controls, and lunged at Jake, extending sharp claws that dripped the same caustic fluid.

As the clawed hand clamped down on his left arm, Jakes entire body reacted, shooting waves of pain through over-stimulated nerves along his spine to his head. Jake groaned. His eyes blurred, and his arm began to jerk, as tiny jolts of electricity racked his body. He felt his legs tremble and knew he could not keep the fight up much longer. Somehow he managed to raise his hand and press the laser against the alien's side. His grasp weakening, he pulled the trigger.

The alien screamed.

Jake kept his finger locked on the trigger as he moved the weapon upward, burning completely through the body along a path similar to a human's spine. He didn't notice when the screams stopped, continuing upward until the laser had bisected the head. Then he collapsed in the vacant pilot's chair and turned the ship back toward the river.

Santwan wondered why Jake was going back toward Knoxville until he saw him begin his descent toward the water. He landed on the shore next to the other ship in time to see Jake jump into the river.

"What's wrong?"

"Don't touch anything. That fish-eyed bastard's blood is like acid. My fuckin' hand feels like it's been boiled."

"Water helping?"

"It's helping but it ain't stopped it from hurting. Wait a sec and I'll show you."

Santwan began to dig through his pack, looking for the first aid kit. They all carried baking soda in case they got hit with acid. He hoped it would help neutralize whatever was in the creature's blood that was eating away at Jakes skin.

Jakes hand was bleeding and skin was already peeling away. The fluid had eaten through the thin metallic coating along the arm of his space blanket liner. From the elbow to his wrist the skin was raw and enflamed. The three deep gashes where the claws had dug into his arm looked bad.

"Tell me if this helps," Santwan said as he sprinkled a liberal coating of the alkaline sodium bicarbonate into each wound.

Jake grimaced as the white powder went on but began to relax as the soda neutralized the acidic fluid. "Hell yeah, that's better. Makes me want to bury my arm in the shit. But its gonna have to be enough for now. We need to dump the bodies and look for a place to hide out for a while. I saw it talking to someone. This area is going to be hot as hell in a few minutes."

"Feel up to driving that thing?"

"Yeah, but I'm not gonna sit in that chair until its cleaned. I'll stand until we reach cover."

"Which way?"

"North. We go up into Kentucky. There's a lot of farmland up that way. Make a wide circle and come back toward Knoxville from the eastern side. Taking this second airship changes things." Jake wondered how Erika was doing? He realized it might be a few days before he got back to the compound. She was almost back to full health. That meant she could be leaving any day.

He hoped she hung around, so they could continue the discussion they had started the night before. With the info lockdown on the special op, she would have no idea why he had left or when he would be back. There was no reason for her to hang around.

"Agreed. We can work it out after we find somewhere to lay low." Sant paused. "How the hell are we going to explain all this to Captain Jeffers?"

Chapter 22

Erika wondered why she had bothered to return to the compound. It wasn't as if she could not handle being alone, she'd had plenty of time to adjust to that before Jake had stumbled into her life. She had Chance, Goldie, and all the animals to keep her company. But after being back home less than twenty four hours, she found her eyes being drawn to the ruins atop the mountain. If she squinted, she could just make out Rock City from the meadow behind her family home. When she found out Jake had left without saying goodbye it had hurt. Cody had declared her fit for duty, which basically meant she could do anything she normally did. With Jake gone, she had no reason to hang around. That evening she began riding down the curving mountain road to her hidden hideout.

Chance had been happy to see her, giving her multiple wet kisses and beating her leg black and clue with his tail. She spent the night checking all her traps, locating two that contained rabbits for Chance to chase. One managed to escape and the other was big enough for them both to enjoy.

Goldie had returned to the pasture she shared with Blunt, the gelding and Popcorn, the Shetland she had rescued from a collapsed barn. Now they were waiting impatiently for her to pour the grain they knew she carried in the buckets. She jumped away to avoid being trampled by the three horses as they greedily shuffled for position around the trough.

"Pigs," she muttered, noticing the hay in the racks was getting low. There was no gate on the paddock to prevent them from grazing around the neighborhood but they preferred to stay nearby. She had spotted the paw prints of a dog pack down by the creek and made a mental note to do some hunting. Coyotes like the feral dogs, had no fear of humans but they had learned to fear her bow. By now, they had cut her trail and changed hunting grounds, moving away from this side of the park.

She sat and stared up at the night sky for several hours, wondering why she was so depressed. *Maybe she would feel better if she killed a few Kurs?* They had not flown over the Battlefield in weeks but she had a good idea where to find them. She saddled Goldie and began riding toward Chattanooga, not really paying much attention to where she was headed. Before she noticed, she realized she was heading up Nick-a-jack road. The ride up the mountain hadn't taken more than an hour. She debated turning south and riding toward the cove but turned back toward Ruby Falls instead. Jake owed her an explanation. Regardless of his reason, she would have no closure until she told him how angry and hurt his behavior had made her feel.

She stripped the tack off Goldie and turned her out with the other horses, leaving her riding equipment inside the old dumpster the unit used for tack storage. If anything happened to it, she would replace it, she had found the tack and there was a lot more where it came from. After brushing Goldie she opened a coke, drink it slowly, then ate a candy bar. Nothing helped. She needed to face Jake or ride away. There was still time to go hunting.

A shadow at the edge of the tree line caught her attention. Something in the way it moved convinced her it was an animal…an animal that was closing in for a kill. She pulled her bow and began following it. It was moving away from the pasture toward the secret entrance to the stairway above Ruby Falls. A knot began to form in her stomach as her intuitive mind recognized the way the animal was walking. That funny jerking off kilter hop step. For a second she hesitated, remembering how close she had come to death. No one would blame her for running in the opposite direction. Offering a brief prayer so that her soul would be okay, she dropped her bow and pulled the phaser, running as fast as she could toward the intended victim.

She caught the brief flash of fire as the guard lit something to smoke. In that moment she recognized the beasts target. Danny wasn't a soldier but he often participated in the everyday tasks alongside the enlisted men. She was usually happy to find him on guard because he recognized her, removing the need for an extensive question and answer session a stranger would be put through.

Danny was relaxed, leaning back against the hand-rail puffing a cigarette he'd been smoking on breaks. He'd been trying to quit but after finding several packs in a wrecked car, he was indulging his only vice.

She screamed a warning as the shadow leaped. The beasts front claws took out the side of his face. Its teeth clamped down on the teens neck as she fired, snapping his neck with one savage twist. It was crouched over his lifeless body, red blood glistening on its fur in the moonlight. She knew she was too late for Danny as she continued to rake the creature with the laser.

The beast dropped the boy's body and turned toward her. Several ugly burns showed on its chest and legs but nothing appeared life threatening. The high pitched skittering squeal brought shivers, as memories of the beast that almost killed her returned. Except this wasn't a nightmare. She could see it hesitating, deciding on whether it should go after her or return to its master.

Erika know she had to kill it. If it got away it would return with the Kurs. They would find the hidden entrance. Hundreds could die. She pointed the phaser its head, pulled the trigger and ran toward it, praying it would not lose power before the beast was dead.

Realizing its danger, the beast paused, searching for a way to escape. Enormous granite rocks rose twenty foot high on both sides of the hidden entrance. The heavy metal door required a passcode. It had one option, get past Erika.

Faster than she imagined it reversed its course, running straight toward her. Her hand was shaking but she kept firing. Somehow, she had also pulled her pistol and was firing the small handgun at the same time. The clip held ten bullets. One must have hit its spine. It tumbled to the ground less than five feet from her. She continued to fire the laser, slicing sections away from its head until there was not much left.

She stopped firing when a hand grasped the gun from behind and pried it out of her fingers.

"It's dead, Hun. You can't kill it no more than you did already." Beth put her arm around her, pulling her close as she cried. There were several uniforms standing nearby, but her eyes were too blurry to recognize who was who.

"Are you okay?" Cody had appeared and was making sure she was unhurt. He had already examined Danny and covered his body with one of the space blankets. Two men she did not recognize was examining the remains of the beast.

"Mikey heard the gunshots and knew something was wrong. He was near the stairs and hit the alarm, then ran this way. He arrived too late to help. You had already killed the beast." She smiled and Erika felt the weight on her chest fade away. "Why don't we go inside and let them clean up this mess. It's going to be daylight soon."

Erika hesitated. "I dropped my bow and backpack, back along the trail. I promised Jeffers I would drop off a few things I'd picked up."

Mikey perked up at her words. "If that's what I think it is, Captain will be happy to see you. Things have been crazy since you left."

"Really? Anything I should be aware of?"

Her voice sounded so hopeful. Mikey regretted what he had to say. "Better wait and let the Captain fill you in. You know how it is." Mikey knew without her saying anything she was asking if Jake was involved. The Captain had a lid on the op, so he could not say anything. He was certain the Captain would talk to her when she saw him.

"Gotcha. I will walk back with Beth. Be careful, there may be more of them around." Beth supported her as she limped toward the open door. She must have turned her ankle while running.

Mikey grinned and nodded, keeping one eye on her as she walked away. Jake didn't know how lucky he was...

***

When the two women arrived at the transition point of the tunnel, there were three strangers already waiting for the golf cart. They were all dressed in the same uniform that Jake and his friends wore.

Erika wasn't concerned, just curious about the new arrivals. Her intention was to be polite but remain reserved.

When Hunk pulled up in the golf cart he blew that. The lovable weightlifter grabbed her around the waist and swung her like her father used to do when she was three. "Erika! When did you get back? Damn, you weigh a ton. Whatcha got in the backpack. Lead weights?"

"More toys for Captain Jeffers."

"All right! Celebration time! Meet us in the break room later?"

"Sounds good. Maybe I can win some of my money back."

She gave him a quick hug and nodded to the three strangers who offered them space in the cart. No one talked during the short trip down the tunnel. Beth helped her from the cart and they began walking toward Captain Jeffers's office.

She heard some laughter and a few ribald com-ments as she hobbled away but decided it wasn't worth reacting to them. There was two strangers waiting when they reached the desk in front of Captain Jeffers office. She could see the question in the adjutants eyes but he didn't ask.

"Hi, Thomas. Captain in?" Beth said, "Erika wants to see him."

"For Erika, I'm sure he is. But he's not alone. Captain Armstrong is with him. Since you were the subject they were discussing I don't expect him to get upset when we interrupt." He knocked on the door and then announced her after the captain acknowledged the knock.

Captain Jeffers grinned. "Come in, come in. Were your ears burning?"

"Toasted to a crisp," she replied. "I'm going to need to wear long hair to cover the ashes." She ignored the glares the two soldiers did their best to hide, thanked Beth and walked into the room behind him.

Captain Jeffers said something to Thomas and shut the flap behind him.

Erika could hear faint voices then the sound of footsteps fading into the distance and realized Thomas had sent the two men away.

"Pull up a seat. Let me introduce you to Captain Ben Armstrong. Ben this is Erika... you know, I don't know your last name."

"Hicks. Erika Hicks."

"Nice to meet you, Erika. I have heard a lot about you in a very short time."

"Don't believe any of it." Captain Armstrong was exactly how she pictured a military officer in her mind. About six foot two and heavily muscled. Dark haired and tanned, he wore a flattop haircut liberally sprinkled with grey, giving him a distinctive air of mature strength. Even without asking, she could tell he had been in the service a long time.

She picked up her pack and set it on Capt. Jeffers already overloaded desk. "Brought you something."

His eyes lit up as he moved to open the pack. "Is that what I think it is? Yes!" He began to unload the alien weapons, laying them out in a line.

Both men were like kids with new toys at Christmas. After examining the three distinctive sizes and shapes, Captain Armstrong asked if there was a big difference in power.

"Not that I noticed. They all seen to burn anything you point them at. And the force field does not stop them."

"I hear you had a run in with a beast on the way in."

Captain Jeffers knew Danny had died but he did not mention it, so Erika didn't. "Killing them is much harder than the Kurs. It took the phaser and a pistol to stop it."

"Finding it on our back doorstep worries me."

"Me too. I don't know if it was random, or if it was searching for survivors. I've never killed anything on the mountain."

Captain Armstrong shifted his weight and cleared his throat. " There are seven guns here. Royce said you had already given him two. Are you telling me you have killed nine aliens yourself."

"Not nine," she said.

"So you had help?"

"No. I killed them all."

"But you just said" Captain Armstrong appeared skeptical.

"No. I said not nine. I've actually killed fourteen." Erika crossed her arms and offered him a defiant stare, daring him to question her numbers.

"Fourteen? By yourself?"

"Yeah. Well, one fell out of the aircar when the pilot died. But yeah, thirteen definite. And two tracker beasts. They are much harder to kill."

"The tracker beast. Is that what injured Sargent Anderson?" He still looked unconvinced but was willing to accept her answer, given the evidence lying on the desk.

Captain Jeffers quickly answered the question. "No. That's the new one. Kind of a cross between a fish and an owl. They are using them as pilots after dark."

"So what is this beast she's talking about?"

Jeffers grinned. " I can tell this conversation is going to take longer than I planned. We might as well send out for something to eat. Once you hear the story you are going to need a strong drink and it's not good to drink alcohol on an empty stomach."

Two things stuck out in Erika's mind as she listened to the two men talk. There was a new alien. And she was pretty sure Jake's last name was Anderson.

***

Dinner was over and most of the soldiers remaining in the break room were playing cards when she arrived. She scanned the room, looking for her friends, listening to bits of conversation. It was hard not to laugh.

"…burned his legs off and splat, the rest hit the ground."

"Let the bodies hit the …

"Give me two…"

"…of her melons. I could barely get my"

"About damn time! I'm was about to start taking off clothes to pay my debt."

Erika had been invited to have dinner with the Captains, a delicious roast chicken served with rice, fresh tomatoes, and sweet baby carrots, the kind of food she had only dreamed about since the restaurant had burned. The fresh vegetables were sublime. The inhabitants of the compound had scattered small garden patches around the mountain and had recently begun early harvesting, making the succulent treats available for everyone. Then Thomas had brought in Blackberry cobbler for dessert. It had been hard not to lick the bowl clean.

Spotting her by the door, Mikey waved his hand overhead and Erika made her way through the crowd to their table. One of the men vacated his place and she settled down in the chair; dumping her change on the table, eager to win some of her losses back. Something Captain Armstrong had said was chipping away at her subconscious mind. Captain Jeffers had mentioned how difficult it was to bring down the beasts with the standard armament the men carried on patrol.

Captain Armstrong had answered, "We gotta get a bigger gun." Both men had laughed.

She had no idea why that sentence was nagging at her, it was a famous line from an old movie, nothing that should have struck a nerve. Military men were always going on about something crazy. Most of it made no sense to non-enlisted people, all those letters. She shrugged and took two cards, then settled down to play some serious poker.

She was laughing about something Mikey had said and missed Jake and Santwan when they walked into the room.

Jake did not miss her.

Sant laid his hand on Jakes shoulder and shook his head, signaling with his eyes that Jake should go to a table on the opposite side of the room. This was not the place for a public display of emotions, good or bad. The conversation could wait for a better time and place.

Jake grunted and slow walked his way to the table, keeping his ears cocked the entire time. Erika was laughing at something Mikey had said, something that had flushed her face and his.

Jake shifted in his chair and began to rise. "

Santwan stopped him. "Slow your roll, Romeo, you're losing the ability to reason. The woman is already pissed, and you are number one on the *why the fuck should I care* list. Think of her like that Chance dog you told me about. Get you hand too close and you may draw back a bloody stump."

Jakes shoulders fell but she settled back into the chair. Sant was right. He needed to talk to Erika but this was not the right place to do it. He tried to study his cards but his mind wasn't on the game.

***

Erika tossed her coins into the pot and arranged her cards in the latest hand. She had spotted Santwan by the snack area and followed him back to the table with her eyes.

Now she was torn between acknowledging Jakes's presence and pretending she had no idea he was in the room. His presence set off a new wave of emotions. Erika fought to retain control of her turbulent reaction. It had hurt her feelings when he left without saying goodbye. She had shared parts of her life with him, parts she had never told anyone. He had seemed to listen and understand how hard it was to drop her barriers. Knowing that he had returned and not bothered to seek her out made it even worse. The idea that he could be thirty feet away and she wasn't even worth acknowledging mad her mad. She decided to go with that.

***

Jake had hesitated when he spotted Erika playing cards with several of the men in his unit. It was evident his buddies had become comfortable with her during his absence. When Sant laid a hand on his shoulder to stop him the second time, it made him angry. But he knew Santwan was right even though he wanted him to be wrong.

T-Jax noticed his interest and answered his unspoken question as he dealt the cards. "She came in earlier today. Had a long shut-in with both the captains before showing up here about an hour ago."

Jake nodded as he picked up his next hand. He studied the cards he had been dealt with and made his opening bid. His eyes kept going to the other table. Erica looked sexy as hell in fatigues. Firm champagne glass breasts, a slim waist, soft rounded buttocks, and lightly muscled hips. She was only average in height but her long legs would not have looked out of place on a much taller girl. The sun had lightened her auburn hair adding a blush of red that made her skin glow. Sexy and smart.

He took two cards on the draw and folded, his mind not a hundred percent on the game. Mikey was doing his best to charm her, leaning closer and whispering things that made her laugh and Jake wonder what was being said.

Jake wasn't sure if she felt his gaze or not, but she glanced over at him, offered him a *eat shit and die* stare, and then went back to the card game. Yep. She knew he was here. There was no question of that now. She was probably pissed about the way he had disappeared without saying goodbye. She had already left for home when they returned the first time. Since then Santwan and he had made the same trip three additional times. He was a soldier. It was his job to keep the people under his care safe, not to run after some girl, no matter how much he wanted to. He tossed in a few coins and took three cards, then folded. There was no way he would be able to concentrate until he got that issue settled between them. He was ready to go and strike up a conversation, and at least make sure she knew he wanted to talk to her.

"I'll be right back."

"Not good man, let her cool off."

"No. She saw me. I need to go and at least say hello."

He was sliding his chair back from the table when the. breakroom door opened and Destiny walked in. She looked around the room and then made a beeline directly for him. *Damn.*

***

Erika was surprised to see Destiny come through the door. Her antagonist had lost a few pounds and if anything was even prettier than she had been back in high school. She was wearing a slinky red dress that followed every curve, so she was probably here to meet someone. Destiny had been one of the popular crowd, but not especially adept at anything, preferring that the boys at school fawn over her and fulfill her every whim. It made Erika wonder how the pampered cheerleader had survived the invasion. She had met and spoken to most of the cavern's inhabitants and had no memory of seeing anyone resembling her. Maybe she came down with Captain Armstrong's group?

Destiny seemed to know where she was going, taking seconds to spot the table and walking directly to it. She said something to Santwan and one of the other men, and then she kissed Jake on the cheek.

Erika's face fell, her heart began to slam against her ribs and her stomach rebelled. She could imagine how pale her face must be.

"Is it just me or did someone let one rip?" Erika's smart-ass comment was a nasty snipe at Destiny and Jake. Her mouth had gone completely dry. She fought the urge to retch and tried to swallow but found out she was unable to do it with her throat tight and constricted. Why did the idea of Jake talking to Destiny bother her? That's what girls like her did. She smiled and batted those eyelashes and every male within a hundred yards lost all sense. It wasn't as if it hadn't happened before. She had just thought Jake was different.

Screw this, I don't need this kind of crap.

"Sorry guys, but I think I'm really gonna be sick." She stood up from the table and walked toward the door, fists balled, trying not to cry and hating her high school tormentor more and more with each passing second.

The four men at the table exchanged amused

glances as she walked away. There had been rumors of something between Jake and Erika since the first time her name came up in a meeting. No one had any idea of what she looked like until she collapsed in the parking lot. Now there were several men interested in stepping up since it appeared Jakes's interest was elsewhere.

Despite every mental control method, she tried Erika knew there was no way she would make it to the bathroom area. Her stomach continued to clench and roil and she realized she was really going to hurl. As she was passing through the exit flaps her churning stomach won the battle and she left a pool of sour liquid on the floor. She retched several times adding to the mess until the only thing coming up was clear green bile. She felt childish wiping her mouth on her arm but at that point did not care. Her body was cold and shaky but she had a better grip on her emotions.

"Sorry," she mumbled to the young girl with the mop who had arrived after receiving some mysterious signal. She didn't offer to help to clean up the mess on the floor. Instead, she stumbled her way to the room she had been assigned for the duration of her stay.

"Why does it always have to be her?" Once the door shut behind her, Erika released her pent-up emotions. Blinded by her tears, she shuffled back and forth between the bed and the door flap, unable see where she was walking through the salty blur. It was late, she really should chalk it up to another proof of her stupidity and go to bed. She had no business being in the unit's break area at this time of night anyway. Karma kicked her in the ass.

She flopped down on the narrow cot and closed her eyes but she couldn't sleep. Her mind was running wide open and no matter how many times she told herself to let it go, it refused to listen. Instead, she berated herself over and over, and then added a few mental curses for good measure.

After eight months Destiny just happens to mysteriously reappear. Of course, of all the men inside the survivor's camp, the bitch had to pick the only one she had any interest in. She felt as if someone had put one of those "Kick Me" signs on her back. Her brother would have never let her live it down. This was just another reason why she didn't do close relationships. She'd learned by middle school that people couldn't be trusted. Women were catty backstabbers and a man would look you right in the eye and lie. It didn't matter who they were. One too many bad experiences had taught her that. She had thought Jake was different but he was just better at lying.

Was this love? If it was, it sucked. Storybooks made it sound so wonderful. Wonderful was not the word she would use to describe what she was feeling. If this is what love felt like, they could keep it. Her heart could only handle so much pain

The location of her room was not a secret. Even so,

she was surprised when someone knocked on her door.

"Erika? Can I come in."

Wonderful. Venom fairly dripped from her words as she snapped out a response. "Your presence is duly noted."

Jake waited for her to open the door.

She didn't open it.

"Are you going to let me in?"

"Nope." A note of bitterness overshadowed the sweet sexiness of her voice.

He winced. *Yep. She was pissed.*

"I'm coming in to talk whether you like it or not." There were no locks on the doors. The universal signal for '*do not disturb*' was a sock hanging on the doorknob. There was no doorknob and no sock so he would not be breaking house rules. Not that he was going to get too close to her. Erika was fast and knew how to throw a knife. He considered going to get his flak jacket and decided that might make her madder. If that was possible.

He opened the door, poked his head in, and jerked it back outside as the wooden bolt hit the jamb beside him. *Cross bow. Damn.*

"I just want to talk to you. Without losing a pint of blood."

"Looked like you had plenty of volunteers in the break room."

"I'm here, not there. I'm coming in." He peeked inside, making sure she didn't have a loaded crossbow in her hands before entering the room. After ensuring himself there was no immediate threat he walked over and sat on the end of the bed near her feet. And waited.

Erika lay there looking irate and sullen as she continued to ignore his existence.

"Hello, Jake. What do you want?"

"I was worried about you. Are you feeling any better?"

Hell no, you're an ass. I want to hit you, call you a few choice names, and scratch your eyes out. Then I might feel better. He shifted uncomfortably, making her wonder if she had said that out loud. "I'm fine. You can leave now. Thanks for checking on me." After observing the confusion on his face she was overcome by remorse. It took all of her concentration not to respond to that kicked puppy dog expression. Then Destiny's smug face popped into her mind and she hardened herself.

Jake's initial response was *thanks for nothing.* He couldn't understand Erika's behavior. First, she rescues him, and then she hunts him up. Everything seemed fine the other night but now she disses him. Maybe she didn't like the kiss? He could do better. He liked the idea. She had exceptional lips, soft pink, with a saucy curve that drew his eyes. What does she expect, anyway, some type of commitment? He would have to talk to her about it. But first…

"Whoa, whoa, whoa!" Jake reacted by holding up his hands and spreading his fingers wide. "Wait a minute and hear-me-out."

"There's nothing we need to talk about."

"Yes, there is. I wanted to tell you bye, but I couldn't. It was an order. The captain had us leave without anyone knowing we were gone or when we would be back."

She had no snappy comeback. "Okay. Orders trump feelings. Got it."

Shit. She was still mad. It wasn't him leaving. It was Destiny. He had to make her understand there was nothing there. "Look, we need to talk. There are a few things I need to explain. I have to report to the Captain but once the brief is over I will be back."

"Maybe we should goodbye now in case you disappear again…"

Jakes's mouth quirked upward. Saying goodbye sounded good to him. He slid down the bed, pulled her into his arms, and kissed her. She struggled for a moment and then began kissing him back. All thoughts of the meeting vanished.

When he finally came up for air, she had to remind him of the meeting. *Damn.* "We still need to talk. But that will have to wait for a better time. I got to run. I'm going to be late." He gave her one more quick kiss and took off. They would have that talk. First the meeting and then he had to deal with Destiny.

Erika smiled as the door closed behind him. She lay back on the bed thinking *He was really running.*

Her mind was flooded with endorphins, leaving her feeling pretty good for a change. She tried not to dwell on things too much, but with all this free time at her disposal, her mind tended to go places she would never contemplate under normal circumstances.

Like Jake. She was looking forward to their discussion. He was attractive, in a long-legged, rough around the edges, coltish kind of way, but she couldn't read his signals. He might be telling the truth but his secretive attitude mystified her. It could be her foolish pride but it had hurt when he left that way. She had been certain there was something growing between them.

Obviously, she was wrong.

Maybe it was her?

She was certain he wasn't gay. Nor did he behave like an inexperienced teenager who had never had anything to do with a woman. Did he consider her too young? He was at least three or four years older than her. Or ugly? Did he have doubts because she was a virgin? Wasn't she worth waiting for?

A horrible thought crossed her mind. Maybe he was in a relationship…even married. Could Destiny be his wife? That would make her his side piece. Her parents would have killed her. No, that didn't fit. He hadn't done anything except kiss her. She was overreacting. She took a deep breath and tried to calm her nerves. She was the inexperienced one, not Jake. He had been halfway around the world and fought in a war. He was past the game stage.

The only thing she knew for certain was what she had seen. Destiny had seemed comfortable with him. That kiss was her way of marking her territory. Everyone in the room saw it. She sighed and fluffed her pillow again.

Of all the women in the world, why did it have to be her? At one time they had been best friends. She had changed once they reached high school, moving on to a new circle as if Erika had never been a part of her life. Destiny stopped coming to the skating rink and after becoming a cheerleader had stopped hanging out after the weekly football games. Her hateful attitude in school had often prompted shouting matches during which Erika wanted the earth to open up and swallow her.

Those days were gone. She was no longer the immature science nerd that took it all and never fought back. The thought of the malicious bitch queen of RidgeEric High ending up with the one man remaining on earth she was interested in, seemed like too big a price for her to pay.

She wiped a few stray tears away with her sleeve. There was no use dwelling on something she could not control. Girls like Destiny always got what they wanted. Girls like her got ignored.

Erika had always known she was different. In school, she had always been *that girl*. The smart one. The one who understood the math problems the first time the teacher explained them. The one who read because she enjoyed it, not because it was an assignment to suffer through. She kept to herself because she could not understand why no one else understood what was completely logical as long as you looked at it the right way. Not just because she was smart, but because she had no idea how to dumb herself down to their level. It had not been a problem when she was younger, everyone assumed she was shy. As long as Erika could remember she preferred to be alone instead of in a crowd. She had one or two friends throughout school and was perfectly fine with that. Most drifted away as they paired off in high school, becoming a couple instead of two friends. By tenth grade she realized there was no one in school she was attracted to, male or female, so she devoted her time to get the best education possible, taking every science and tech class offered. She could design a house and build it herself by the end of ninth grade. By the night of the attack, she had completed all high school graduation requirements and started college classes in robotics. She didn't have time for dating and knew no one would notice as long as she didn't allow them to get to close. Seemed like all that practice would have prepared her for disappointment. A dark shadow swept across her features, obscuring her unusual beauty as her inner rage worked itself out.

She sighed and fluffed her pillow for the twentieth time. Despite being a couple of hundred feet below ground in a cavern it was too hot to get comfortable. She was sweating, and her clothes stuck to her skin. She had hoped she would wear herself playing cards after a long day with the two Captains but it didn't look like that's was gonna happen. Though almost healed the slashes in her side ached. She was suffering from nightmares. When she managed to grab an hour or two of sleep, she'd toss and turn as her body reenacted the aliens' attack in her dreams. She opened the drawer of the nightstand, looking at the small horde of pills she'd hidden. One pill would relax her, two would probably knock her out. It wasn't a good idea to take them after drinking alcohol but no one needed to know. Just once, she needed a good night's sleep. She took two and finished off the glass of water. Then she lay down and waited for oblivion. The last thing she remembered was turning the wet pillow over to the dry side.

Chapter 23

When Destiny finally released him, Jake had gone looking for Erika knowing she wouldn't be glad to see him. He had a sinking suspicion that he'd made a serious error in judgment by spending any time with Destiny. She was assuming feelings he didn't have and a relationship he didn't want. Somehow, he had to get Erika to understand it was all one sided.

The military respected privacy, treating any barrier like a door. The thin strips of plastic that acted as the door to the small offshoot in the cavern she was using did nothing to prevent him from hearing. The heartrending sounds of her sobbing tore him up. He had stood before the door, trying to gather his courage to knock.

She wasn't having any. The crossbow bolt had been a warning, the girl could hit a quarter from across a field.

He sighed and headed back toward the break room. Somehow he had to convince Destiny to leave him alone, without starting a dramatic meltdown. He had no intention of walking away from Erika without a fight. It was too bad the Captain had laid down the law, making it clear that he had to pull his little red wagon out of the fire on his own time. He was leaving for Nashville as soon as the sun set. This gave him just enough time to say goodbye to Erika before he had to meet Santwan at the stables. He was not going to leave without telling her again.

Erika was unusual. She had a rare personality, she actually listened when he spoke, instead of trying to talk over him. She didn't chatter aimlessly when she didn't have anything to say. And she was smart. She had taken the limited info she'd gathered on the aliens and found a way to defeat them. Most women would have pulled their knees up under their chin and receded from reality, refusing to accept what their eyes had seen.

Destiny was another thing entirely. He had been wasted when he hooked up with her, but that excuse would not save his ass if Destiny kept up her machinations. She was a master manipulator. Mikey's overt flirting was payback for his indiscretion, and he had brought it on himself.

There was no way he could ignore the Destiny problem and hope it went away. That wasn't going to happen if he hoped to salvage any kind of relationship with Erika. He wanted to tell her what happened… about the mission, the secrecy required, and what had kept him away for so long. But first, he had to finish this mission. Sant was piloting and he was navigating. They would be following a hand drawn map in an area neither had ever visited before. They could find the base, just across the state line in Kentucky. But the survivors were hiding out in Lost River Caverns about ten miles east of Fort Campbell.

He sighed. Any plan was better than no plan.

Chapter 24

"You are weak, weak, weak, "Erika told herself as she brushed her wavy auburn hair and pulled it back into a ponytail. It was getting so long. She had always kept it cut boyishly short in school, preferring something she could wash and go with without needed upkeep or styling. She had never realized how much the dark red color brought out the soft green tints in her hazel eyes. The length of her hair and the loose waves softened her face, lending a sultry allure to a face she had always considered plain.

Just about an hour earlier she had opened her door to a knock to find a young girl, about ten or so standing with a bouquet of wildflowers and a note from Jake asking her to forgive him for being an ass, asking her to meet him at sunset for a picnic. She was happy to find out he was back from his latest mission but peeved that he had not come to see her as soon as he arrived. The note had mentioned the exit at top of Ruby Falls. She had thanked the girl, then watched as she dashed off down the hall toward the tunnel back to the main cavern. At eight, she was probably willing to run any errands that allowed her to drive the golf cart and get away from her parents. Whatever Jake had paid her to deliver his message was a bonus.

The next two hours had strained her nerves, seeming to pass so slowly she could hear the tick of each passing second. She had emptied her pack on the bed and examined every article of clothing inside it. There was nothing she could do about the jean shorts and tank top she was wearing since everything decent was still wet from an earlier wash. Finally, she gave up looking for excuses to delay and headed for the stairs to the top of the falls. About halfway to the top, she moved to the side to let a messenger go past her. Her respect for the military training program had grown. Until she began climbing up and down these stairs she had thought herself in reasonably good shape. The private that had passed her on the way up wasn't even breathing hard.

By the time she reached the top, she was shaking. This would be the first time she had been through this door since watching Danny die. Visions of the beast attack haunted her dreams. She had paid one of the younger boys to feed and brush Goldie, allowing her to avoid the area. Now she had no remaining excuses.

Jake was waiting by the door when she arrived. He had the decency to look sheepish, as he shifted his weight from foot to foot. He reminded her of Brianna's little brother after he got caught sneaking quarters from his mama's pocketbook. Almost all of her anger had faded and this display of remorse helped push away the remaining bits of anger.

He had picked a romantic spot inside Point Park to set up the picnic. There was a tarp stretched out between two tall pines, and he had lain two thick quilts on top of the tarp. The items in the picnic basket must have cost him a fortune. Fresh berries, a sweet cake, and a real chocolate bar. As she settled on the quilt, he popped the cork on a bottle of champagne, surprising her, anything alcoholic had vanished within days of the Kur's arrival. An old fashioned MP3 player was playing a romantic songs, rather outdated but even the older ones were a welcome change.

Jake must have seen the question in her eyes because he answered her unspoken question.

"I got it from Mikey. He has a small solar charger. It works on quite a few things. The battery in the player isn't unlimited but it should last until the end of our picnic."

"It was nice of him to loan it to you."

Jake laughed. "Trust me, it's not a loan, more like a rental. Mikey doesn't do anything without some personal incentive." He didn't go into details about his agreement and luckily she didn't ask. Even Destiny's name could screw up the evening, but it was something he needed to explain. He decided to switch the subject and get the hard part done while she was feeling the effects of the champagne she'd been drinking. He explained how they had found Destiny on the river and how they had kept her isolated in the cave for over a month before the Captain would allow her into the compound. That Mikey was crazy about her, and how she tried to play them off one another. "I have never given her any reason to think I was interested in anything except a casual friendship."

She rolled her eyes and he winced. "You don't believe me?"

"I believe that's what you want me to believe." She had heard the rumors while Jake was gone. She made it a point to discuss details of a tattoo that was covered by his boxers with one of the other girls. Her voice carried. Knowing Destiny's story doesn't make what happened any easier to accept how she acted toward Jake. If anything it made it harder.

Jake was an honest man and as far as she knew he had never lied to her before. Maybe she had lashed out at the wrong person? She decided enough was enough. "Why don't we just write this off as a summer spat between friends and forget it ever happened?"

Jake hesitated just enough to catch her attention before answering. For some reason, the words between friends bothered him more than he expected them to. He glanced at her hand, thinking that he was taking a big chance by reaching for hers. Erika was the type of woman that would leave you with a bloody stump if you touched her when she did not want to be touched. Instead, he laid his hand by hers and waited to see how she would react.

Erika's skin began to prickle even though he had not touched it. She wondered if he would consider her to forward if she kissed him? That brief spat had shown her how much she did care about him. One day they needed to have a serious discussion about relationships. And possible futures. For now, she would be happy to know they had a future to look forward to.

***

For the next few days Santwan and Jake swapped off with two pilots from the Knoxville unit, travelling back and forth between the Cavern in Kentucky and Lookout Mountain, transferring men to Chattanooga. The biggest obstacle they faced on a daily basis was the inability to communicate over long distances. The satellites had gone first, then any land based radio tower. Telephones and computers were worthless without an active internet system. With face to face communication the only option, old fashioned coded messages were the norm. That had required a human to travel overland from one point to another. Operational cars and trucks were almost impossible to find. Occasionally, they would come across a motorcycle that would crank up and run, but no wanted to risk the heat signature being discovered and tracked to a survival compound. That left the old fashioned Pony Express until Erika captured the aircar. The aircar had led to three additional captures, allowing them to shuttle men from one location to another.

No one was certain what the Captains had in mind; they only knew it involved the military. It was need to know.

They didn't.

***

Four nights later, Jake, Erika, and Santwan were sitting on the cliff side by Lovers Leap watching a trio of ducks swim around in the pool on the side of the mountain. They had planned on cooling off in the waterfall inside Rock City but the ducks looked so happy no one had the heart to disturb them. Which was a shame since it was sweltering hot outside the cavern.

Once she had overcome her initial fears of being on the side of a mountain, the pool had become the perfect place for the trio to hang out. In the beginning, there had been no way to climb back up once you slid down the rope to the pool beneath the tiny waterfall. Reece had solved the problem when he found an emergency fire escape ladder while salvaging the ruins of a local fire station. Using steel brackets and lag bolts they had mounted the roll-out ladder into the enormous rocks above the pool. The ladder made it simple to climb back to the top, ensuring it would become a favorite hangout on a hot summer night.

Something had been nagging at the edge of her subconscious since her meeting with the two Captains, and she had no idea why. She decided it might have something to do with being in the military. Maybe one of the guys would know. "Have you ever seen a movie where they said I got to get a bigger gun?"

Jake grinned "Yeah, Split second. This guy named Dick Durkin said it. Well. he said we got to get bigger guns."

Sant turned to him and they both said, "BFG." Then they broke out laughing.

Erika had no idea what was so funny.

Finally, Jake got himself together and cleared up the mystery. "BFG. Big Fucking Guns. It's a favorite Rotten Tomato cult movie."

"What made you ask that," Sant asked. "You don't strike me as the type to like really bad movies."

"It was something Captain Armstrong said to Captain Jeffers," she replied. "Needing bigger guns. It's been stuck in my mind ever since I heard it."

"Don't know why he would say something like that. None of our weapons can pass through the force shield. We have tried bazookas, rockets, even a few bombs. The only thing that works is wood and rocks." Sant stopped talking, a funny look on his face. Could it be that simple? "Hey, bro. Gotta bounce. I need to go talk to Captain Jeffers." He didn't wait for Jake or Erika to say goodbye and was up the ladder and out of sight before it really registered that he was gone.

Erika sighed. Now it was gonna drive her crazy.

***

"If anything, it's a real Hail Mary. We have tried everything else without success." Captain Jeffers looked at the map, making mental calculations of distance. If they could find a good location it might possibly work. They would get one, maybe two chances before the aliens retaliated. The decision to give it a try was a no-brainer, but like everything that seemed to be too good to be true, there always had to be a downside. This could turn out to be an enormous disaster or the turning point of the battle to save Earth.

So far, nothing about this invasion had gone by the books. Traditional weapons are useless. Unlike the War of the Worlds, the aliens had not caught a virus and died off. After landing they had destroyed most of the buildings and killed or captured the majority of humanity. The survivors had absolutely no idea how many alien the ships were in the area much less on the planet. Unless humanity was willing to go meekly into the invaders ships like sheep following one by one, then they had to do something before the option to try was taken away from them.

"I agree we have to give it a try. It's just crazy enough to work." Captain Armstrong ran his fingers through his thinning hair. It was already going grey at the temples. At this rate, by the time he reached forty, he would be pure white...if he reached forty. The life he had planned with his wife and children had ended abruptly when the first wave had destroyed Knoxville. He had been working in his office when the first strike occurred. Like most military officers, he had moved directly to the underground bunkers. An elaborate underground base had been built after 9-11, establishing a safe headquarters from which they could conduct military operations in case of foreign attack. He doubted anyone had considered someone from so far away. The bunker had withstood the effects of the Kurs attack exactly as it had been designed. Originally a source for Manganese and iron ore, the old mine presented a ready-made subterranean tunnel system that only needed slight modifications to make it operational. He grinned, thinking about all the mole men around the country living in similar habitats. It would be wonderful to find a way to bring the survivors into the light once more.

Captain Armstrong paused, letting his mind run through all the tidbits of information they had gathered over the last few weeks. "We need some specifics. Someone needs to get close enough to the Kurs to map out the force field generator and decide what is its weakest point. We also have to consider the recovery of any prisoners. There hasn't been a transport ship for several months. They may be waiting to capture enough warm bodies to make it feasible to send the ship. Or it could show up today. We have no idea why they are taking prisoners off-world. Or what happens to the ones that do not go on the ship."

Major Eric Whitten had arrived on the latest transport run. Theoretically, he was the highest ranking officer and should have command of the small military unit. However, as a West Point Graduate, he had entered the service as a Captain and less than a year later had been promoted. He had spent his active duty time in the United States working with drone technology and had zero combat experience. Under the circumstances, he had conceded the necessity of deferring command to the older, more experienced Captains. He had no idea how to even begin to develop a plan using the primitive weapons the two men had been fighting with. "What about the weapon? Do you think it's possible it could take out the ships power source ?"

"We are concentrating in the force field generator. At this time, we have no idea what powers the ships. It would be redundant to destroy the ship and find out we had destroyed the state in the process."

Major Whitton nodded. "I might be able to get a drone close enough to photograph the area. The trick will be getting it back here safely with the camara intact."

"You would need to find a place to land it away from the compound. Maybe we could have a man pick it up down in Saint Elmo. With the Fisheyes piloting after dark, our restrictions have increased. You would need to fly it by sight, and that means going into the red zone."

"Wont your man need to go into the Red Zone to make a drawing?"

"Yes. But they know the ground. And they all have combat experience with the Kurs. If you are certain you want to give it a try, I will talk with Anderson and arrange an op for tonight."

Major Whitten nodded yes.

Captain Jeffers grinned. "That takes care of one issue. We have men working on the weapon now. We are also collecting raw materials to create a way to deliver it." He turned to Captain Armstrong, "Who's your best engineer ?"

"I have two good ones with me. I will have them report here at…he glances at his watch, 1300. That okay with you?"

"1300 sounds good. He turned to Thomas, "Who's the best we have."

"Stone, sir."

"Have him report at 1300. Get me, Anderson, too."

"Sir, yes sir." He paused as if he had something else to say.

"You have something to add?"

"Yes sir. I suggest you talk to one of the McGowan boys. They are into re-enactments. I've seen some of the equipment they have built, and it could come in handy."

"Equipment?"

"Yes sir. Have you ever heard of a trebuchet?"

He looked puzzled but Captain Armstrong's face was split by a beaming grin. His mind was working a mile a minute as the images the young aide had generated opened up new possibilities.

As Thomas disappeared through the plastic strips that acted as a door on the alcove Captain Jeffers used as an office, he noticed the two men had already bent their heads together and Captain Armstrong was sketching something on a pad.

Chapter 25

"We are really going to do this. We are going to destroy the force field generator." Erika could scarcely contain her excitement. From the overlook she could use binoculars and see across the river easily, noting increased activity around the mother ship as the aliens prepared the airships for their daily surveillance of the area. She didn't see any of the new night pilots but that wasn't unusual since they only were seen after dark. Unfortunately, she spotted three more of the tracking beasts.

"We are going to give it a try. There's really no way to know it will work. We will only get two clear shots. Maybe three. With luck, that's all it will take. " Jake was feeling good himself. The attack was a longshot, but there was no way they could overlook this once in a lifetime opportunity to make a difference for every human left on Earth. His eyes drifted to the two pine trees a few feet beyond the overlook. Work was ongoing but it was taking longer than anyone expected. It was clear they'd never get a chance to complete the weapon during the daytime. That much activity would draw the attention of the Kur's scouts and they would be all over the mountain looking for any sign of human activity. The engineers had set up a similar apparatus on the back side of the mountain and were testing for range and accuracy. It was harder to do after dark so they had been testing at dawn and dusk. So far, it had not drawn the attention of the Kurs. That was only a matter of time.

However, it was a risk everyone was willing to take.

Santwan disagreed. "It's going to take more than luck. We are going to need a diversion, a big one. Something that will keep all the available Kurs attention while we fire the bow." Sant was feeling pretty good about his project. After his unexpected epitome, he had rushed to explain his idea to Captain Jeffers. He had been surprised when his idea was not only acknowledged, both Jeffers and Captain Armstrong seemed excited over the plan.

Earlier in the campaign Armstrong had tried using the arrows to deliver dynamite and plastique explosives into the Knoxville Red Zone with little success. Since only natural materials would pass through the barrier they were ineffective and the explosions have done no harm. Any modification to the raw material, no matter how small, would prevent access. Santwan's plan was crazy but so far no one had found anything to prevent it from working.

Jake nodded. "I'm curious what they plan to do to save the captives. Tony has been in that hellhole for three weeks now. It can't be long before another transport arrives. We are trained to believe no one gets left behind. No one ever planned for an alien invasion."

"I know it was your plan, but do you really think it will work? It's such a crazy idea." Erika tried to sound optimistic but her face betrayed her inner turmoil.

Sant hesitated, deciding whether to offer a snappy comeback or not when he heard her doubts. He thought it was a brilliant plan. Of course, if he had not been the one to come up with the idea, he might be skeptical, too. "The engineers seem to think so. They are still working out the details but everyone appears excited about the possibility of taking out the main generator."

Jake knew there were a thousand things that could go wrong. He studied the Tennessee River that swept by in a wide band along the base of Lookout Mountain. It had seen a lot of Hail Mary's over the years. He preferred to reserve judgment on the feasibility of the plan until after the tech boys had a chance to check their figures. "It's a calculated risk, but one worth taking. I figure the biggest problem will be developing a way to deliver the payload. That's a lot of weight to propel through the force field with enough power to damage or destroy the mother ship." He grinned. "At least gravity is on our side."

There had been limited places in which they could build the frame of the weapon. Point Park being located in such a great position seemed like a gift from God. The engineers were already constructing the framework atop the brow of Lookout Mountain. A lot of thought had gone into designing a weapon capable of destroying the spaceship. There was plenty of elevation at the point and a clear view of the target. The only problem was they had no way of testing the idea.

The Kurs had the edge in advanced technology. For all intents and purposes, the force field had stopped any physical weapon they had fired at it. Chances are the Kurs had never considered humanity capable of fighting back with the level of technology they had currently developed. Surprise would be in their favor since no one at the ship seemed to be paying any attention whatsoever.

Erika thought the contraption looked like something her brothers would build with tinker toys. The salvage team had searched the ruins of a truck stop looking for materials. Groups of engineers had carefully chosen the best weight and size. They had three spares. Four chances to save humanity.

"At least we are doing something," Jake added. "Any plan is better than no plan at all."

"When will be ready?"

"We should find out more at the meeting. Captain Jeffers called it for 1300. If we want to have time for lunch, we need to start heading that way. There's gonna be a line for the golf cart."

***

"Erika, so happy you could join us. Please, take a seat." He waved his hand toward the only empty chair in the room.

Erika smiled. Captain Jeffers always made her feel

as if he were glad to see her. She walked to the chair he had indicated and sat. waiting to see what would happen next. She had bever been in a military briefing and had no idea what the protocol if any, was.

Santwan and Jake remained standing before the desk, waiting for orders. Being called in to discuss what he had seen was expected. Both he and Santwan had been through the drill multiple times. Having Erika in the room with him was different and for some reason, made him nervous. He concentrated on what Captain Jeffers was saying and tried to keep him mind off Erika.

"We are fighting an unknown enemy with extremely limited information. We don't know where they came from, what they want from us, or how to communicate with them. So far, they have shown zero willingness to negotiate. After almost a year we have no idea what makes them tick. Hopefully, Lt. Anderson can fill in a few gaps.

Jake cleared his throat before he began to speak, using the time to let his mind run back through the mental images, making sure he had not forgotten any important detail. He had an idea of what needed to be done, but the final decision would come from someone higher up the chain.

The night before last, he had taken Major Whitten into the city and stayed with him as he used the probe to take photos of the Kur ship and surroundings. Afterward he waited in the rubble of a nearby building as Jake made a visual survey of the stadium, ensuring he had all the necessary info available before he had to report what he saw. There was no room for errors. The people being held inside had no way of knowing the survivors were planning the rescue. Knowing they could expect limited help from anyone inside, he had taken a chance and entered the stadium to get a closer look.

Ordinarily, a soldier has specific orders to complete the mission and report back. As a scout, Jake had more flexibility. If he saw something he felt he needed to investigate, he didn't need to get orders before checking it out. This had allowed him to get a clearer picture of the aliens than the average patrol would be able to see. If things had gone south, he would be on his own. There would be no rescue attempt. Chances are he would have cost the prisoners any likelihood of escape as well.

It was on the fly decisions like these that had earned him his position, but the wrong one could easily take it away. The Kur guard could not see him but the beast on the leash was looking his way. So far it had not alerted on his presence, but Jake wasn't about to take a chance. He had slipped back out the way he had come in.

Jakes' report today was as straightforward and factual as the engineer who spoke before him. He described the tracking beasts, using Erika's sharp-toothed, furry praying mantis description to help with a visual image. Then he went on to describe the fished eyed alien the Kurs had brought in to pilot the airships after dark. He could see the questions in their eyes and was ready to answer as needed.

Major Whitten listened without comment before speaking. "Thank you for the information. It makes it easier for me to picture the opposition if I can visualize them through the eyes of others. You three have a unique outlook due to the hands-on interaction you have with the aliens. Captain Jeffers has done extremely well with the limited assistance he has received, no doubt in part because of your input. Now we are here to help carry out the plan you developed.

Captain Jeffers had listened as Whitten spoke without interrupting. Now he stood and moved to a dry erase board someone had salvaged. There was a basic drawing on the board showing the key components of the plan, the weapon, the stadium, and the mother ship. "It's extremely hard to develop a working plan with inadequate information. That's why I asked all of you to be here. I need input. Jake's report answered many of my questions but added a lot more."

For the next hour, the officers fired questions, and one of the three managed to have an answer for each one. Afterwards they sat and talked about options, looking for answers but not getting any. There was no simple solution. One of the biggest difficulties was communication. Walkie talkies worked over short distances but the signal could be easily traced and blocked. They were also limited because the signal would not transmit through stone. Over the past year, the resistance had set up a person to person transport similar to the old pony express used before electronic transmittal. A message sent at sunset could reach Nashville before dawn. The addition of the nighttime fish pilots had put a stop to anything except very important missives. With the addition of the two aircars, they were able to make a trip up and back within a few hours but no one was certain how long the power cells would last. Running out of power while five hundred feet in the air would challenge the nerve of the most stalwart warrior.

The conversation had shifted to the newest alien presence, the fish eyed pilots.

Jake was speaking about his experience. "They sure are ugly muthas. I had nightmares for weeks after my first run-in with one. Took me weeks before my have was normal."

"Something about the bulging eyes remind me of one the demons from Dante's version of hell."

Erika was surprised by Captain Armstrong's statement. It wasn't the physical appearance of the aliens that bothered her. Or the acid in their blood. It was not knowing what they wanted, or what they would do to her if she was captured that frightened her. She no longer feared fighting them. The fishmen died relatively fast. Killing one was easier than killing a Kur, who seemed to have few critical points. Without the force shield a bullet to the brain worked, so did removing the head completely. The heart was center of the chest and lower than a humans but they could not survive a direct hit from close range. Distance shots tended to deflect off the bone or cartilage that protected the area. Chopping at the extremities was a waste of time, they could shake off losing an arm with no effort.

"It would be best to work in teams of two. One to use the bow to take out the breather and one with a phaser in case the arrow missed." Santwan had listened quietly as the others talked without comment but decided they needed to take a few things into consideration.

"Why not just using the phasers?" Whitten asked.

"The limits of the power cell have not been established and we have no way to charge them. Best to save them for emergency situations instead of using then up with kills a traditional weapons can handle."

Captain Armstrong nodded his agreement. They had been careful with the aircars for a similar reason. They had no idea what powered them or how long the power supply would last. He was afraid that once the main generator went down, the aircars would no longer work. Losing that means of transportation would be a small price to pay if they could take out the Kurs shields.

"Another thing we need to take into consideration. Even without the generator, we will still have to face the Kurs. We assume their weapons will still work, since the ones we captured are not affected by distance. So we will need heavy armaments as well. Once the shield is down a couple of rockets should keep the ship on the ground."

"Agreed. We will need teams to take care of that and any other unexpected issues that arise."

"Like the beasts," Erika added. "I saw three definite and possibly more that I could not be certain were different animals. If they are loose they can locate and attack at will. We have no defense against them." She still had nightmares about the attack that killed Danny. Despite the care she had received, she still favored her left side. The scars were a visible reminder of how close she had come to dying.

Captain Jeffers turned to Major Whitten, "They breathe air as we do. You can shoot one of them multiple times and they keep coming. And they hunt by smell so the suits do not hide us."

Jake agreed. "The phasers work, but we need to save them if possible."

"How many flamethrowers do we have?" Armstrong asked.

"Not enough. Seven workings. Three out of fuel."

"We could do like the female mantis. I bet a machete across the neck will stop them." Santwan was trying to ease some of the tension in the room. The more they talked, the more it seemed like an impossible task.

Luckily, Captain Jeffers realized what he was doing and laughed. "With our luck, we could take off the head and they would keep coming. We have no idea where their heart or brain is. They may even have two of them."

"Yeah. But the alien's guns have no problems dealing with them. Erika brought in ten more, giving use thirteen total. Too bad we don't have a few more of them." He looked right at Erika.

She blushed and shrugged her shoulders. "I may have three or four still hidden around the area but that's it. If that will help we can go and get them."

"They would be appreciated," Jeffers said.

Jake had been thinking about something and this seemed like a good time to ask. "What about Washington? Do you think the President survived?"

Captain Armstrong appeared unsurprised by Jake's question as he had thought about the same thing himself. "It depends on how they hit the city. The Whitehouse did not look especially important. If they had the time to get unto the bunkers there could be a lot of high-level officials alive. The same could be said of the Pentagon. Washington is a maze of underground tunnels. That was the idea behind our Knoxville bunker system."

Captain Jeffers decided the meeting had run its course. "I don't know about you, but I'm ready to head over to the break area and see what's for dinner. We all have a lot to think about. I would like you both to go with Erika to retrieve the remaining phasers. We want to be moving to the stadium in less than forty-eight hours."

Chapter 26

The cows and goats were happy to see Erika as she poured the sweet feed and grain into the various troughs. It had been almost two weeks since she had been home. One cow had a new calf by her side and there were several colorful kids playing on top of anything they could climb on. The clatter of hoofs against wood drew their eyes to a tricolor billy who had figured a way to get on top of the collapsed section of the barn and was proudly surveying his kingdom as the trio entered the paddock.

Erika pointed to the left fence line. "Dig next to the third pole from the far end. One of the guns is buried there."

Jake smiled at her crazy system of hiding. He stepped back to get more room to dig and cursed as his foot came down in a pile of steaming dog crap. A really big pile.

"Oops. Chance doesn't respect boundaries. I try to get him to understand but one spot of grass is as good as another to him." She started to shake as she fought back the laughter and failed.

Santwan's angelic expression did nothing to disguise his amusement. He chuckled, then laughed as Jake hopped around on one foot and tried to rake the vile substance from the heel of his boot without having to touch it.

"I haven't even met your dog and he hates me already," Jake snarled. After three or four tries he had removed enough on the grass to satisfy the immediate needs and returned to his friends.

He chunked the alien gun to Santwan, who easily plucked it out of the air. Santwan examined it, liking the way it fit in his hand. He had been surprised by the variety of shapes and sizes the weapons came in. He wrapped it in a tee shirt and placed it in his backpack, making himself a mental note to try and swap his currently assigned phaser for the new one.

Jake ducked his head in the water trough and shook it spraying droplets of water on both of his friends. Felling refreshed by the cool water, he decided it was a good time to follow up on an earlier discussion.

He walked over to a clear spot in what used to be the front lawn of the house and called Erika over. "Guns are great but if you are going with us, everyone on the team has to feel like they can trust you to have their back in any situation. I need to make sure you can survive hand to hand with a bigger opponent. Try to hit me—if you can."

She immediately swung a fast blow to his head. He easily sidestepped it and kicked her legs out from under her. He tried to ease the sting to her ego as he pulled her up.

"It helps if you know where your opponent's vulnerable spots are located. With humans, it's simple, the eyes, the mouth, thethroat, and their testicles. With Aliens it guesswork. If you have to, punch under their armpits."

"Armpits?"

"Yeah. It seems to be a soft spot on most bi-pedal creatures. A knife is a great choice. Hitting a human hard enough can paralyze their arm, or if you are lucky it might even stop their heart. It won't work on every species, but it's worth considering. Don't be afraid of fighting dirty. Your opponents won'tthink twice about it. We have no idea how they reproduce but give a kick to the groin a try. Ready to try again?"

She nodded.

Jake stepped back and planted his feet, waiting for her to rush at him. Before he could Kur an eye, Erika launched a surprisingly fast punch to his solar plexus, laying him out on the ground. He curled up on the grass, one hand on his stomach, the other trying to cover his mouth and prevent him from spewing all over the ground. Once again he had underestimated her. His attention had been on protecting his groin, the typical target. It was all he could do to keep the tears from his eyes. The girl had quite a punch. It wasn't as if he'd never been hit that hard before, he had. It was he had never expected to be hit that hard by a woman half his size.

Erika tried to keep the triumph from her voice as spoke but Jake could see the sparkle in her eyes. "That was my first fighting lesson. The one who hits first often wins. He stressed it several times, it doesn't matter how strong you are, if you hit them in the right place, they are going down." She snapped out the answer, as if she'd been asked the question umpteen times before.

Jake ducked his head to hide the quirk of his lips. He loved the way she got all awkward and embarrassed whenever she spoke of anything personal.

He? Now Jake was Curious. "How did you learn your fighting techniques? I know you are too young to have military training. Were you in ROTC ?"

"Nope. No ROTC. I survived four big brothers," Erika laughed aloud as she walked alongside him. "Fighting was a normal way of life in my family, you learned how to win or you suffered."

"You fought with men?" Santwan asked.

"I know it sounds crazy, but that's how I was brought up. On a farm, the girls are not treated any differently than the boys. I had to show them that just because they were up against someone smaller, they can't take the win for granted. And they taught me how to fight someone who's bigger, and not automatically believe I was going to lose."

"It doesn't seem like a fair fight. What, they must have had fifty pounds or more on you?"

"Sure, I was smaller than them but it didn't matter. My father didn't play favorites. I had to haul bales of hay and carry water buckets just like my brothers. After school, we all worked at the restaurant." She paused and took a drink of water. "My brothers helped me adapt what they did for my use. Although I did learn a few moves from my mother they would never have considered using on each other."

Jake laughed and let her help him up off the ground. "Let's go again." He moved into a crouching position, watching for her first move.

Erika was strong and she was quick. Despite everything he tried a few punches of hers got through. They hurt more than Jake expected, but a perverse sense of pride made him not admit it out loud.

After about an hour they were both huffing and covered with sweat. Santwan decided to call it a day before one of them was seriously hurt. "We better get back before someone declares us AWOL."

Jake nodded. He had to admit he felt better knowing how well Erika could fight. The horror of the Kurs was not the advanced technology or the weapons. It was the unknown, the not knowing what they wanted or the lengths they were willing to go to, to achieve their objective. They were going to need every advantage if they hoped to succeed.

Chapter 27

The heavily loaded aircars left the mustering site as soon as the evening sky darkened sufficiently for the Kurs to become inactive. There was still a small chance they could cross paths with fisheye pilot, but they had decided it was worth taking the risk to keep the op on schedule. The unit planned to cross the river downstream from the hidden exit below Point Park, on the lower end of Moccasin Bend. The water in that area was three hundred to three hundred and fifty yards wide, deep, swiftly flowing, and heavily wooded on the opposite shore, making it difficult to swim but flying across was no problem. Moccasin Bend had been designated as a historical reserve so no homes had been built, making the area unattractive to the invaders. The heavy growth allowed an abundance of natural cover, mostly gigantic oaks and willows, eight to twelve feet around. Through careful maintenance the park had restricted the trees from first few feet of the shoreline, however, by eight feet from of the water's edge the forest was all old growth timber that continued throughout the preserve. Unless someone was directly above them, the forest would hide the two aircars, removing the fear of a patrol spotting them and alerting the Kurs to their presence.

Less than half an hour later Jakes unit exited the

preserve across from the old Siskin Steel plant, crossing the Tennessee River again before hiding the two air cars in a small overgrown area that at one time was a park and flower garden. This gave them easy access to Main Street and a direct walk to Finley Stadium.

Hiding twenty heavily armed men proved easier than expected. There was sufficient rubble scattered along the route that Jake would have felt comfortable moving a hundred or more along that route.

The team's initial order was to reach the old Eureka Foundry, find a secure base, and then send out two scouts to check the next section of the route. This was the most dangerous point of the rescue. The Kurs had paired the Fish-faces with the beasts, then assigned them to guard the prisoners after dark. Despite several nights of surveillance, they still had no idea how far the nocturnal aliens could see. There had been several of the teams walking the perimeter of the stadium during Jakes's scouting mission. If one of the beasts had picked up his scent after he had finished scouting the route, they could easily be waiting for their next attempt.

Jake signaled for a break." Spread out in groups of three and find shelter among the ruins. Sant! I need you and Malone to hang back." Santwan was an easy choice. Jake would trust him with his life and often had. The second man, one of two good ol' boys from Kentucky, was young but tough, a marine tracker and scout who had been visiting Gatlinburg during the invasion. His partner, now commanding one of the other teams, was a Marine Raider. The two men had been walking toward their base in Virginia when they ran into the survivors outside of Knoxville.

The rest of the men moved quietly, leaving two men waiting for orders. Within seconds they were swallowed up by the darkness.

"You two need to scout ahead and make sure nothing had changed in the past twenty-four hours. I hate to risk it, but we have to assume the beasts got a whiff of me, and they are on alert. We have no idea if they can communicate that information to the Kurs. They might be intelligent or just canny like a dog or wolf. Quiet and sneaky. So keep all your senses on high."

"How close you want us to get?" Malone asked.

"Close enough to get a good view of the back of Findley. I climbed the fence and went in from the upper level."

"You said they have four feet and two front limbs? It's possible the damn things can climb."

"It's possible they control the Kurs. Not likely but hell, we are going on instinct anyway."

"So we will all go in together?" Sant checked his weapons for the tenth time. He was certain he had forgotten something important.

"Correct. It's 22:09. Captain Jeffers plans on attacking at midnight. We need to be in place by then."

He saw Erika waiting with her team and walked

over as Sant and Malone disappeared into the shadows. She pulled him to the side before he had a chance to move out of reach, breaking every protocol on the books as she kissed him. The others began looking upward, and to the side, anywhere except toward the embracing couple.

Erika didn't care what the others thought. Despite her trust in Jake, the idea of him going into the Kurs territory scared her more than she wanted to admit. His team had to infiltrate the stadium and get the prisoners out while remaining undetected by any of the Kur's guards. She was startled by how much it bothered her to know Jake was going into the stadium with all the beasts.

"What is the chance of us succeeding?" she asked as he stepped back.

"Thirty, maybe thirty-five percent," he said. "But it's a better chance than we had yesterday." There was no easy way to say it. Fourteen men carrying alien guns were not enough, but they would make it work. A lot of people were depending on them. Hell, the entire human race was depending on them.

She tried to remain calm. "Well, stay safe. This may be my last chance to say that. I gonna be pissed at you if you get yourself killed. I don't do funerals."

"I'm sure they will be happy to cremate me for you. All you have to do is find the right pile of ashes." He had hoped to make her smile, but the joke flopped.

She lifted her hand in the universal three-fingered reply and headed off to join her team. Time was counting down. She began praying that the weapon would work. That they could take out the generator, leaving the aliens unprotected from their weapons. Three chances did not seem like enough.

***

Sant lay beneath the shelter of a burned-out pickup truck about fifty feet beyond the area lit by the stadium lights. Somehow the Aliens had gotten several of the light panels working. Since Jake had not mentioned working lights during the briefing, he could only assume this was a new development. For almost an hour he lay motionless, watching the fishmen patrol the perimeter of the stadium. Something must have spooked them. Now two fishmen walked together, along with one of the beasts on a long leash. Sant was upwind from the patrol, but he had no idea how sensitive the beasts senses were. His almost motionless body was concealed by overgrown brush, a heavy scattering of busted cement and the hulks of charred cars and trucks. Even so, he dared not shift or stretch, knowing any unexpected sound or movement would draw the eyes of the patrolling groups.

Over an hour earlier Malone had returned to report the change in situation. It was now a quarter to midnight. Jake would have moved his men into position around the back side of the stadium. He would trust him to take care of himself. The damn thing had better hit the generator. Sant had already mapped out his route in his mind. Once the shot was made there could be no hesitation. If things went as planned the first shot would take out the generator. The second should seriously cripple the Kurs ship, and hopefully keep it from lifting off. Most if not all of the Kurs would be killed in the ensuing barrage of rockets. If not killed immediately, many would suffocate. The fishmen could survive without a breather, but it slowed them down. Without the force-field they were vulnerable to traditional weapons. He had excellent concealment, he knew where he was going and what he would face when he arrived. All he had to do was to remain hidden until midnight.

Suddenly he tensed. Moving toward him at a slow shamble was one of the beasts. It was not on a leash. Fascinated by something it was tracking, the creature had stopped, staring straight ahead past the truck remains Sant was using for cover. Something in its manner led him to believe it was closing in a kill. But he was not the target.

Sant was relatively certain its intended victim was not one of the men with his unit. More than likely it was human making it worth risking his location, and even his life. His watch read 23:57. Three minutes before the attack began. The hidden stranger may not have three minutes.

Damn. Resting one hand on the pommel of the

phaser, Sant rose to his feet and began following the beast. Within seconds he spotted both the alien animal and its intended target. About twenty feet beyond the crouching creature stood a woman, facing in the opposite direction. Sant was torn between stopping the beast and throwing off the attack. By interfering he could be risking the safety of everyone in the stadium. The decision became unnecessary as the beast turned and rushed straight for him. It leaped and landed, throwing it entire weight against Santwan, slamming his body up against the back of the truck. Barehanded Sant struggled to keep the beast's teeth away from his throat. The beasts back claws raked at his legs and stomach, tearing narrow gashes in the Kevlar and the muscles of his thighs. Somehow, he managed to unsnap his knife belt and withdraw his hunting blade, jabbing it over and over into the side of the beasts neck. They were both covered in his blood and the creature's acidic body fluids. Desperately he grabbed for the bloody handle as a sharp twist of the beasts' body, snatched the slick knife from his hand.

Instead of running away, the young woman had moved closer. Holding a sharp-edged rock above her head, she brought it smashing down upon the creatures' head.

The beast turned away from Sant to look at the woman. Acidic spittle dribbled between the double rows of teeth, turning the creature's fur a strange greyish white near his mouth.

The woman screamed.

Santwan used the momentary distraction to try for his phaser. His blood slicked fingers struggled to grasp the metal only to fumble and drop it onto the cracked pavement.

The beast turned back to Santwan at the sound of the metal gun hitting the parking lot. Santwan's alarm began to beep. And the night turned into day as the alien's generator exploded.

***

"Move! Everyone up the fence." Jake began climbing, knowing all the guards' attention would be drawn to the mothership and what was going on there. He was relatively certain that the generator was no longer working. He had no idea how long the ship could maintain the force field without it. Nor did he know how long the personal shields would work. They had come prepared for either possibility, but there were only twenty of them.

Two groups of three were making their way around the outside of the stadium perimeter with instructions to take out anything not human. Each man was armed with all three weapons, bow, gun, and phaser. One way or another they were determined to get the prisoners free.

Wire cutters made short work of the zip ties he had used to close the hold he had made in the fence. He led his team to the right once they reached the upper level at the top of the fence. It was only a short walk to the stairs going down. Understanding the aliens may decide to eliminate the prisoners to prevent the possibly of escape they were practically running between levels. After three flights Jake began to wonder where everyone was. He knew the chances of discovery increased the lower to the ground they went.

A slash of grey from the shadows was all the warning they had before the beast was among them. The man next to him jerked up his gun and began firing. There was no hesitation as multiple bullets slammed into the creatures' body.

Jakes's face blanched as he saw what was coming. He opened his mouth to scream a warning. One second the man was pulling the trigger, the next the gun was lying on the ground and his hands were clasped to his neck as blood sprayed from four deep gashes. He staggered a few steps and fell to the ground, dead in seconds.

The beast wheeled, turning his attention on Joel, one of the ROTC cadets. Jake fired his phaser and the beast howled, flames engulfing his body. He continued to hold the control until there little more than charred ashes on the ground.

Joel was still shaking but he was doing his best not to show how much it had affected him. He didn't know the dead man well, only that his name was Javier, and that he was from Oaxaca, Mexico. He had died bravely, yet they had no one except Captain Armstrong to notify. Jake took one of the dog tags and slid it between two of his teeth, then slipped the chain around his neck. The attack was just beginning and Javier would not be the last casualty.

***

The earth heaved under them, throwing them all to the ground as a rain of sparks and dirt began to fall. Santwan knew if he were going to have a chance to escape death, it would be now. He dove for the phaser. Holding the alien weapon with both hands he pointed it at the creature and pulled the trigger. The beast screamed as its body was engulfed with bluish-colored flames. He howled and began to roll but Sant kept the bean locked on its body. Finally it jumped up and began running into the darkness.

Santwan watched it until he could no longer see the fire in the darkness. Then he checked on the young woman. She appeared to be unhurt other than a few scrapes from falling on the cement.

Sant wished he could say the same. His leg was killing him. He had at least three gashes on his hip. He tottered a few steps and almost fell. "You are okay for now but we need to hurry. My unit is breaking everyone out of the stadium right now. I need to reach them to get help. I don't think I can make it on my own."

She was surprised that he would even think she

would leave him alone after what had just happened. "My sister is in there. So is my next-door neighbor. If you think there is any way we can get them out, let's go." She put his arm around her neck, using her weight to support him as he hobbled along. Together they began working their way toward the front of the stadium.

****

A phaser fired and Mikey dived behind the shattered base of a lamp post. Just as they had hoped, the alien's protection shields had failed along with the destruction of the generator. He had no idea if the ship had been damaged in the explosion, however, in the distance, he could see that at least one, and possibly two, of the thirty foot tree trunks, had breached the shell of the spacecraft. He doubted the ship was taking off without repairs. His team carried a rocket launcher that would guarantee it. Every so often he could see smaller explosions light up the darkness. This was the result of the trebuchet tossing granite boulders at various targets.

As ordered his unit had swung east after the explosion, making their way to the area surrounding the damaged mother ship. Along the way, they had several short skirmishes with the Kurs. All had taken some type of wounds from their phasers but there had been no problem taking the aliens out. Only one man had been seriously wounded. He had sent that man back with one of the cadets assigned to his unit, removing them both from further injury.

Santwan's crazy "Big Gun" had worked. The giant arrows had flown through the shields like hot knife in butter. The first had missed the target but it had punctured the otter skin of the ship. The second one was a direct hit and took out the generator. The final arrow had centered the door into the ship, plowing deep inside before something solid had stopped its progression. The door was unable to close and with no generator the artificial atmosphere was quickly replaced by Earths. Without the shields, one bullet easily destroyed their breathing apparatus. Each man was now carrying several phasers as well as their M-16. Without a shield, it was easier to carry the bow across their back beside the quiver.

The fish-faces turned out to be harder to kill than the Kurs. Bullets were worthless, that passed through their thick gelatinous bodies leaving wounds that closed behind them. They could breathe our atmosphere, so destroying the breathers only irritated them. Unlike the Kurs, they did not catch fire. It was necessary to use the phaser, holding the weapon on them until their body had melted into a thin liquid puddle on the ground. This could take several minutes during which they continued to return fire. The smarter men learned to burn away the head, hands and arms before attempting to kill the body.

Other than a second run-in with a praying mantis

beast, no one in Erika's team had been seriously hurt. Unfortunately, it had sliced open Jermaine's stomach like jelly. They had wrapped it the best they could, then hid him in the basement of a burnt-out building, promising to bring the aircar and pick him up. Erika had surprised Malone by volunteering to go back on her own to fetch help.

Malone figured he would catch hell from Jake later. He was going to be pissed but it was really the most logical option. She wasn't carrying any heavy weaponry and could move faster on her own. Plus she was the most experienced fighter in his group. He had stared in awe as she had taken out the beast that attacked Jermaine before anyone else could react.

***

Jake and his men entered the prisoner holding area from the rear, unsurprised to find there was no one now watching the prisoners. They had all heard and felt the explosion. Any Kur or Fish-face able to leave had rushed toward the mothership to find out what had happened.

"Spread out. Make sure they are all dead. No prisoners."

Six of the remaining men broke into three men teams, leaving one to back up Jake.

Jake moved to address the first group of prisoners. "We are here to get you to safety. Do any of you have military or police training?"

" I do." A tall middle aged woman stepped forward.

" Good. I need you to help separate the captives into Wounded, Walking Wounded and Physically able to help." He looked at the twenty odd in the first group, shaking his head at the sad condition most were in.

"We need food and water more than anything. Some have not eaten in days."

Jake nodded and removed his backpack. Inside was his emergency rations, a couple of packs of crackers and trail mix. He handed it over to the woman along with his canteen. The soldier from Nashville had moved to the next group of prisoners and had located someone to help organize. The man who had stepped forward spoke Spanish, which helped since most of the captives in this group was Latino. He repeated Jakes actions with his store of food and water.

"Looks like the cleanup is complete. He comes the others."

"Good. These people are starving. Have everyone released from the chains. Make sure they have all been given something to eat and drink and are ready to be transported."

There number of people being held inside the stadium surprised him. They had expected a dozen. Instead there were closer to two hundred. Most were in bad shape, having eaten very little during their captivity. The meager amount of water they had been supplied had kept them alive but little more than that. Jake was reminded of a movie he had seen, about a Georgia prisoner of war camp. Many of the prisoners in the movie had looked like walking skeletons. The captives they released did not look much better.

Everyone in his unit was digging through their packs, pulling out anything edible, and passing it out. The older survivors insisted that the younger ones eat what was there, insisting they would be alright until they reached safety and could enjoy their food.

Jake wondered what was taking Santwan so long? He should have been waiting outside the gate to let them out. He sent one of his new recruits to check to see if the gate was still locked. It was.

Something serious must have happened to Santwan. He needed to get these people to safety and go and find him. He had lost everyone else in his family. Sant was all he had left. Erika was a possible future, but that was a *might be one day*. Something to dream about.

"Jarnigan, take a phaser and cut through that lock. I want to start moving these people toward transport immediately." He thought about and changed his mind.

"Rescind that order. Hopkins, you are trained to pilot the aircar, aren't you?"

"Yes sir. So is Sargent Hicks."

"Forget cutting through the lock. You two go and get the aircars. We will lift them out from here." He saw the fear grow on the faces of the people waiting to be taken to safety. "Hurry. I want everyone out before the Kurs recover. If any of them survived, they may have a way to call for help."

Jake used his bandana to wipe the sweat and ash from his face before collapsing down beside his pack on the filthy synthetic turf. He could just make out the faint numbering and grinned. The last time he'd collapsed on the twenty yard line he'd shattered his ankle, ruining any possibility of an NFL future. Sant had played for the other team and had also been injured in that game. They had laughed about it together. The doctors had rebuilt his ankle sufficiently to pass military standards and three years later he was able to sign up for the National Guard. He'd never regretted that decision.

So why was he so upset now? He was surprised by the film of tears in his eyes. Where was Sant?

Chapter 28

Santwan woke to a smiling face lying next to him and bright sunshine thru a window, something he had not experienced in a long time. His eyes watered and blinked rapidly for a moment, as they adjusted to being woken by the sun. The air was crisp and clear, letting him see that they were not in the same location as his memory insisted was the place that he died. That thought startled him. Was he dead? This wasn't his idea of Heaven but then again no one had ever returned to say what Heaven really looked like.

The woman before him was tiny, with a slender but curvaceous body and slightly oval eyes. Native American or Latino he figured, her complexion was dark, but not as dark as his with more of a red undertone. She wore her raven-colored hair in a single thick braid that reached past the middle of her back. She was certainly attractive. That was made more evident by the scraps of clothing that left little to the imagination. The only flaw he could see was that she didn't appear to speak much English.

"Where am I?" he asked.

"No entiendo? Hoblas Español?" She looked just as aggravated by the communication problem as he was.

"No. Do you speak English?

"Muy Poca….leetle bit."

Sant grinned. He could work with that. He had no idea how long he'd been there. It must have a while, the gashes in his stomach were closed and beginning to heal. Someone had done an excellent job of stitching him up. He had no idea where his shirt and flak jacket was. He would catch hell if he lost that jacket.

Jake and the others would be looking for him. They may even think he was dead. Hell, he had thought he was dead. Somehow he had to get word to his unit that he was alive. It was not going to be easy to get her to understand what he needed without saying the words. But he was looking forward to trying.

Chapter 29

Jake barely looked up as a pair of aircars passed overhead. The rescued prisoners were gradually being shuttled to safety. The more serious injuries had been transported directly to the Cavern while the others were taken to Rock City atop Lookout Mountain where they were fed, given an opportunity to bathe and tucked into warm beds for the first time in months. The transfer had not been without incident.

Destiny had been present when one of the ships arrived at Rock City if hopes of spotting someone she had been friends with. At the sight of one of the former prisoners she had begun to scream and tried to grab a phaser away from one of the returning men. "No! Not her. She works for them. She is not even human. Look at her neck. She has gills."

Mikey had immediately grabbed for the woman, only to realize she had somehow slipped out of his grasp. Not only that, she now had his knife in her hand and had pulled one of the other women in front of her, using her as a shield.

"Everyone stay calm. She has a hostage." Mikey waved the others back, while addressing the woman in soft tones, "We don't want to hurt you. Just drop the knife and we can talk." He kept his eyes locked on her hand as he spoke, not trusting her to react as a human would.

She shook her head but did not try to speak. Her eyes darted here and there as if she were looking for a weakness, an opening she could utilize in an escape. It was clear she understood the language. The brass would want to have a long talk with her. He had to make sure she didn't escape.

Mikey noticed the gills that Destiny had mentioned. She was probably afraid, after watching them decimate the invaders and taking no prisoners. She expected similar treatment now that her secret was exposed. He caught a glimpse of two bodies inching closer to her from the doorway behind her position but did nothing to indicate what he had seen to the woman. She was fast. Much faster than he was, and that knife was razor sharp. He wasn't sure the three of them would be enough to take her out. He slowly worked himself into a better position to assist when she unexpectedly darted forward and sliced the blade across his chest.

At the sight of Mikey's blood, Destiny gasped. Then she surprised them all by leaping off the top of a table onto the alien girls back. She jerked the woman's head back by her hair and began stabbing at her neck with a fork.

The alien woman's hostage was forgotten as she fought to remove the berserk woman clinging to her back. Each jab of the fork brought another spirt of coppery brown fluid but did not appear to do any serious damage.

While Destiny proceeded to distract the woman, one of the men dove for her knees, driving her to the floor and the second grabbed one of her hands, twisting it up behind her back. She screamed and cursed as the muscles were pulled from their normal position. Mikey immediately grabbed her other arm, twisting it back beside the other one. He recognized Cody as being the one holding her other arm. "Quick, grab this one and hold her. I'll get a zip tie around them."

"Better hurry, she's a lot stronger than she looks. And her skin is slick. It's like holding on to an eel."

"Yeah, but she seemed to understand what we are saying. The Captain will want to talk to her." The woman continued to struggle as additional zip toes were added to her arms, ankles, and knees. Mikey insisted on adding extra ties in case the woman was like an eel and could contort her body. Once there were zip ties every six inches and he decided she was reasonably secured; Mikey pulled the bent fork from her shoulder. Most of the bleeding had already stopped. The injuries had to be painful but did not seem to be life-threatening.

Cody had applied a dry pad to her shoulder but no one seemed worried about her comfort. He sent a cadet for a gurney to carry her to a secure room. He thought about removing some of the restraints once she was on the bed but decided to let someone with more seniority make that decision.

The sound of familiar voices approaching was a welcome relief for both men. The three officers looked tired but happy, so Cody and Mikey relaxed.

Major Whitten blanched at the number of fork holes in her neck but did not remark on it.

Captain Armstrong addressed her directly, "Do you have a name we can call you?"

"Xika,"she snarled.

Jeffers wondered if that was her name or the aliens version of Fuck you. There was no way to know for sure, however he was certain she knew exactly what they were talking about. "Someone get me Anderson."

***

Jake was beginning to show signs of stress after the last few days and looked like he was about to collapse.

Hunk wondered if his team leader had gotten any rest at all over the last few days. He thought about it and realized this was the first time he'd seen him since the attack began. Erika had asked about him earlier, mentioning she had not talked to him since they had begun the advance on the stadium three days earlier. He was about to mention it when a cadet approached him and Jake walked away without another word.

Hunk got busy and forgot all about it.

***

Jake passed through the plastic door divider and went directly to Captain Jeffers, spoke for a moment, and then walked over to get a better look at the captive. "I don't know how we missed her."

"She looks human. At least until you get a really close look. Destiny recognized her and went ballistic. We had to pull her off, she was doing her best to fork her to death. I get the impression that she had something to do with why Destiny had been placed on that raft."

Jake had been surprised when Captain Jeffers filled him in on the capture. Destiny had always seemed the type run away from anything larger than a caterpillar. He smiled, thinking the alien woman's attack on Mikey might have had something to do with Destiny's unusual behavior. "Looks like you are gonna need a couple of stitches."

Mikey looked up at Jake's comment and nodded. He had let Cody use a stack of paper napkins to stop the flow of blood but every time he moved it began seeping again. He was tired, and the strain of the last few days was beginning to show on his face. Destiny had one arm clamped around Destiny, ensuring she would not attempt to murder the alien woman again.

Dealing with the headstrong blonde had been surprisingly simple. She had agreed to have her injuries looked at, as long as Mikey promised to come with her.

As soon as they figured out what to do with their new acquisition he could get his own wounds taken care of. Captain Armstrong was talking to Jake and from the few words he overheard it would not be long before they could leave. He was not surprised that they had called in Jake. Losing Santwan had left a void in his chest where his heart should have been. The alien woman had no idea what she was facing. He turned to Destiny, "Come on. Let's go get these wounds taken care of."

Jake listened to all three men for a moment, then nodded and stepped toward the female captive. His eyes were dark and hooded, his lips frozen in a tight lines. Any compassion he might have felt was long gone. He approached the alien woman, picked up one hand and snipped two of the zip ties away before sliding a metal tray beneath her hand.

"I am going to ask you a few questions. You will answer these questions. The choice of whether you ask them before or after I begin to burn your fingers and toes off is up to you."

Cody pushed a rolling table over beside the bed. Lying atop a white clothe was a small handheld phaser.

Jake left it sitting where she could see it and turned to the three officers. "What would you like to know first?"

Chapter 30

Erika shoved the last of her clothing in her pack and looked around the room for anything she might have missed.

Three days earlier the jubilant soldiers had entered the damaged mother ship and quickly cleared up any survivors. There had been a possibility that some of the beasts had escaped, but without knowing how many the Kurs had been brought to the planet, there was no way to be sure. After an intense grid search, the men were reasonably sure they had accounted for all the Kurs and any Fisheyes that might have survived the initial assault. They would need to be on guard for any of the beasts. The possibility of a mated pair surviving and reproducing had everyone on alert.

Techs had been brought in to examine the control system of the mother ship, hoping to understand enough to be able to move the vessel to a location where they could delve deeper into its secrets. When one tech suggested Area 51, it had been met with laughter, a sure sign that spirits had been eased by the success of the strike.

Captain Armstrong had returned hours later, congratulated the team on a successful operation, made notations of the MIA and KIA. Jake had immediately been reassigned to the team heading north to Knoxville. A second team was going to Nashville. Humanity was fighting back.

Erika had watched him leave with a heavy heart. He had not spoken to anyone. She had heard from Hunk about Santwan being MIA and decided it was not a good time for them to work on their possible relationship.

She could wait.

***

Jake had a lot on his mind. He was supposed to be feeling jubilant over the destruction of the mother ship. Instead, he was fighting back multiple waves of depression. It was all he could do to keep his personal misery from reflecting in his work. It had been four days since the end of the attack. No trace of Santwan had been found. There had been several unidentified piles of ash around the stadium, any of which might be the remains of his best friend.

One of the prisoners had mentioned seeing a Fisheye with two beasts leaving the stadium moments before they had begun climbing up the back fence.

Captain Jeffers had taken his report, raising his eyebrow when the list of casualties was read but refrained from making any comment. Earlier that day a fleet of aircars had appeared from the south, moving to examine the wreckage. The one that landed had been surrounded by 4 aircars carrying heavy armament. The aliens had not expected the loss of the force field.

Just as they expected, the Kurs from Atlanta had no idea that they were vulnerable to the ancient weapons. The fisheye pilots put up more of a fight but the end result was never in doubt. The army now had five additional aircars.

Jake had caught a glimpse or two of Erika in between his shuttle runs, however, he had not been able to find time to talk to her. He had a lot he wanted to tell her. Only yesterday he had received a field promotion to Captain, an honor he had not expected but was happy to receive. In fact, all of the men in the attack force had received promotions. Impromptu celebrations had broken out around the compound. The addition of a hundred and twenty extra bodies to the facility was already straining the available resources. They had discussed the need to expand the living quarters deeper into the cave system in the near future. From the behavior he had witnessed since the newcomers had begun to arrive, that would be a priority. There had been a distinct gap between the numbers of male and female survivors. That was no longer an issue since the majority of the rescued had been female.

Observing the intricate dating dance between the men in the unit and the new civilian woman made him grin. A few short months ago he would have been right in the midst of the pack, doing his best to line up some female companionship for the night-- if not longer. Now he could not contemplate being with any woman besides Erika. As soon as he returned from Atlanta he intended to see her. They had a lot to talk about.

He was practically running down the passage that led to the small offset Erika had been assigned for her use.

He almost forgot protocol and had to stop before barreling into the room. He rapped on the piece of wood and called out her name.

"Erika?"

No one answered. Maybe she was asleep. He decided to throw caution to the wind and poke his head inside. Maybe she wouldn't shoot at him this time.

The bed was neatly made. The room was empty. Her packs were gone.

His stomach clenched and he suddenly felt nervous. He thought back on the casualty list, going over the names in his mind. Hers was not there. So where was she?

He began walking back toward the breakroom. Someone there would know. She might even be there herself.

The room was crowded when he arrived, but it only took a moment for him to realize Erika was not inside. He spotted Cody playing poker with some of the guys from Knoxville.

"Cody, you seen Erika?"

"Yeah, a little while ago. I think she was heading home; she had her pack with her. I saw her walking towards the transport tunnel. Her horse is in the upper pasture, you might catch her there."

Jake was overcome by a pang of sadness and anger, the latter emotion directed toward himself for being such an inconsiderate fool. He took off running toward the access tunnel to Ruby Falls. When he arrived at the tunnel exit he realized she had quite a head start on him. Someone had already returned the second golf cart. He considered returning to the Captain and requesting the use of an airship but knew that request would be denied. They had no way of knowing how long the power supply would last. Use of the airships was restricted to very important missions only.

He mentally urged the golf cart along the tunnel, hoping that Goldie was being stubborn and refusing to leave the herd. He took the stairs two at a time, knowing that it was probably too late to catch her but unwilling to give up without trying.

Sara was on duty at the gift shop exit. As he exited the staircase, she looked at him with his eyes too bright to be dry. Jake knew the tears were for him.

He felt the lump in his chest grow almost too large for him to catch a breath. Erika was already gone.

"She wasn't riding fast, and she's heading for the gap road instead of taking the shorter route through Saint Elmo. Take Jupiter. He's the fastest horse we have. You can catch her.

Jake threw the saddle on the big gelding and took

off at a gallop trying to catch her before she reached the road down the mountain. Surprisingly, she was not hard to catch up with. Less than a mile down the road he found her, walking Goldie slowly along down Lula Lake road. She must have detoured by Rock City.

She seemed surprised to see him.

"You came to tell me goodbye. You didn't have to do that. I figured you would come to see me when you found the time."

Jake shook his head. "No. Never goodbye. Not again." His voice finally cracked and she could hear the pain he was hiding.

She turned to look directly into his eyes. " I heard about Santwan. I'm sorry. I know how close you were."

"More than close. He was family." His voice shook as emotion threatened to break down the barriers he was fighting to hold on to.

She nodded. "You should not blame yourself. Sant knew the risk and choose to be there. He would expect nothing more from you." Unsure what she should say next, she sat quietly on Goldie and waited to hear his words.

He seemed to pause, taking a deep breath before continuing. "Listen Erika. It's true, we still have a long road before us. Word is spreading of our success and humanity is striking back. We have already destroyed three of the big mother ships and captured a dozen aircars. We also found a storage locker full of bigger, heavier phasers. The techs think they might be what the Kurs used to blow up everything. They definitely helped take out the mother ships."

"So the Knoxville raid was a success. That's good."

"Yes. The unit is leaving for Atlanta soon. There are two ships there, one north of the city near Stone Mountain and the other down at Hartsfield Airport. We hope to muster at least a hundred men for the attack. There are no convenient trees nearby but we have a volunteer willing to fly one the airships into the red zone and blow up the generator from inside the force field."

"And you are commanding one of the details?"

"Yes."

"Then I don't need to keep you. I'm sure you have a thousand things to do before you leave."

"They can wait. I have something important to do first. I need to talk to you."

"I'm pretty sure everything we needed to say was said before the raid. At least everything I needed to say. My part in this war is over. I see no reason to remain."

"Damn it, Erika, a man needs time to decide how to respond to these things! You surprised me. You're the bravest person I ever knew--the most graceful—the most honest. The idea of loving you scared me. I wasn't sure if I was ready for that kind of a relationship."

"Have you decided?" she asked.

"I came after you, didn't I," he snapped.

"That doesn't answer my question. What are you

trying to say?"

"I don't want you to leave. Well, I understand if you want to go get Chance and bring him back. Maybe the cows and goats too. But I want you to come back to me."

"Sometimes we don't get everything we want." Her voice was soft and full of sadness. But it was clear she was still leaving.

Jake knew he was missing something. Something important." Look, Erika. I'm not very good at this. I need to make you understand how much you mean to me, and I don't know the words..." he paused, finally realizing what was missing in the conversation.

He swung down off Jupiter and walked over to Goldie. Reached up and lifted her from the saddle, setting her on the ground before him. Her mouth, close at hand, was too tempting to ignore. His kiss was fiercely demanding, possessive and territorial, leaving no doubt in her mind of his intentions.

She jumped away, startled, then uttered a little breathless laugh." Well, that was different."

"Woman you talk to much."

She started to reply and he kissed her. "We haven't got time to fight, and I'm going to catch hell for leaving without permission as it is."

"But--"

He kissed her again. "No buts. I love you. You love me. The rest we can work out later. We are going to be busy between organizing and rebuilding society, ensuring there is enough food for everyone, and continuing the fight against the alien invaders. But I promise I will somehow find the time for you."

The eastern sky was beginning to turn pink and gold as the morning sun began to rise over the distant mountains. Jake pulled her into his arms and held her as they watched the sun come up together for the first time. Humanity had taken the first step toward a new future. It was not going to be easy, but with her by his side, he knew it would somehow turn out alright.

"Damn. I have got to go now. I doubt Sara and Hunk can make up enough excuses to cover my absence."

He went to swing up onto Jupiter and paused, staring at the horizon, unsure of what he had glimpsed in the distance. His face was pale, his eyes damp.

Erika turned Goldie to see what he was staring at. In the distance, she could see two figures walking slowly up the road. The taller woman appeared to wobble, leaning against the second, smaller woman for support. As they drew closer, Erika smiled when she realized what she thought was a woman was actually a man, a skinny black man with long dreads, wearing camo pants and a flak jacket with no shirt. He wasn't moving very fast.

But Santwan was coming home.

MAKING
MEMORY
V.C. SANFORD

Bell, Book and Claw

V.C. Sanford

To Crown
A Chimera
V C Sanford